THE SUPREME CRIME

"As she sat thus before him, wreathed in the trails that made a sort of clumsy imitation of vine leaves, he seemed to be looking upon a Bacchante."—*Page 78.*

THE
SUPREME CRIME

BY

DOROTHEA GERARD

(MADAME LONGARD DE LONGGARDE)

DER SCHLIMMSTE WURM, DES ZWEIFELS DOLCHGEDANKEN'
HEINE

Fredonia Books
Amsterdam, The Netherlands

The Supreme Crime

by
Dorothea Gerard

ISBN: 1-4101-0114-2

Reprinted from the 1901 edition

Fredonia Books
Amsterdam, The Netherlands
http://www.fredoniabooks.com

In order to make original editions of historical works available to scholars at an economical price, this facsimile of the original edition of 1901 is reproduced from the best available copy and has been digitally enhanced to improve legibility, but the text remains unaltered to retain historical authenticity.

NOTE

FOR the enlightenment of English readers little acquainted with the religious customs of Eastern Europe, it is as well to point out, at the beginning of this story of Ruthenian life in Austria, that the representatives of this class belong to the branch of the Greek Church united to Rome, in which matrimony, although not absolutely obligatory for the clergy, is the almost universal condition. An aspirant not married at his ordination must be celibate for life—a rule which results in all Ruthenian priests, with very rare exceptions, being married men.

CHAPTER I

GREGOR PETROW settled his cravat before the little glass on the wall, looking at himself critically the while. What he saw there was a young, narrow, rather hollow-cheeked face, above which the reddish fair hair showed an inclination to stand up. The eyes were of a clear, transparent blue, and a trifle too wide open, which, in conjunction with the upright hair, gave him a slightly startled expression. About the large, mobile, and well-shaped mouth there was a suggestion of harshness, corrected by something sunny in the depth of those transparent blue eyes—the eyes of a boy who has not yet done wondering at the place he finds himself in. A fine young fellow, taken all in all, despite a slight stoop in the shoulders, and with the hand and foot of a woman—delicate, narrow, and yet strongly moulded.

But the picture did not please him ; with a sigh of discouragement he turned from the glass and made a few irresolute steps about the room. It was a small, low apartment, with white-washed walls, a brick stove in one corner, and a mud floor ; for furniture a cast-iron bedstead, a deal table, and a

A

bench on which lay a cushion stuffed with maize straw, and which did duty as sofa.   But for the primitive book-shelf on the wall, and the absence of chickens and pigs, it might have passed for an exceptionally clean peasant room.   Both the small windows were wide open on to the village street. Gregor Petrow stopped beside one of them, and with widened nostrils drank in the syringa scent which the spring air carried in with it, for this was May, and straight opposite there grew a tall syringa bush which leaned as impetuously over the wicker-work paling as though bent upon casting itself down into the road.   Beetles on the wing skimmed past, with open-beaked swallows hard on their trail.   The air was full of minute, floating things, such as the petals of overblown flowers, tiny seedlings, and almost invisible clouds of green or yellow pollen, which the breeze was conveying about the country as is its mission during this busiest of Nature's seasons.

Gregor Petrow's brow cleared as he stood there gazing before him, and when he turned from the window it was with a more resolute movement, as though the syringa scent had been a strong wine, drowning the doubts which, a minute before, still disturbed him.   He went back again to the glass and finished settling his cravat, gave one touch of the brush to his black Sunday coat (and yet this was Wednesday), and, picking up his best hat, left the house with the step of a man whose mind is made up.

It was the hour at which the cows were being

driven home from pasture, and Gregor was scarcely out in the narrow lane which did duty as street, before he had to range himself against the wattled paling, in order to save his only decent pair of trousers from being unduly spattered. As a rule his attire was the thing in the world which occupied him the least, but this was a solemn occasion, and it would not do to present himself before the *Pope* (parish priest) in soiled garments. The disadvantage of these pauses in his progress was that it exposed him helpless to the attacks of the small cowherds, who could not think of letting slip so good an opportunity of kissing somebody's hand. A monotonous ceremony this, and a slightly grimy one; but Gregor bore it with an equanimity which at moments looked like pleasure. Sometimes, at the sight of some familiar shaggy head, the light which dwelt at the back of his blue eyes would look out suddenly, and the way in which his severe mouth relaxed in answering to each separate ''Slawas' (greeting) spoke of the existence of some bond between the fair-haired youth and the ragged urchins.

At last he was free of the lane and out on a green common sprinkled with white geese, where hobbled horses were patiently grazing, and round which the huts squatted in an irregular circle, each with a few apple-trees beside it, in full blossom at this moment, and giving the impression of a huge, straggly white wreath. Just now it was a picture painted almost entirely in green and white, for the birchwood which stood up to the very edge of the common was in its first and most vivid leaf. Only the blue of the mountain line to the west contrasted with the universal tints.

At one spot—it was the spot where stood the only building that was not a hut—the white wreath seemed to thicken to a knot, and towards that point Gregor took his direction, following the cart-track— two ribbons of dust divided by a rib of green, where the grass grew obstinately between the marks of the wheels. Gregor's hand shook slightly as he pushed open the wooden gate which stood hospitably ajar. The wave of perfume which met him inside was almost overpowering, for the house barely looked out of a tangle of lilac bushes, and on the grass plot before it narcissus and lily of the valley, in full prime, ran riot at their sweet pleasure. Hens and ducks walked about, also at their pleasure, and at Gregor's approach a pig fled squealing round the corner, for the garden melted indefinitely into the farm-yard, and that again into an ancient orchard, where more moss grew on the trunks than fruit on the branches.

A small wooden porch, jutting out right into the sea of lilac blossoms, formed the entrance, and having mounted the five or six steps which led to it, Gregor found himself abruptly in presence of the eldest daughter of the house. She was busy gathering a bunch of lilacs—she had only to lean over the wooden balustrade to do so—and at sound of his step turned round in the very act of breaking a branch.

'Panna Zenobia!' said Gregor, in sudden confusion, for he had not counted on finding himself alone with her—it did not fit into his programme.

The girl evidently was as surprised as he, though she did not speak at once. It would have been difficult to tell her age, as is usually the case with very dark women, but in reality she was scarcely twenty. Perhaps it would have been almost as difficult to decide whether she was handsome or plain. To an eye unused to the physiognomies of the country, the Semitic strain would probably have appeared too pronounced to be agreeable, for her mother was of Armenian blood, and Zenobia Mostewicz undoubtedly showed a reversal to the Armenian type. The first flush of surprise once passed it became clear that her rather long face was habitually pale, with that sort of opaque pallor which is peculiar to some orientals. The eyes were long, and dark, and seldom quite open, as though the eyelids were too heavy to be completely raised. A certain heaviness altogether marked the features which yet were almost quite regular. Her magnificent coal-black hair was of the sleek, shiny order, and her thick eye-brows almost met at the root of a well-cut nose. With this an almost majestic stature, and a fine, supple figure, carried somewhat too languidly.

'Can I speak to the Pope?' asked Gregor, rather precipitately, after a moment's pause.

'My father is not yet back, but my mother is at home.'

From under her heavy eyelids she had, before answering, thrown a wonderfully rapid glance at his holiday attire.

'No, thank you, I will not disturb the Popadia' (the usual designation for a priest's wife), said Gregor, if possible more precipitately.

'I forgot, you could not speak to her now, at any rate; she is busy, arranging about Jerena Rylko's marriage, I believe.'

'I will not disturb her. Where are you going to put these flowers?'

'I meant them for the Matka Boska (Mother of God), in the orchard. It is her month, you know.'

'Are you going to take them there now?'

She looked at him again furtively, and did not answer at once. It was evident that if she took the flowers to the orchard, he would accompany her, and there seemed to be something disturbing in the thought. From him her eyes wandered down to the garden and fell straight upon the identical pig which had fled at Gregor's arrival, now flying back round the corner, followed by two girls in short frocks, whose stockings were half-way down their bare legs. Zenobia's face cleared; the problem was solved.

'Yes, I shall take the flowers. Wasylya, Paraska!' she called over the balustrade. 'Come and help me to carry the flowers to the Matka Boska! We shall just have time before supper.'

With a shriek of delight Wasylya and Paraska complied, to the evident relief of the pig, who returned, grunting, to his revels in the onion beds. They were two black-haired brats of respectively ten and thirteen years of age, with dancing black eyes, vividly pink cheeks, and cotton frocks which ought to have been in the wash at least three days ago. Wasylya, the elder of the two, had stuck a row of narcissus into her dense black hair, hooked two small twigs of lilac over her ears in the guise of somewhat barbarous earrings, and hung a necklace of pansies round her neck. She seemed in high spirits at her artistic invention.

'You must take these off,' said the elder sister severely, as—the two girls having first lustily fought for the biggest bunch to carry—they were crossing the yard towards the orchard. 'You cannot go to the Matka Boska in these ridiculous ornaments.'

'Ridiculous ornaments!' echoed Wasylya in shrill-toned indignation. 'What is there ridiculous about narcissus and lilac? You don't find them ridiculous in the garden?'

'But on your head, I do. You would not go to church like that on Sunday, would you?'

'Perhaps not; and yet I *know* they look well there. All right!' she laughed gaily, 'I'll throw them to the ducks, and gather new ones after supper!' And gleefully pulling off her flower necklace she shied it at a passing hen.

It was clear that the orchard had not always been an orchard; the stone urn standing under an apple-tree, with a pair of stone legs beside it which had probably once belonged to a weeping angel, a mouldy cross aslant, and a fragment of iron railing which, just visible above the nettles, leaned in one corner—all this, together with the slightly undulating surface of the ground, was enough to point out its original destination. But the thought of the bones mouldering underfoot never seemed to spoil anybody's appetite for the pears and apples growing overhead.

'There is a good show of blossoms this year,' said Gregor, looking up at the dense canopy, and rather at a loss for a subject of conversation.

Zenobia made some indifferent answer and walked on straight in front of him along the narrow path. He gazed at the back of her head, and in the nervousness of the moment the amber shades at the roots of her black hair seemed to touch his imagination as they had never done before. He did not know whether to be provoked or glad at the presence of the two younger sisters; with them away he felt almost certain that he would at that moment, and quite contrary to his original resolution, have put his fate to the touch, but with Wasylya and Paraska flying backwards and forwards across the path, throwing their hats over beetles and butterflies and making ineffectual grabs at their limp garters, everything but commonplaces became an impossibility.

The Matka Boska herself was obviously a former grave monument, though all that remained legible of the inscription on the battered pillar on which she stood was the date of some forty years back. Zenobia began to pull off the faded lilacs of yesterday,

which festooned the pillar, and Gregor coming to her
assistance it happened not unnaturally that their
bare hands more than once came in contact, at which
moments he was astonished to see her shiver and
draw her black brows together, as though in pain;
was he then so disagreeable to her? A bad prospect
for his errand of to-day.

When the flowers had been arranged there was
a pause.

'I think we ought to say a prayer,' said Zenobia
at last, a little diffidently.

'Very well; but who is to say it?'

'You, I think; you are accustomed to pray with
the children in the school.'

'I?' he hesitated. 'Very well, I will say it'; and
as they all knelt down on the short grass, he folded
his hands as simply as a child might have done and
spoke the 'Our Father' in a slightly tremulous but
wonderfully melodious voice, and in that accent in
which it is too seldom heard—the accent of deep
conviction. The thought that this day was to be a
turning-point in his life put an earnestness into his
appeal for help which moved even the two children,
who, as the little congregation again stood up,
measured him with awe-stricken glances, just as
though they had discovered a new person.

No one had spoken yet when a shrill call was
heard from the house.

'The Mamusia (little mother) is calling us to
supper!' said Paraska, racing off, while Wasylya
lingered to pick up the remains of the flowers, with

which she immediately began to replace the necklace and earrings recently discarded.

On the doorstep of the back entrance which faced towards the orchard stood a long, lean woman in a dirty dressing-jacket. Her face could be called either dark-yellow or light-brown, according to individual opinion, and presented a large amount of tough, leathery surface. She had a haggard, tired-looking appearance, and the quick-moving eyes of a person on whose shoulders rest many cares. Just at present she was pulling violently at the buttons of her dressing-jacket—no wonder that there were only two remaining—from which symptom Zenobia knew that her mother was in a temper.

'Ah, Gregor Petrow!' she said, in an unpleasantly rasping voice; 'so you have remembered that we are still alive? That's right!' But she said it as though it were all wrong. 'The Pope will be glad to see you,' she added, about as sweetly as though she were swallowing a spoonful of vinegar.

'Is the Pope come home?'

'Yes, he is home,' and, with a new contraction of her sunken chin, she led the way into the house.

CHAPTER II

IN a low-ceilinged room, whose windows even by day were darkened by the lilac bushes, a petroleum lamp was already burning, and the frugal evening fare spread—the *kolesha* of the country (a sort of maize porridge), supplemented by a tureen-full of sour cream. Father Nikodem, whose appetite, brought back from the afternoon's excursion, would brook no delay, was hard at work already. He was a big, stout man, as dark as the rest of the family, with black hair sprinkled in pepper and salt style, and whose almost perfectly round face was supplemented by a handsome double chin. The eyes were likewise quite round, and set in such thick lashes that when he turned them suddenly upon a person they gave the impression of being touched up with charcoal. His parishioners approved of him, not because he was one of those good average priests who, unhampered by higher ideals, fulfil their duties in a punctual, business-like fashion, but because he talked and laughed loudly, told good stories, even during his sermons, and made the bargaining about the price of a funeral or a wedding an almost amusing, if unprofitable, practice. In the very tone in which

11

he boisterously welcomed Gregor to his board the whole man was reflected, a coarse-grained but genuine nature; and, indeed, the jovial Pope never looked more in place than when receiving a guest on his doorstep, or filling his glass at table. Whatever cause had cast a gloom upon the Popadia's humour had obviously had no effect upon his, or rather had produced a contrary one. From the first moment it had been evident that some joke was tickling him vastly, which nothing but the warning glances of his wife kept him from making public—but not for long. The company had been eating *kolesha* for hardly three minutes when the Pope exploded, unfortunately just as he was in the act of ladling another spoonful of cream into his ample mouth.

'It's no use, Justina, it's no use!' he gasped, wiping the traces of the catastrophe from the breast of his black soutane. 'It won't be suppressed. To keep it from Gregor Petrow would be to cheat him of a good story, and that's a thing which has always gone against my conscience; just think how precious an honest laugh is in this valley of tears!'

'I don't see anything good in the story,' said the Popadia, savagely hacking at her *kolesha*. 'And how a priest of God can find pleasure in exposing himself to ridicule——'

Father Nikodem made a funny grimace. 'If priests of God did nothing worse than that—But there! let Gregor Petrow judge for himself! You must know'—and he turned his round, merry eyes upon his guest—'that Mitru Skribnek was buried this afternoon.' He laughed again till he choked, as though the fact mentioned were quite irresistibly comical. 'He had fifteen head of cattle, so not unnaturally we counted on getting something handsome for the funeral. Yesterday Jurko Skribnek was here to settle matters, and it was Justina there who undertook to speak to him. She's a far better hand at it generally than I am—*generally*, I say, but not always.' The Pope winked across knowingly at his wife's gloomy face. 'Well, Justina had taken it into her head that, all things considered, we had a right to expect the best price ever to be had, so naturally she began by asking fifty florins, while they started off with fifteen. At the end of an hour they had got no nearer than twenty, while Justina had come down to forty. There the matter stuck. "If the Pope can't come and fetch him for less, then we shan't trouble him to come so far," said Jurko, who always was one of your pert ones for answering. "We shall be content if he meets us in the churchyard and seals up the grave; he's bound to do that, and, of course, we'll pay him the regulation tax."

'Upon this they went, and Justina let them go, never doubting to see them back again. Was it likely that a family with fifteen cows would let their head be carried to his grave without candles and song? A mere sealing-up is what the very pauper gets. But yesterday evening passed, and so did this morning, and by midday Justina began to grow seriously restless. "Fifty florins is a fine thing," she said to me at last, "but twenty florins is better than nothing. It almost seems as though these godless people were going to stick by their word." "So it does," I said; "and I've often thought that you're apt to hang the basket a bit too high; but it's too late now to make an outcry." "I don't know about that," said Justina—she's got a wonderfully inventive mind, you know—"I fancy something might be done yet. I've got an idea, Nikodem. They can't have got him to the village yet, and no doubt they would be glad of a chance of making up matters, but they just don't know how to begin. We've got some potatoes in that direction—it's a fine day—supposing you were to go over and have a look at those potatoes. You'll take the little cart, of course, as two miles is a good bit to walk, and if you put your vestment at the bottom, who is to be the wiser? It may very well chance that you meet the corpse on the way, and if you don't manage to put matters right then, why, you're not worthy the name of Pope."

'Well, the plan struck me as grand, and off I went in the cart, my vestments well buried in the straw. And up to a certain point it all happened exactly as Justina had foreseen. Just a quarter of a mile before the hut I met the funeral procession, and scarcely had they caught sight of me than I saw them consulting, and finally standing still. "Good-afternoon to you, Pope," they say, in quite a friendly way. "You seem in a hurry?" "In no special hurry," I reply, chuckling with satisfaction as I think of that chasuble in the straw, and blessing Justina's foresight. "I'm just having a look at my potatoes over there; they tell me they're late in coming up."

'"They *are* a bit late," says Jurko Skribnek; "but if you're in no hurry you'll take a mouthful of *wódki* before going farther, won't you?"

'"If it please you," I say, seeming to feel those twenty florins in my pocket already.

'I drank one glass, I drank two glasses, I'm not sure that I didn't drink a third and a fourth; we talked of the potatoes, of the maize, of the apples, but never a word of the funeral so far. I was beginning to feel just a little queer, but I kept saying to myself, It must be coming, why else should they have stopped me? It was not until the bottle had gone round several times that Jurko seemed to remember what they were there for.

'"Well, Pope," he says, hammering the cork down with his fist, "I fancy that we've all had about enough. If you take much more you won't be able to reach your potatoes, and even if you do get there you'll see two growing for every one there is; and if we take much more we'll as likely as not tumble into the grave when we get there. And your time for getting there and back is short, too, for remember, you've promised to seal up the grave for us."

'That was all; in another minute I was alone on the road; and all I regret is that I had not got a pocket mirror with me, for my face must have been a sight to see. It's a bitter thing to lose twenty florins through trying to get fifty, but the devil take me if I can help laughing at the trick they played me! Justina there can't see the joke at all; and it's true that the new carpet she had meant to buy is gone with those fifty florins; you can't buy a carpet for two florins, I suppose, and that's what the sealing-up brought me : fifty kreutzers for the incense, and fifty kreutzers for the chanting, and so on according to the tax. There are the fruits of my afternoon!' And throwing the loose coins on to the table, the Pope leant back again, gently shaking with laughter. The two younger girls, infected by their father's mirth, shrieked a delighted chorus, while Zenobia's dark, serious face betrayed by its pre-occupation that her thoughts had been elsewhere.

Gregor, too, had lent but half an ear, but in that which he had heard, and in spite of his mind being of quite a different fibre from that of Father Niko-dem's, there was nothing which directly offended him. The chronic bargaining between Pope and parishioners was a thing far too familiar to disturb him seriously ; it was one of the conditions of life, just as rain and sunshine are conditions, and although of a distinctly religious turn of mind, to imagine a state of things in which this element was absent had not yet come to him. Popes have to live as well as other people, and to bring up their families, which, by a special dispensation of Providence, are usually more numerous than those of other people, and, the government provisions being a mockery, it naturally follows that each wedding and funeral becomes, in the first place, a business transaction. Gregor also knew that this particular Pope was not nearly so black as the story just told appeared to paint him, and that, while making as good bargains of his duties as circumstances permitted, he yet fulfilled them conscientiously. Despite his business-like shrewdness, his heart was anything but hard nor his hand close; many a kindly act could the village tell of him. But as for letting down his charges for his priestly functions, even one florin below what he felt to be his due, such a thing never occurred to him. Of these contests, custom had made a species of legalised sport, a constant trial of strength between him and his parishioners, which he could not think of missing, and which gave a certain zest to an otherwise monotonous existence. True, it was the Popadia who usually began the transaction, not only because she had an almost superior talent in this direction, but also because some fragment of traditional etiquette demanded that a third person should intervene between the priest and the parishioner; but it was rare that any word of interest should escape him, and not infrequently, at the hottest moment of the debate, the door beside which he had been lending an attentive ear would burst open, and his last clinching word to the bargain be successfully put in.

Gregor knew all this, and yet smiled at the conclusion of the narrative, as though he had heard something merely amusing. His thoughts were anxiously bent in another direction.

'Can I speak to you alone?' he asked in a low voice, as the company rose from table, and while the Popadia was carefully collecting the remains of the

B

kolesha, presumably for the hens' breakfast next morning.

Father Nikodem, growing suddenly grave, looked at him keenly, and something like understanding flashed up in his black eyes.

'Come in here,' he said shortly, opening a door close beside which they stood.

CHAPTER III

THIS room was smaller and almost quite dark when they entered it. During the minute which passed while the Pope, still in silence, groped for the matches, Gregor had time to decide what his first words should be. These words were ready even before two candles, on a large table much spotted with ink, had been kindled, but even after the Pope had said in a distinctly encouraging tone of voice : ' Sit down, my son,' they refused to cross his lips.

' Is it I who am to begin, or you ?' asked his host at last, occupied in kindling some vile - smelling tobacco in the bowl of his cherrywood pipe.

' I fear you may think me preposterous——'

' If I ask leave to pay my addresses to your daughter,' finished the Pope, forcing his deep baritone voice into an imitation of Gregor's higher tones. ' Don't open your eyes wider than they are by nature. Have I hit it off or not ? It's Zenia you're after, aren't you ? I'm always for taking the shortest road everywhere.'

' It certainly is Panna Zenobia whom I had hoped——'

' To call my own some day; that's it, isn't it ? And you ask me whether I think you presumptuous ?

I should rather think I do—as confoundedly presumptuous as people only succeed in being at your age.   How could you for a moment suppose that I could give my daughter to a village schoolmaster?'

Gregor listened aghast, but also puzzled, for there was that in the Pope's merry black eyes which seemed to belie the harshness of the words.

'And you're not only presumptuous, you're also improvident.   What do you propose to live on? Your twenty-five florins a month?   Perhaps you expect me to give a portion with my daughter?   It will have to be a confoundedly small one, so long as we are all alive.'

'I had not thought of the portion,' said Gregor, reddening.

'Shows you're more of a fool than I took you for.   You expected to live on baked air, I suppose; it's a fare that some lovers manage on for a time.   Tell me, Gregor Petrow, are you fond of the girl?'

'I—yes; I would not think of marrying her if I did not esteem her highly.'

'Esteem?   Hem—and yet no thought of a portion, really it's beyond me how you came to think of marrying her at all.'

'Then I must consider myself rejected?' said Gregor, after a moment's silence, and making an ineffectual effort to rise.

'Sit still!' growled the Pope through the clouds of tobacco smoke which enveloped him.   'Where's the hurry? I'm not inclined to move so soon after supper, and politeness would demand of me to show you to the door. It's a very bad habit to jump to conclusions. Who told you you were rejected? What I said was that I could not give my daughter to a village schoolmaster.'

'Well, but since I am——'

'You are, you are; but must one always be what one is? You weren't born as a schoolmaster, were you? and need you die as one?'

Gregor stared uncomprehendingly; his wide-open eyes and upright hair giving to his puzzled countenance so unique an expression of astonishment that the Pope, tickled by the spectacle, felt half inclined to prolong the torture.

'No doubt your profession is a most honourable one, but no one can assert of it that it feeds its men fat; your own countenance is enough to knock that idea down flat. At twenty-one no man has a right to have such shadows under his cheek-bones, and do you think I want to see such dark blotches under Zenia's eyes? But there, I dare say you've had enough of it by now; let's talk seriously, my son. You have not surprised me, Gregor Petrow, I've seen this coming; and that which I am going to say to you now, I have had it ready to say to you for weeks past. From the moment I began to perceive that you and Zenia seemed to be drawing together, I set to ask myself how it could be possible to arrange the thing—for I like you, my son—I may as well tell you so at once, and I wish all my girls had a chance of as good husbands as Zenia seems to have. To let her marry a schoolmaster is out of the question, but if you could make yourself into some one else there is no saying what might happen.'

'Make myself into some one else?'

'Yes; it's much simpler than it sounds, especially if one happens to have a leaning for books, such as you have. Now, listen to my plan. Instead of paying your addresses to Zenia, you say good-bye to her for a time, and pack yourself straight off to the seminary at Lemberg. The studies will take you four years, but at your age one can manage to give up four years, and at the end of that time you have only to come back and fetch Zenia, and you will be all ready to take orders. She too can afford those four years, since she is only nineteen.'

'A priest? *I*, a priest?' said Gregor, half starting from his chair, and with eyes which had grown suddenly wild with astonishment.

'Yes; why do you stare as though I were pro-posing to you to become a highwayman? Can you give me a valid reason why you shouldn't be a priest just as well as dozens of other youngsters who haven't got half your steadiness and industry? Positively it seems to me your only chance of ever getting out of the school-house and of having at least enough *kolesha* to eat. I don't say it's a brilliant prospect—the beginning especially is hard—I 've been through it all myself, but unless you 're as blessed with children as I was, and if you learn to work the fees properly—and I can give you a few hints in that direction—there will always at least be *kolesha*. You would have a good figure for a vestment, if you could learn to hold yourself straighter —and the people like a priest who can be seen above the heads of the front rows—and you've got a good tenor voice which they'll train at the seminary, and which will make a grand effect at High Mass.'

Gregor had sunk back into his chair, listening breathlessly, and still astonished to the point of consternation.

'But I cannot—I have never thought of it before,' he stammered, pale with excitement.

'Haven't I told you that there is plenty of time to think of it now?' said the Pope, a trifle impatiently. 'I know several parish priests who at your age had not thought of it either. Out with it now. What's your opinion of my plan?'

'It's impossible; I have not the means for the studies.'

'But I have; and if I choose to go to the expense of procuring for my daughter the sort of husband I approve of—a son-in-law who will not be likely to send her back to me because he cannot feed her— then I should like to know what objection you can possibly make? You'll pay me back in time, no doubt, and in the meantime the money I advance will stand in place of the portion which it would be far more inconvenient for me to give.'

'But could I accept?' said Gregor doubtfully.

'If you could not, then we have been wasting our time, and I can only go back to what I said at the beginning of our talk : I cannot give my daughter to a village schoolmaster. And now, Gregor Petrow, if we end here it won't be my fault.'

Under the Pope's shrewd gaze the young man had sunk his face into his hands, and sat thus for a minute, beaten upon by a flood of emotions which made clear thought impossible.

'There is nothing so alarming about the idea as seems to you just at first,' the Pope's voice was heard saying rather more gently. 'And as for the money, why, it's just my way of making an investment, don't you see ? When one has got daughters to marry one can't expect to do so without putting one's hand in one's pocket. If one of my sons had grown up he would certainly have been a priest—it's the safest thing on the whole, as I've always maintained— you're to take the place of that son, don't you see ? The chance isn't a bad one for you, and I advise you to think over it before saying No.'

'I will think over it,' said Gregor, uncovering his face. 'It has been too sudden ; I will come back when I have thought.'

'That's right! Come back to-morrow, or take a week, if you like. There's plenty of time before the beginning of the term. But mind—not a word to Zenia meanwhile ! It's the one condition I make.'

'I will say nothing,' said Gregor, as he rose in a great hurry. 'I do not want to see anybody to-night. Will you let me out at this side, please? I should like to go home at once.'

'Without saying good-night to the ladies? Well, have your way, and may you be well inspired in your reflections!'

CHAPTER IV

OUTSIDE it was already so dark that Gregor, in his hurry, half stumbled down the wooden steps of the porch. Once free of the lilac bushes and out upon the common it was astonishing to discover that the night was star-lit and transparent. Gregor began by walking very fast along the ghostly-looking ribbons of grey dust, but he had not got to the middle of the wide space before the stillness of the night seemed to lay hands upon him. Why was he hurrying on? He knew quite well that he would not be able to sleep when he got home, and if all he wanted to do was to think, surely this spot was more congenial to thought than the four mud walls of his tiny chamber? All around him the village was asleep already; the Pope's house and the Jewish tavern alone still showed lights behind their windows, and the only sound to be heard just now was the uneasy lowing of a cow whose calf had been driven to market that day. As Gregor's face relaxed, his eyes turned instinctively to the line of mountains on the horizon, dimly visible even now, for he loved to look on them and to imagine himself in their richly wooded depths. On the other side there was the plain, easily to be over-

looked for miles from the raised ground on which
the village stood, and nearer at hand the stems of
the birch trees shone through the shadows like white
marble columns. Here and there a dark, inexplicable sort of phantom limped across the scene—the
hobbled horses which had been left out for the night
and were still apparently more hungry than sleepy.
Passing close beside one of them Gregor could hear
its deep breath. When he came to a chance log
which lay on the grass it seemed to him quite natural
to sit down, with his face towards the mountains.
That feeling of astonishment, almost consternation,
which had been the first effect of the Pope's proposition was still upon him.

'A priest! *I* a priest!" he said aloud. The words
had been ringing in his ears all the time as he walked,
and to speak them aloud was almost a necessity.

Considering his natural piety it was perhaps strange
that such an idea should never have presented itself
to his mind, not even in the shape of a hopeless wish ;
but ambition did not lie in his nature, and the thought
appeared to him, at first sight, purely ambitious.
Except for an uncle whom the opinion of the world
(that is, of his neighbours) had driven into paying for
his schooling—such as it had been—and who bore
him a grudge in consequence, Gregor had always
stood quite alone. Scarcely could he be said to have
comrades, for his sickly health as a child had shut him
out of all rough sports. The uncle was a bachelor,
but this circumstance could not diminish the grudge
towards Gregor ; in fact it rather aggravated it, for

when a man out of sheer reasonableness renounces the comforts and pleasures of family life, it is all the harder upon him to have to pay the cost of his brother's improvidence. At the earliest possible moment Gregor was therefore told to look out for his own living. If at that time he felt an inclination of any sort it was towards the career of a doctor, but since studies were quite out of the question, and a post of schoolmaster being available, it became inevitable to accept it. Within a few months he had got fond of his work. By dint of impressing upon him the fact that he was an absolutely superfluous personage, his uncle had succeeded in training his natural diffidence to excess, and the sensation of being looked up to—even if only by village *gamins*, and after having been so persistently looked down upon—was so new as to be almost entrancing. At first nothing could exceed his astonishment at seeing his own tremulous orders obeyed, his recommendations followed, his approval coveted. A feeling of gratitude towards these little beings who thus helped him to find his footing, not only in life, but also in his own mind, so to say, was the first phase through which the new schoolmaster passed. Pity came next—an acute and aching pity for these children, who yet were no poorer than himself, and certainly far better framed for resisting the miseries of poverty. Out of all this there grew a real affection for his pupils, which for the first time made life appear interesting, instead of only endurable.

For very long, however, this interest could not

suffice. His days were full enough, but the evenings were long, and the holiday times painfully empty. A family life had always appeared to him as the ideal of existence—probably because he had never known it—and when he sat alone in his bare chamber he would listen enviously to the clamour which the peasant children made alongside, and wonder in how many years he would be able to think of marriage. As yet he had scarcely spoken to a woman, and in the village of Hlobaki, the only women, not peasants, were to be found in the family of the Pope. It was inevitable that a certain intimacy should arise. For a year past Gregor had spent all his Sundays at Father Nikodem's house, and for half a year past had become aware of being attracted by Zenobia Mostewicz. Whether he was in love with her or not he could not have himself said; she did not dazzle him, but she pleased him; to be with her did not excite, but soothed him. Their frequent talks had been extraordinarily serious for two people of their ages, and if he had felt drawn towards her it had no doubt been in part because of the contrast which her reflective mood presented to the commonplace superficiality of the rest of the family. Beside the father's boisterousness, the mother's acidity, and the younger girl's tomboyishness, Zenobia's chronic calmness of demeanour, even her apparent apathy, exercised a charm of its own.

But to think of aspiring to her hand did not occur to him for long, and occurred only at first to be rejected as a piece of presumptuous folly. Many months of further intercourse, and many more solitary evenings were required before he found in himself the courage to put his case before the Pope. He had expected either Yes or No; and now, instead of getting either, there was a new problem to face.

'*I* a priest!' This one idea absorbed his mind, pushing the thought of his marriage entirely into the background. Why, after all, did the idea terrify him so? The various priests he had known had not, either by the exaltation of their ideas or their mode of life, impressed him as presenting something unattainable in the matter of Christian perfection. What they did, would he not be able to do it too? Whence, then, this feeling of unworthiness which seemed to bow him to the ground? Even the story he had heard that afternoon was not calculated to exalt the thought of priesthood in his mind, and yet Father Nikodem undoubtedly was counted among the more conscientious of his class.

What they did,—yes, but would he be content to do as they did? It was there that the difficulty lay. Strange that there should be such a difference between his manner of viewing priesthood as exercised by others, and of this same priesthood when contemplating the possibility of taking its duties upon himself. He had even thought himself quite resigned to the low standard prevailing, until called upon to make that standard his own. Together with the mass of his co-religionists, he had grown up used to see the priests of his church live the commonplace lives of other people, to be priests only within the walls of their church, to lay aside their sacred character with their vestments, becoming again everyday-men, with the interests, the pleasures, the petty anxieties, and even the vices of everyday-men. Scarcely had such sights offended a soul whom tradition had taught sharply to distinguish between Religion and its official representative—the blessings of the church and the hand that chances to dispense them ; and never for a moment had his childlike faith suffered from the sight of the personal unworthiness of an individual. 'My words, not my deeds !' is the principle of the great mass of Ruthenian priests when exhorting their flocks, and hitherto Gregor had accepted it. How was it then that he now discovered in his heart a quite different ideal of priesthood ? Whence could it have come, since he was certain of never having met its representative in the flesh ? That, indeed, would be as hard to say as it would be to explain how an isolated flower comes to grow in a country where none of its species exist ; how trace the breeze which has carried hither the one frail seed ? Gregor could not know how the thing had come, but only that it was there, and being there it would not let him lightly accept the chance offered him, merely because it was 'the safest thing, on the whole,' nor allow him to recognise the possession of a figure that would do well in a vestment, and a tenor voice which might be useful at High Mass, as valid grounds for taking orders.

All this time, and in the midst of his doubts, there

was slowly growing up in him a hot, hungry desire
for the thing which he yet did not dare to grasp at.
When he looked round him again the stars seemed
to him to be shining brighter, and the common to
have grown as large as the plain. The lights, both in
the priest's and in the Jew's house, had disappeared ;
and only the voice of the bereaved cow broke the
silence of the sleeping village.

Was it not possible that the Pope had been inspired
by Heaven to make him this offer ? It sounded too
marvellous to come from a mere earthly source. But
was it quite certain that he actually meant it ? Father
Nikodem was fond of jokes—was he not only amusing himself at the naïve young man's expense ? An
ugly shadow crossed Gregor's fair face. The instinctive spirit of distrust, which is the bane of the
Ruthenian peasant, was at work within him, for it
was not yet two generations since his ancestors had
walked behind the plough, and peasant instincts are
as hard to kill as the thistles in their own fields.
Centuries of oppression, of being overreached and
played upon at every turn, have made of the Ruthenian
peasant the most mistrustful of human beings, not
only towards his oppressor the Pole, but even towards
his own kind. In Gregor this national vice—for it
deserves this qualification — was counteracted by
other qualities, in especial by his own innate candour,
which now came to his aid, dispersing the suggestion
of false play, clearing the cloud from his forehead,
and leaving the flood of exultation, that was gaining
on him, free to rise.

'I a priest!' But he said it already in an accent of hope. He was beginning to discover within himself all sorts of reasons why this thing should be possible. His first conscious desire had been to be a doctor; and now, if he would, he might be a doctor of souls, and dispense heavenly medicine! Now, also, he began to understand why his school work had taken such immediate possession of him; there also his mission had been to guide, to support, to plant good seed in ready ground—and this mission, how much greater?

His eyes sought the star-spangled sky exultingly, but immediately dropped, once more his head sank upon his breast. The feeling of his unworthiness was upon him again, heavier than ever.

'A priest of the God who built those mountains!' he groaned aloud. 'A priest of the God who lit those stars! Oh, never! It can never be!' And a desire to make himself smaller still, to prostrate himself on the earth and press his face into the grass, came over him almost irresistibly. It was as though the whole firmament and all its wonders were weighing him down to the ground.

He had sat for long when something soft pushed his shoulder, and he heard a breath drawn in his very ear. Then he turned with a start, to become aware of one of the hobbled horses curiously sniffing him. He discovered now that he was shivering, and that out in the plain the mists were beginning to rise. He had come to no conclusion, and yet it was clear that he had sat here long enough, for the nights were

C

still cool at this season. Tired out with the useless debate, he rose and resumed his way. He had
reached the other side of the common, and was
about to plunge into the dark lane, when a sound,
which was something between a groan and a snore,
startled him by its vicinity. Bending down he saw
a dark mass on the ground, lying in the shadow of
the paling, and at the same time became aware of an
unpleasantly strong smell of *wódki*. When his eyes
had got accustomed to the light he saw that a woman
was sleeping there, evidently dead-drunk. Another
moment and he had recognised her,—it was Marka
Ritzko, a well-known incorrigible drunkard, who
carried all her earnings to the Jewish tavern. The
natural thing seemed to be to awaken her, but all
the vigour at Gregor's command succeeded only in
shaking a few inarticulate sounds out of her. He
was about to turn away in disgust, when a small,
bare foot, sticking almost straight into the air,
attracted his attention. That foot could not belong
to Marka; it proved to belong to her two-year-old
son, who was sleeping beside her, in imminent danger
of being suffocated by his insensible mother. Gregor
knelt down quickly, and deftly extricating the child
from its mother's drunken embrace, lifted it in his
arms. The boy's head was thrown back, and from
his half-open mouth the same overpowering smell of
wódki, which had made Gregor almost sick in the
moment of bending down, met him again. With a
mixture of horror and pity he recognised that the
child was as drunk as the mother. Gathering it

carefully in his arms he entered the lane, and, as he felt his way along in the dark, it seemed to him that out of the night some words were being spoken in his ear—

'It is not my Father's will that one of these little ones should be lost.'

Through the shadows he peered at the face of the poor little outcast which lay upturned upon his arm, and a new flood of warmth rose deliciously in his heart. The shepherd who had left his ninety-nine sheep to find the one that was lost, must he not have known this same joy as he carried it back over the hills?

Arrived at home, and having managed with one hand to kindle a light, he laid the insensible child in his own bed, then stretching himself on the bench, exhausted both physically and mentally, fell into a deep sleep. When he awoke in broad daylight he could not at once explain this new feeling of contentment and joy which pervaded him. It was only when his eyes fell on the child, sitting up in the bed and playing with his Sunday cravat, that the details of yesterday came back to him.

'Worthy I am not,' he mused; 'but who is worthy? Was Peter worthy when he was told to leave his fishing-nets and to come? Did he not afterwards prove himself to be a coward? And yet God, who knew the bottom of this weakness, made him into the first of His apostles. Does He not take His instruments where He chooses?'

The school hours seemed very long that day, and

scarcely were they over when Gregor, just as he was, and without making the careful toilet of yesterday, almost ran across the common, and straight into the room where he knew that he would be most likely to find the Pope alone.

Father Nikodem's round eyes grew rounder still at his visitor's unannounced and somewhat impetuous entrance.

'Anything wrong at the school, Gregor Petrow?' he began, and then, after a good look at his face—

'Oh, I see; so you haven't taken a week about it after all?'

'No, Father Nikodem. I have come to tell you that I accept your offer, and am more grateful for your generosity than I can say!'

'Indeed! Why, *this* is quite a different tune from yesterday. What has brought you round so quickly?'

'It has just come to me.'

'That's right, my son! You've got more sense in you than I dared to hope for. Make your preparations so as to be ready for the term; mind you pass your examinations, and then come back and be welcome to take your choice among my daughters —there will be three of them to choose from by that time, you know,' and the Pope laughed rather knowingly.

'I shall do everything I can to requite your magnanimity,' said Gregor, with a fervour which rather disconcerted the Pope.

'Well, well: but mind, not a word to Zenia. The

arrangement remains between you and me. No
love-making in advance! There is no use in turning her head now—time enough for that when the
examinations are safely passed. Do you promise
me that?'

Gregor promised readily, and almost without a
pang. From an end Zenia had all at once become
only a means to an end.

'That was a good idea,' said the Pope to himself,
left alone once more, and thoughtfully stroking his
comfortable double chin. 'It is quite as likely as
not that before the time is over she may have picked
up another husband for herself, which she might not
do if she felt herself bound. But my money won't
be wasted on that account, since he'll do just as well
for one of the younger girls.'

For Father Nikodem was a practical man, and
had long since recognised that Gregor was worth
securing as a son-in-law.

CHAPTER V

THERE is a street in Lemberg winding up in easy curves from the centre of the town, and in which a long white building, flanked on one side by a weather-beaten church, on the other by a stretch of high garden wall, forms the chief feature. From out of the church, as well as from behind a long row of windows, there are, at certain hours of the day, to be heard the sound of many voices chanting in unison—men's voices and young voices, as not even the thickness of the walls can conceal. Those who lodge in the neighbourhood, inasmuch as they have ears for music, are people to be envied, for whoever leads that invisible choir understands his business, and the innate musical genius of his nation bends his pupils to his will. In summer more especially, when the many windows stand open, even the passers-by are apt to slacken their pace at this point; amid the glare of pavement and sunlit wall, and high above the rattle of passing vehicles, there are snatches of song to be heard which rejoice the town-weary heart, and make it dream itself far away in the shadow of some sacred grove or at the door of some rustic church! But it is at evening, when traffic is over in this fortunately not much frequented street, that the best moments come. Then the possessors of balconies take place therein as though they were settling themselves in a theatre box. And though these informal concerts are almost invariably religious in character, they are not for that monotonous, since the splendours of an *Alleluia* or a *Gloria* are continually varied by the sombreness of a *Miserere* or the poignancy of a *Stabat Mater*. To listen to the voices of these unseen singers, so young, so clear, so vigorous, and yet all pierced by that supreme note of pain which seems inseparable from the musical Ruthenian, is to come to believe that you are listening to a choir—if not of angels, at least of youthful saints. It would keep the illusion better if they never left their walls; but the sight of all these robust, and anything but æsthetic-looking youths, streaming out at given hours, on their way to the theological lectures at the university, and evidently finding some difficulty in giving to their general demeanour the soberness demanded by their clerical attire, is apt to quite destroy that vision of singing angels. No trace on the majority of these dark or fair faces, with eyes that will roam in spite of themselves, of that 'divine despair' which the voices seem to betray, and which, far more generally than not, lies in some mere quality of tone. Their tall hats and long black sashes notwithstanding, these young candidates of the priesthood look, generally speaking, remarkably like other young men.

But not all. Sometimes, though rarely, the visible individual answers to the picture that has been made of the invisible one ; and whoever had met a certain fair-haired seminarist, at that time to be seen in the streets of Lemberg, whose wide-open blue eyes seemed to look at things without seeing them, would have suffered no disappointment of his ideals.

Gregor had reached his fourth year of studies without having quite lost that sense of rapturous astonishment with which he had first received the proposition made to him by Zenia's father. He was passing through what would probably be the happiest period of his life. Not that he found his surroundings as congenial to him as might reasonably have been expected, but that early isolation had given him the faculty of making to himself a world apart. At first, indeed, he had naïvely attempted to share some of his thoughts with other minds, and had allowed a little of the eagerness which filled him to overflow, but he was too sensitive not quickly to comprehend where sympathy failed, and finding his timid remarks, concerning the exaltation of their common vacation, received either with polite indifference or else with barely veiled amusement, he had withdrawn within himself and henceforward lived there contentedly, almost forgetting that he had companions. A very brief trial had sufficed to convince him that he could have nothing in common with men who regarded the priesthood they aspired to as a good appointment and nothing more, who shirked what they could of its obligations, were not unwilling to exchange glances with the young ladies who on the summer evenings sat on their balconies, who bribed the porters to smuggle in wine and cold pasties, and of whom many kept *taroc* cards hidden under their mattresses, and played half the nights, with a sentinel at the door ready to warn them of approaching danger. If there were congenial spirits among his companions, both his natural diffidence and his inherent mistrustfulness prevented him discovering them. Having been disappointed in his first attempts, he somewhat too abruptly lost hope.

'You make a mistake, my son,' one of his superiors said to him on more than one occasion. Father Spiridion was a keen-eyed old priest, who, being the leader of the choir, not unnaturally took an interest in the possessor of the best tenor voice under his guidance, and observed him more than he would under other circumstances have done. 'To live alone is not good for any soul. To speak too little is sometimes to think too much, and these solitary thoughts are not always as full of charity as they should be. There is much zeal in your isolation, but there is also pride—spiritual pride, which is the most ensnaring of all, for you are apt to believe evil too readily. It is good to hold your vocation high, but beware lest this very upholding should not be the ruin of your humility, and of your charity too. I find in you many qualities, but the quality of mercy I do not find as much developed as I love to see it. Doubtless you have many frivolous companions, but you have also some earnest ones ; you do not find them out because you look upon all alike with suspicion.'

But Gregor's individuality proved stronger than these wise words, and he went on living alone as before. The access to many things hitherto unattainable—for instance, to books and to music—entirely sufficed for his happiness ; and the thought of opportunities never again to be enjoyed kept him from wasting even one hour of these precious four years. Never did he lose the consciousness that he was preparing for battle, and that the better he armed himself the better would he be able to fight that fight to which he was determined to consecrate all his energies. On the whole, he was the quietest and least noticed of all the seminarists, only on one or two occasions being roused out of his serene isolation by some rough mental contact, and flaring out into almost passionate protestation. Thus any too broad compliment paid to him on his voice was apt to irritate his sense of the fitness of things.

'If I had a voice like that, it is the stage I would go in for, and not the church,' a merry-eyed seminarist once said to him laughingly. 'We can do with less than that for High Mass, but you would make a glorious *Trovatore*.'

'That is just what Panna Halka was saying,' put in a stander-by, 'when she inquired who it was that sung the solo in the *Agnus Dei* we were practising last week.'

Gregor reddened angrily. 'If my voice is good

enough for the theatre, that does not mean that it is too good for the church, does it?' he asked, with unwonted sharpness. 'What is it to any man or woman how I use it?'

Another time it was some talk about his hands, which have already been mentioned as white and narrow as those of a woman, which put him into one of his rare rages.

Those who were getting near the end of their term had been going through the practice of various priestly functions, amongst others that of dispensing the blessing to the congregation, and among all the hands raised in this species of rehearsal—plump and lean, robust and frail, those of Gregor were undoubtedly the ones most likely to meet the approval of a sculptor.

'How is it that hands and hands can be so different?' sighed a certain youthful possessor of a pair of regular bear's paws; 'mine might be boiled beetroots, while yours are living ivory. What hands to give the blessing with! If I were a woman, it would give me distractions during Mass. Anyway, you can count on a large female congregation,' and he sighed enviously.

Gregor looked at him for a moment, silent with indignation, then he burst out.—Was this Pawel Prokup, a future priest, who spoke thus of hands? Had not God made all hands, and could white hands be more pleasing to Him than red ones? Was not the whiteness of the heart, wherewith the blessing was given, the only thing to be considered; and must

everything, everything be viewed from the earthly
point of view, and turned into a snare for the eyes,
and a pitfall for the soul ?   These and several other
things he said, and perhaps would have said more,
but, looking round with glittering eyes, he read
astonishment on every face, and remembered that
they could not understand him.

During all this time he had not again seen Zenobia,
nor any one of the family except Father Nikodem,
whom ecclesiastical business had once or twice
brought to Lemberg, and who never failed to present
his portly person and cheerful countenance at the
seminary.

'That's right, my son,' he would say, with one
of those pats on the back which were apt to make
Gregor's teeth rattle, 'nothing but good accounts of
you ; we'll make a famous Pope of you yet !'

It was probably also to keep in touch with this
promising son-in-law that the Pope pressed him more
than once to spend his vacation at Hlobaki; but
Gregor, who had no money for the journey, and was
ashamed to ask for more help, made vague promises,
and ended by spending his vacation-time almost
alone at the seminary, wandering contentedly under
the big trees of the garden, and more at ease than
when sharing its cool alleys with uncongenial companions.

In this way four years passed without another
meeting, and without Gregor feeling the urgent need
of one, for his priesthood engrossed his thoughts far
more than did his marriage.   When he thought of

Zenobia it was chiefly with a feeling of gratitude that through her he was going to be spared all that unavoidable exercising of mind over the future which seemed to absorb so much of the mental energy of his companions. His matrimonial programme being thus mercifully fixed, he could spare his thoughts for higher objects.

How deeply occupied his fellow-students were with exactly the matrimonial part of the arrangement, was proved to him in more than one way, but more especially by the existence of a volume which went by the name of the 'matrimonial album,' but which showed many of the characteristics of a catalogue, containing as it did a collection of photographs—procured in all sorts of official and unofficial ways—of all the marriageable priests' daughters in the east of Galicia, for it is an exception when the candidate for orders takes to himself a secular wife. Below the photographs the names of the originals were neatly inscribed in round-hand, and not only the names, but the ages, probable marriage portions, and any salient detail regarding the family, which might influence a possible choice. Thus Sidonia Burlewicz would be described as aged nineteen, worth two thousand florins, and possessing six feather pillows,—musical, lively, but with the counterpoise of a mother who was known to drink; while Rosa Beleps had more money, more pillows, and perfectly unobjectionable parents, but also more years behind her, as the photograph alone, without the help of the baptismal register, was able to testify.

Over this album many warm discussions were wont to take place, more especially on Sunday evenings when the services were all over. But, seeing that it was worldly prudence and not sentiment that guided them, these debates seldom grew more than just warm, and occasionally jocular. Since marriage has to precede ordination it was naturally wiser to have one's plans fixed before the end of one's term. Indeed it often proved necessary to fix them far earlier than that; for the seminarist who finds himself at the end of his means, has frequently no resource but to engage himself to a priest's daughter, and finish his studies at the expense of his future father-in-law, just as Gregor was doing. At the beginning of each new term a certain number would come back from their vacations irrevocably betrothed, upon which a corresponding number of photographs would be removed from the album, as being 'off the lists.' Collisions were rare, a long-established custom having left the decision in these matters to a friendly understanding.

'I will take Leona Chrotofis,' one of the seniors would say. 'She gets a thousand florins less than Marya Markew, but she has a good face. I leave Marya to you, Franek, if you fancy her.'

'Thank you,' laughed Franek, 'I prefer the little Stepanski girl. Let me see—how do matters stand there? Five sisters, ah mercy! and the mother died of consumption—no, that won't do. I think I shall try for one of the Bordewicz girls.'

'The Bordewicz girls are put off the list,' said

another, 'you know, since the eldest sister eloped
with Paskew.'

'That's a pity!' sighed several voices, for the
Bordewicz girls were good-looking; but nevertheless
it would not occur to any one present to go to that
house with matrimonial intentions, for these young
men, though not necessarily saints themselves, are
strict moralists when it came to choosing a wife.
The game has its rules as well as any other, and
to visit a tabooed house is considered as unfair a
move as to cross each other's plans by wooing
the wife whom common consent has allotted to
another.

Gregor, who was understood to be disposed of
otherwise, had never hitherto been drawn into the
discussion. The arrangement, though supposed to
rest between him and Father Nikodem, had not failed
to leak out, and had caused Zenobia's photograph to
be kept out of the album. Accordingly, one Sunday
evening in the spring of his last year, he was not
a little surprised, while passing through the large
recreation hall, to hear the remark—

'Why, that is Petrow's one, surely! Who put her
in here?'

Hearing his name he stood still for a moment.

'Look here, Petrow, is it not the Mostewicz girl
who is to be your wife?'

With a certain feeling of curiosity Gregor approached the table. If Zenobia's photograph was
there he would certainly remove it; that was not its
place. The album lay open on the table and a finger

pointed to a freshly-inserted photograph. It was the portrait of a very young girl, whose eyes and lips were laughing straight out of the picture, and with a white rose shining like a star in the black cloud of her hair; her dress was cut out at the neck and a second rose nestled among the lace that touched the skin. In face and expression nothing more unlike Zenobia could be conceived.

'No, that is not her,' said Gregor, after a moment.

'Then who has put a wrong name? Where is Barnuk? It is he who keeps the album.'

'The name is not wrong,' said Barnuk, stepping up. 'It is the elder Mostewicz girl whom Petrow is to marry, and this is the younger one, Wasylya Mostewicz.'

'Wasylya?' said Gregor. 'But that cannot be—she is a child.'

'She was a child once upon a time, no doubt. When did you see her last?'

Gregor thought for a moment. 'To be sure—that was four years ago.'

'There you are! No wonder you did not recognise her.'

'No, I did not recognise her,' said Gregor, looking with more attention at the photograph.

'So this one is still free?' asked some one.

'So it seems. I wonder if she really is as pretty as that?'

'I'm not sure that I should risk it,' said another critically. 'I've often remarked that it's a particular sort of girl that is so apt to stick flowers in her hair.'

'Oh, you know all about it, of course,' laughed a chorus of voices, and Gregor, finding that the conversation was turning a way that was not congenial to him, glided out of the group and went back to his room.

CHAPTER VI

THE sun was pouring down upon the maize-fields, causing the yellow grain to swell hourly, and laying a thicker coating of gold upon the pumpkins that crawled about their feet, when Gregor again saw Hlobaki. Except that here and there some hut had got a new roof and some piece of paling been freshly plaited, four years had not changed much about the village, but the man who came back to it was not quite the same that had left. Successful studies had given him a new confidence in his own powers and done much to wipe away that diffidence which had clung to him since boyhood. He had found his place in the world, and the consciousness of this altered his appearance incredibly. Despite the many hours spent over books, he held himself straighter than he had done four years ago, there was no more doubt in his clear eyes, no more hesitation in his speech; he had even gained enough flesh to save him from the epithet of 'lanky'—formerly applied to him not infrequently—and this was not astonishing, seeing that for the first time in his life he had had enough to eat. The long robe of the

seminarist sat well upon his youthful figure, and on
the serious young face the dignity of priesthood
seemed already to have set its stamp. The examination had been passed not only satisfactorily but
brilliantly, and with buoyant heart he came to claim
the bride who was to make it possible for him to
receive orders. Once outside the seminary his
thoughts had turned with a sort of rebound towards
Zenia, as towards the woman who was to be his companion in his new life, and with whom he longed to
share his hopes and aspirations. Now only he felt
free to dwell on what would doubtless be the
amenities of his future. He did not come straight
from Lemberg, for his uncle, suddenly remembering
the existence of a nephew who promised to be a
credit to the family, and whom, moreover, he was
going to be successfully rid of for ever, had actually
waylaid him on the journey and insisted on a few
weeks of his company. Since the ordination would
not take place until November, Gregor had resigned
himself to paying what he considered to be a debt
to family feeling, but it was only when his face was
turned towards Hlobaki that he began to feel on the
right road.

As, somewhat stiff from the long drive, he clam-
bered out of the cart which had brought him from
the station, he almost fell into Father Nikodem's
arms.

'At last, my son, at last! You've kept us hanging on long enough; there have been impatient
people here, I can tell you! You'll find one of them

on the verandah up there! But let's have a look at you; you've made another stride since I saw you last!'

The Pope himself was much the same in appearance as on the day when he had propounded his plan to Gregor, except that the double chin had grown almost triple, and that in his pepper-and-salt hair there was now more salt than pepper.

On the little wooden verandah which jutted out among the lilac-trees, and was now almost smothered by four years' additional growth, the female part of the family was already assembled. As Gregor ascended the well-known creaking steps—which creaked far worse than he remembered—it seemed to him that it was quite full of women; but in reality there were only four of them. Before he had begun to distinguish between them he found himself enclosed in a pair of arms whose angles he could feel right through the cloth of his coat, while the quality of the kiss which the Popadia applied to his forehead was enough to show him that he was already regarded as a son. Then he felt himself handed over to the next person, who, however, did not embrace him, but held out her hand, murmuring something. Was this Zenobia? The green twilight, which reigned on the verandah even at midday, made it necessary to look twice; yes, he supposed it was Zenobia, though he had never before noted this likeness to her mother; and she looked tired, too, despite the unwonted brightness of her eyes; perhaps these four years had appeared longer to her than to him—the thought crossed his mind while he instinctively raised her hand to his lips.

The next in the row was a half-grown girl, sallow and dark.

'Wasylya?' said he inquiringly, but at the same moment he remembered the photograph in the album and got confused. There was an audible titter behind him; he turned that way, and straightway met that same pair of laughing eyes he had failed to recognise at the seminary, but which were now regarding him with undisguised curiosity, as well as evident approval. It seemed to him that he had been aware of these eyes, even while mounting the steps, and that they had followed him while he made his round of greetings.

'I'm not Zenia and I'm not Paraska, so who can I be?' said the owner of these eyes, with a smile that was ravishingly impertinent.

'Wasylya?' he said again in increased wonder; while a vision of the short-frocked tomboy, whom he had last seen chasing pigs, flitted across his remembrance.

'How clever he is!' she laughed. 'That's what they make of people at Lemberg!'

'You are quite different,' murmured Gregor.

'So are you,' she said shortly, and then with demure lips but a spark of mischief in the extreme corners of her black eyes, 'I'm quite old enough to have my hand kissed, Gregor Petrow.'

Every one laughed at what was evidently considered an excellent joke.

'I beg your pardon,' murmured Gregor in confusion. He felt extraordinarily hot as he carried the
small, plump hand to his lips, no doubt because he
was ashamed of his own remissness.

In the dining-room, to which the Popadia now led
the way, there was spread a meal whose ampleness
testified to the solemnity of the occasion. Besides
the national beetroot soup, there were *pirogi* (a sort
of small dumplings) which absolutely swam in butter,
and the most artistic sour cream dumplings which
the Popadia had ever fabricated; there were also
some of her famous maize-fattened ducks and a
bottle of that sacred *hydromel* (a sweet drink in
which honey is the chief ingredient), which never
appeared except on some family feast. And that
this was considered to be a family feast was made
evident by everybody being in their best clothes,
even the Popadia, whom Gregor had hitherto known
chiefly in a dressing-jacket, and with fingers generally stained with the juice of some fruit she was
preserving, and who looked almost like a stranger
in a stiff, silk gown, recently dyed corn-blue. And
there were other symptoms as well—to wit, the
significant turn given to the conversation, and the
place ostentatiously assigned to him, by Zenobia's
side. Evidently the Pope had not succeeded in
keeping the secret entirely between himself and
Gregor. Here, out of the green twilight, and in full
face of the window, he could see her better than on
the verandah. No, really she was not as much
changed as he had supposed at first sight; probably

it was only the vicinity of her younger sister which was unfavourable to her. She had always looked more than her age, and beside Wasylya's fuller and fresher face which, with its dazzling teeth, bright cheeks, and impertinently square little nose, might have stood for the very link between childhood and youth, Zenobia's pale, dark face became almost elderly. Although both sisters were brunettes, they belonged to quite different types; the one undoubtedly handsome in a sombre, somewhat heavy style, the other all movement, and light, and colour —especially colour: for in the contrast between her black eyes and white teeth, between the pink and creamy tints of her brilliant complexion lay Wasylya's chief charm. She was like a spot of light against the darkness and pallor of the rest of the family. The difference between the two sisters appeared even in the quality of skin and hair; for whereas Zenobia's somewhat opaque skin rarely showed a change, every wave of blood could be noted on Wasylya's transparent face, and while Zenobia's black hair lay in smooth, massive coils about her head, that of Wasylya clouded around her temples, as light and fluffy as black floss silk fresh from the comb.

It was Wasylya who talked most during the family meal, and asked most questions about his stay at Lemberg, even though she had to lean across Zenobia to do so.

A bowl piled with young maize-heads, boiled to the point of perfection, had been placed on the

table amid signs of universal approval, for whoever
has not tasted hot maize with fresh butter has
missed one of the good things of the earth.

'It must have been ever so jolly at Lemberg,'
Wasylya remarked, while tearing away with her
small teeth at the soft, milky maize. 'Do you
know that I felt almost inclined to visit you?—Not
on your account, you know,' with a provoking glance,
'but just to see a real town. Now, do tell me all
you know about it.'

'I know very little of what is outside the seminary.'

'But surely you were at the circus? I know there
was a splendid circus there this summer, because
Hypolit Jarewicz told me all about the horse that
fired a pistol.'

'And the poodle that played ball,' put in the
sallow Paraska, who was a plain likeness of what
Wasylya had been four years ago.

'Oh yes, and I have been waiting to ask you
whether he knocked the ball with his head or with
his paw; that's another reason why I've been so
impatient for your coming.'

'But I did not go to the circus.'

'That deserves a shaking!' remarked the Pope.
'Such a chance of having a good laugh is almost
sinful to waste.'

'Gregor Petrow is too wise a man to spend his
money on empty pleasures,' said the Popadia, with a
reproving glance at her husband and an approving
one at Gregor.

Zenobia alone made no remark and asked no

questions; but if Gregor had been less occupied with answering those of Wasylya, he might have observed that from under their heavy lids her dark eyes strayed often to his face and dwelt there for moments at a time with a deep-felt joy that was unmistakable.

After the maize-heads had been thoroughly done justice to, for rustic appetites are proof against many emotions, there was an adjournment next door, where the same red rep chairs stood in the same place that Gregor remembered them in four years ago—only that they were not red any longer, but faded to a sort of ghastly orange,—and where the blistered old piano was covered with jam-pots, exactly as it had always been. It was towards the piano that Wasylya went straight on entering. She had insisted on having some lessons—principally because the daughters of a Pope of their acquaintance, who served as models of fashion for the ecclesiastical circle of these parts, had learnt music—and was evidently burning to show off her accomplishments.

'Papa says that you sing beautifully,' she said, pushing aside enough pots to make room to open the lid. 'And I have been so curious to hear you. There you have another reason for my wanting you to come!' and she looked at him again with her deliciously impertinent smile. 'Please sing me something!'

'I cannot accompany myself,' said Gregor, looking rather doubtfully at the instrument whose tone he knew of old.

'But perhaps I can ; you know I have had lessons.
But dear me, perhaps you only sing sacred things !'
and she made a little grimace of mock distress, at
which the family again laughed. Wasylya's little
jokes were evidently very popular.

'I sing other things too ; but really to-day I am
so little prepared—and all that dust on the journey——'

'Oh, that's what people always begin by saying !
It's either the dust, or the heat, or they are not in
good voice, or something—I can't imagine why ; I
always begin at once. Look here, I'll give you
courage by going first !' And, striking a rather
uncertain chord, she broke into the sportive tones of
a *Krakowiak*.

Her voice, though thin and childish, was clear and
true, and the gay verses were sung with so much
verve, and the naïve delight in her own performance
was so evident, that Gregor found it quite possible
to condone the faulty accompaniment. As for the
family, they were evidently in ecstasies.

'A perfect little nightingale we've been training
while you were away, haven't we ?' said the Pope,
enchanted at the success of the pet daughter, in
whom he loved to recognise his own high spirits.
Paraska clapped her hands, and the mother made a
set speech of approval. Only Zenobia said nothing,
which struck Gregor as a want of sisterly affection.

'Now it's your turn,' said Wasylya, when she
had drunk in the applause ; but though she said
'Now it's your turn,' she was looking for another

song already, and upon that there followed another and yet another, all of the gay and playful order.

'But I can sing serious things too,' she assured him, flushed with her own success, and, composing her face, she began once more.

This was a song which Gregor knew, the song of the 'Black Eyes,' well known in the country, and set to one of those heartrending popular airs which seem to embody within themselves the sadness of whole generations. To hear the sweet, monotonous plaint falling from lips which seemed intended only to smile, gave Gregor a curiously painful impression. And how readily came the words of a passion which to her surely must be dark as yet, and how the flame in the eyes responded to the sombre, vehement words!—

> ' I walk on the earth,
>   I sail on the water,
> But whether sunshine glitters,
> Whether thunder groans and lightnings flash
> Whether the stars burn in the sky,
> Whether day, whether night surrounds me,
> Whether in the dark, whether in the light.
> Always with me and before me
> Those black eyes shine.

> ' I drink honey and I drink gall,
>   I gather thorns and lilies.
> The honey I press from the wax, but in its taste
> I find neither happiness nor peace.
> Although around me lies the desolate night,
> Although I kiss the holy relics in church,
> Always on my mouth do I feel
> Another coral-red mouth.

' It is because that wicked witch
    The world has bewitched with her face—
With her face and with her black eyes—
The curse God himself cannot take from her.
Everything, everything is transformed into her,
Whichever way I turn she is there.
The man on whom the curse has fallen
Must possess her or must die ! '

When at length Wasylya remembered that it was
for Gregor the piano had been opened, she found
him standing almost in front of her, leaning with his
elbow among the jam-pots.

' Now, something sacred after all this frivolity ! '
she laughed—she had been laughing almost before
the last despairing word had passed her lips.

' Not to-day,' he said brusquely ; ' I am not in the
right disposition to-day.'

' Not feeling holy enough?   How queer !   It isn't
my songs that have demoralised you, I hope?   You
can't imagine how holy you look in that long coat—
that sash alone is tremendously imposing.   May I
look at it nearer ? '   And without waiting for a reply
she took up the end of the long black silk sash that
Gregor, as seminarist, wore round his waist, and
examined its fringe attentively, with a just perceptible
twitch at the corners of her swelling lips.   As she
dropped it she looked up straight into his face.

' A red sash must be prettier, such as they wear in
the Latin seminary—but those are not allowed to
marry.   Aren't you glad that your sash is not red?
Because then, you know, you couldn't marry Zenia.'

Before Gregor could answer, the Popadia's voice

was heard calling Wasylya. In sudden embarrassment he began putting together the music that lay
strewed over the piano, and even on the top of the
jam-pots. He was aware of movements behind him,
and heard the door open and shut. When he looked
round again he saw that he was alone with Zenobia,
and immediately understood the purpose of this.
The little manœuvre had been too childishly transparent to be mistaken. Doubtless the Pope had
thought it time that he and Zenobia should come to
an explanation. And really it was time—it was
even strange that this idea had not occurred to
himself. Zenobia was the cause of his being here,
and yet he was conscious of having thought very
little of Zenobia during the last hour. He must
make that good now.

She was sitting on the only sofa of the room, beside the show-table, on which all the crotchet covers
and wool-work mats, which represented the feast-day
gifts of the last decade, were crowded together; and
all the outward composure of her demeanour could
not conceal that she was nervous. There was plenty
of room on the sofa, and Gregor, as he went resolutely
towards her, meant to make the bold move of sitting
down by her side, but when he got close he took his
place on one of the rep chairs instead.

'It is a long time since I went away,' he began,
quite at random, and thinking to himself how absolutely commonplace his remark sounded.

'Has it really seemed to you long?' asked Zenobia,
raising her eyes for a moment from the crotchet cover

with which her slender brown fingers were nervously playing, but he was too preoccupied to read the reproach in that glance.

'Of course—that is to say,' he added truthfully, 'these years have been very pleasant, and study makes the time pass quickly. In some ways these four years seem to me like four months only.'

'I can believe that study makes the time pass faster than preserving fruit and feeding the hens,' she said with a touch of bitterness, and then was silent again.

Gregor racked his brain. He had known that this moment would come; even this morning he had asked himself hopefully whether it would come to-day; and yet now that it was here he found that he had nothing to say to her. The sensation was so unforeseen as to fill him with alarm. He knew exactly what she expected of him—she and her whole family, but he felt an unaccountable desire to put back the final word for a little longer, to keep his liberty for just a few hours more, and with this desire upon him, plunged recklessly, and much more volubly than usual, into a description of his life at the seminary; giving her the plan of hours in detail, and being very particular about giving them right, and yet all the time listening for sounds in the passage, as though he were expecting something. And he was not conscious of any embarrassment either, but rather of a new sort of excitement, a kind of excitement which he had not known before. He himself was aware of this unwonted exaltation of spirits, and once or twice as he talked put up the back of his hand to feel his hot cheek, wondering what was the matter with him, and whether he had not perhaps drunk too much of the *hydromel* at dinner.

And while he spoke, Zenobia's fingers were pressed convulsively against each other, and her face grew more colourless as she bent her head, listening. When, at the end of half an hour, Paraska burst in to say that they were going to drink coffee in the orchard, they had come to no explanation, and spoken no word which might not have been said before the whole family.

That evening Gregor was alone with the Pope in the room where stood the ink-spotted table, now more spotted than ever.

'Anything to tell me?' said Father Nikodem, with his comfortable smile. 'All square between you and Zenia?'

Gregor felt suddenly guilty. 'I have not spoken to her yet,' he almost stammered. 'It seemed to me so sudden—we have not seen each other for so long——'

Father Nikodem looked at him curiously; possibly he had made his own observations in the course of the afternoon.

'Well, well—take your time, by all means. There is no special hurry. You may be sure of your answer, I think. For a moment I thought that Hypolit Jarewicz was going to cut you out, but it came to nothing, after all.'

Hypolit Jarewicz was the son of the well-to-do

Pope at Lussyatyn, and the brother of the musical sisters whom Wasylya strove to emulate.

'Did he make her an offer?' asked Gregor, with a deepening sense of guilt.

'He would have made her one if she had let him—but he's gone back to his studies, and off the cards for the present. Let's see—this is Monday, is it not? Take till Sunday to renew acquaintance, and after High Mass we'll celebrate the engagement. That will suit, won't it?

'Yes, yes, that will do,' said Gregor, with a sense of respite which was inexplicable to himself; and he listened with a lighter heart as the Pope went on to speak of the steps he had taken to secure for Gregor an appointment in this part of the country, in a parish where, as he said, the fees were all that could be expected for a beginning. Gregor agreed to everything, surprised that the subject did not interest him so intensely as it had hitherto done, and again aware of listening to the sounds in the passage.

During the interval before the marriage he was to remain in the village, lodging in the same hut where he had lodged as schoolmaster, and when after dark he crossed the common, on which he had held his vigil and had found Marka Ritzko lying beside the paling, it seemed to him as though he had never been away. And yet, yes, he had certainly been away, for although everything was the same, everything was also changed. When before had he felt this disturbance in his blood? Had anything but religious emotion ever moved him as he now felt moved? Was it his way to keep the air of a secular song so obstinately in his head, and why did it seem to him that out of the shadows all around eyes were looking at him, and all the eyes were black?'

It was to get away from those eyes that he almost ran home, and yet he found them again in his dreams, and knew all the time that, although Zenobia's eyes too were black, these were not Zenobia's eyes.

* * * * *

Five days more until Sunday—with this thought Gregor awoke next morning. It was natural in the circumstances that the greater part of these five days should be spent in the Pope's house. Very rapidly he resumed his old habits of intimacy. On that second day already the Popadia, dropping all show of ceremony, had gone back to her dressing-jacket and her stained fingers. It was the season for preserving plums, and in her housewifely eyes no number of future sons-in-law were worth missing it ; and there were also the apples to be gathered and garnered and a dozen other things to be seen about, touching winter provisions, of which she always laid in as large a store as though she were preparing for a six months' siege. No wonder that on the poor Popadia's haggard face the wrinkles had a way of deepening at this season. For so great a portion of her life had Justina Mostewicz been forced to pinch, and scrape, and turn over every kreutzer that passed through her meagre hands, that even now, when scraping was no longer a necessity, she remained a slave to the habit. A chronic anxiety had stamped

E

itself upon her brown leather face, and was no more to be eradicated than is the mark of a seal. She had buried as many children as she had reared, and she had loved them too, and yet it was not these losses which formed the tragedy of her existence and had eaten all the buoyancy out of her soul—it was the ever-standing fear of the larder growing empty, of the beans not being gathered at the right moment, nor the cucumbers salted in time.

For years past Zenobia had been her right hand, and despite Gregor's presence, her aid could not be dispensed with now. Since she was going to lose her so soon it was as well to make use of her while she could. Wasylya was at any rate no great help, seeing that she ate as many plums as she stoned, and made herself ill with licking the sugary spoons. Neither could the mother, whose horizon was bounded by the walls of her store-room, see any necessity for that billing and cooing which usually precedes marriage. Wasylya and Paraska must manage to amuse Gregor meanwhile, and to all appearances they succeeded perfectly in this. Whether the time was spent in the orchard gathering apples—for to this extent even the guest was pressed into service—or at the piano trying over songs, Gregor did not seem to find the hours too slow. Once or twice he remembered with a start that this was scarcely the way to renew acquaintance with Zenobia, and half remorsefully he would go in search of her; but usually he found her occupied in tying up jam-pots, and too busy to give him anything but short and hurried answers, which, as the week advanced, grew shorter and more hurried. Indistinctly he became aware that the distance between them was growing greater instead of smaller, and that she had not again looked at him as she had done on that first day when they had been left alone together. They were never alone now, although, despite the jams, nothing could have been easier than to contrive momentary tête-à-têtes, but Gregor was not ingenious at this sort of thing and Zenobia did not contrive. Slowly she was withdrawing from him, and he was too happy to realise what this meant.

For Gregor was happy in those days, those five strange days that were both so long and so short, and the thing he could not understand was that the rapture of his impending priesthood entered in no way into the composition of his happiness. The pale, pure September sky, the voices of the peasants in the fields busy gathering their maize, even the fragrant heaps of apples that lay piled upon the orchard floor seemed to be part of this new happiness. That apple perfume was so powerful that, in the enclosed space, it became almost oppressive ; and to Gregor it seemed to mount to his head, and at moments to cloud his understanding. What he saw and felt and heard in these days seemed to be seen and felt and heard through a golden haze, which made everything appear a little different from what it really was. But it was the figure of Wasylya which gained the most from this golden haze. Without this haze he might have discovered that she seldom talked of anything but herself, and that her chief occupation was the care of her personal appearance, for the most conspicuous thing about this girl was a perfectly naïve vanity and undisguised pleasure in her own person. That she was considered to be the beauty of the family, not only by others but also by herself, was obvious; but this conviction was aired in so frank and inoffensive a manner, that it was as impossible to take umbrage at it as at a bird that prunes its wings in the sunshine, in undisguised delight at the shimmer of its own feathers. When she was surprised before the glass settling a flower in her hair—despite the lateness of the season she was seldom seen without one—she would make no feint of examining the frame or rubbing off the fly-spots, but would turn round with a radiant smile which seemed to say, 'Am I not worth looking at?'

'I can't understand how Zenia can go and stain her fingers with those plums,' she said to Gregor one day, as they were sorting apples in the orchard. 'I wouldn't spoil my hands so for any money,' and, pulling off her glove, she looked approvingly at her white, well-cushioned little hands.

'It's no wonder it's white, with all the stuffs you use,' broke out Paraska, with a younger sister's mockery.

'Do you know that she even puts glycerine on her face—oh, and other things, too—shall I tell about the bread poultice, Wasylya?'

'I will tell him myself!' laughed the other, with

perfect good humour. 'Know, then, I had chapped my skin last winter, and wanted to get it right again quickly, for I can't stand anything wrong with my face, so I put on bread poultices, and that's what that little goose finds so shocking. Perhaps you find it shocking too?'

'Not shocking, but only uncomfortable,' said the somewhat perplexed Gregor.

'Papa says that Wasylya's face is the only toy she has ever played with,' added Paraska.

At which Wasylya laughingly threw an apple at her sister's head, and a friendly pelting began, which effectually changed the subject of the conversation.

CHAPTER VII

'LET'S all go to the maize-field to-day!' was
the proposition which Wasylya made on
Saturday morning to the family in general.

The maize harvest was far advanced. All day
long the people could be seen coming and going
between the fields, and all night long the sound of a
fiddle or a flute was to be heard at some point of the
village, where the maize-heads, gathered by day, were
being peeled in company, and with as much *wódki*
as was necessary to keep the workers awake. Every
night the festive sounds came from another direction,
and any one who had followed them would have found
half the village assembled, according to the neighbourly custom of exchanging services, for which no
other pay is asked than *wódki*, bread, a little music,
and possibly dancing, if the peeling gets finished in
a reasonable time. The season of the *tolókas* was
the most festive season in Hlobaki, varying in festivity
according to the results of the maize harvest. This
year was a particularly good 'maize year'; and all
hands, from those of mere infants to those of totter-
ing grandfathers, were busy plucking the golden
heads. Masters and servants worked side by side

in order to get the treasure stored before the weather
broke. Wasylya's proposition was therefore both
reasonable and seasonable.

'I have to bake the bread for the *toloka*,' said the
Popadia; 'and there are those pears to be dried. I
can't spare Zenia either; but certainly it would be
good if you girls lent a hand—your father can take
you. But mind you do something beyond chattering
and getting into the workmen's way!'

'Oh, we'll gather mountains of maize!' cried
Paraska, clapping her thin hands, 'so as to have
a good *toloka*!'

'And you, what are you going to do?' asked
Wasylya, looking straight at Gregor. 'Would you
rather gather maize or help to dry pears?'

'He had better go to the maize-field, by all means,'
said the Popadia, who had rapidly calculated that
the number of maize-heads gathered by Gregor would
certainly represent a greater value than any service
he could render her with the pears.

'I will go where I am sent,' said Gregor, thankful
to have the question decided for him.

That afternoon, accordingly, the Pope sallied forth,
at the head of his little party of volunteers, and
was received with many profound inclinations and
welcoming grins by the workmen who had been busy
since morning, as was testified by the mounds of
maize-heads that lay piled at different points, ready
to be transferred to the carts. It was Father Nikodem himself who, after a due exchange of jocular
remarks with his parishioners, gave the signal by

divesting himself of his coat, and, in shirt-sleeves, plunging straight into the forest of high green blades, that was topped by a sea of feathery heads swaying gently in the spicy breeze. The two girls followed in high glee, tucking up the corners of the blue linen aprons put on for the occasion, so as to serve in guise of bags. Gregor, left alone, stared stupidly at the Pope's black coat flung upon the grass, and wondered whether he ought to take off his too. He felt suddenly aware that he ought not to be here, that this was not his right place. Having hesitated for a moment longer, he walked on a few paces and entered the maize-field at a different point. Something like a stone had been lying on his heart all day, and that stone was the thought, 'To-morrow I shall be betrothed to Zenobia.'

If he had but eyes to see, there was enough to look at around him, for a maize-field is not a maize-field alone, but gives shelter to a mixed company of products, colonies of hangers-on that live on the bounty of the real lord of the soil. There are the pumpkins, whose golden balls lie everywhere on the path, and whose long, coarse-leaved trails make a network over the floor, and crawl out of the borders on to the very road; there are the beans, which cling round the straight maize stalks, and drape their festoons from one maize-head to the other; there are the humble turnips and the towering hemp, that have been stuck in to fill a vacant corner; and the sunflower, that suddenly confronts you as you wend your way in this miniature forest, whose rust-

ling blades close above your head, and whose broad
leaves and thick stalks bear a character of almost
tropical richness.   Nor is the gaudiness of tropical
flowers wanting, for although those flashes of red
and yellow between the stalks are no more than the
aprons and headcloths of the gathering women, they
might very well pass for the most gorgeous blossoms
that ever festooned an Indian jungle. The voices
of the gatherers and the continual snapping of stalks
made the afternoon alive, while sometimes was heard
another sound, a gentle rush like that of water, when
a fresh apron or sackful was being poured upon one
of the heaps.

Yet of this gay scene Gregor neither saw nor
heard anything. His inner ear was far too occupied
in listening to the lines of the song which had
haunted him all week, and which was beginning to
be his torment—

> 'Always with me and before me
> Those black eyes shine!'

The words were becoming true with a fearful
truth, and nothing, either, had ever been truer than
that, whichever way he turned *she* was there—that
everything, everything was slowly transforming itself
into her. Was it not she who was peeping out at
him from behind each maize stalk? Was it not her
dress that made the dry blades rustle so sharply?
And immediately, like a cold hand laid upon his
beating heart, the thought would come again : 'To-
morrow I am to be betrothed to Zenobia.'

So busy was he watching the phantom Wasylya that he never saw the real one until she was close beside him.

'Is it your nerves that are so bad, or your conscience?' she asked, laughing, as she stepped out on to a comparatively free spot. 'You started just now as though you were a murderer and I a policeman.'

He turned towards her half reluctantly.

'Show me your maize-heads!' she commanded.

'My maize-heads?' He looked rather helplessly about him. 'I believe I have none. I have looked at several stalks, but somehow I can't find them.'

She broke into her clear, rather shrill laugh.

'Perhaps you don't know what a maize-head is like, in its wrappings? Come, I will show you the way to set about it!'

She was standing close before him now, with one hand holding together the corners of her heavily-laden apron. The hat had been long ago discarded as inconvenient, and her bare head showed only a lilac aster nestling a little above the ear, while round her throat there glistened five or six rows of coloured beads, the necklace of one of the workers, which she had gleefully borrowed.

'Look here! The first thing is to keep to one row, and not go wandering about from side to side, and the next thing is to have something to put them into. Ah, here, by good luck, is a masterless sack! There, put it over your shoulder, and now, look at me well and do just as I do. Remember that the more maize we gather the more we shall have to

peel to-night. It is our night for the *toloka*, you
know, and papa has ordered two fiddlers.'

Gregor turned to the stalk beside him, and broke
off a head in mechanical imitation of her movements.

'Why do you say nothing? Do you not love
music, and dancing, and fun generally? If you don't
get another face before the evening I won't sit beside
you at the *toloka*. One has to be in a good humour
for a *toloka*, and to-day you look positively unhappy.'

'How can I look happy to-day when it is the
last?'

He had taken fright almost before he had spoken,
but she was not looking shocked, nor very much
surprised.

'The last day of what?'

'Of liberty,' said Gregor, almost against his will,
and for a moment their eyes rested on each other,
and above their heads they could hear the feathery
tops sigh and whistle in the wind.

It was Wasylya who spoke first, lightly, and yet
watching him keenly through her lashes.

'Ought not last days to be made the most of?
I have heard——'

'You are right!' said Gregor, suddenly throwing
back his head. It had come over him with the
abruptness of a revelation that there were still
several hours of freedom before him; and, with a
rebound, his spirit leapt up from the depth of de-
pression to an unreasonable exultation. Yes, she
was right! These remaining hours were too precious

to be moped away—he would drain their delights to the dregs, beating all thought of the morrow from him.

'Yes, I am fond of music and dancing,' he said, speaking more loudly, and with a broken laugh that did not sound like his own. 'Let us gather so much maize that the *toloka* must last all night! Am I doing it right now?'

'I have told you that you have only to look at me!' said Wasylya, darting back a significant glance over her shoulder, and they moved on side by side, often busy at the same stalk, their fingers sometimes entangled in the fine, silky threads that burst from the wrappings of the maize—as fine and as silky as a woman's hair—while the shadow of the blades rippled over them in broad stripes. Now and then some small incident varied the monotony of the plucking, as when Wasylya stumbled over a huge pumpkin and caught at his arm for support, or when a green lizard ran over her very toes, and Gregor, making a grab at it, inadvertently touched her foot in its little, worn shoe. She pulled it back with a coquettish laugh, and he stood up straight on the instant, but his heart was beating so fast that he fancied it must choke him. And all the time that he wandered with Wasylya, through what he was now able to recognise as an enchanted forest, he talked and talked in a way he had never talked before, of the most insignificant, the most trivial things, and only for the sake of not being silent; for to be silent for a moment was to hear that voice inside him repeating the monotonous phrase: 'To-morrow I am to be betrothed to Zenobia.'

'I am tired!' said Wasylya, as at last, having come to the end of their row, they stepped out on to the neighbouring meadow. A pile had been begun here on the grass, and, opening her apron, she poured her share on to it, and straightway sat down beside it upon the turfy bank.

'After all, one must keep some strength for the peeling too. Do you not agree with me?'

'I agree with everything you say,' said Gregor, in that tone of artificial jocularity which sat so ill upon him.

'Then why do you not sit down too?'

He hesitated for a moment and then sat down at two paces from her.

From between the stalks of maize, and right over the bank on which they sat with their faces to the setting sun, the long, pumpkin trails, with here and there a belated orange-coloured blossom, were crawl-ing in their clumsy fashion. Wasylya leant towards the one beside her and began dragging it up.

'I never can make up my mind whether I like spring or autumn best. In spring there are flowers, but in autumn there is fruit, and though I like pretty things, I like good things too; and then it is generally warmer in autumn, and I love warmth; and there is music in the village and gay faces, and all that I love.'

'Because you love life in general,' said Gregor, watching her operations with the trail.

'I do, and even its noises, and even its fusses and fatigues, if only it keeps moving and makes a sound, and is—well, just *alive*. I am like papa; I think it is wrong to miss an occasion for laughter. People say so many hard things about life, but if only I have enough to eat, and am not too hot and not too cold, and if nothing hurts me anywhere, I am quite content. After all, it is very good to feel as though one could never be ill.'

While she spoke she had pulled up a long trail, and had begun to wind it round her head in the guise of a sort of monstrous wreath. Even the smallest of the leaves half covered her head.

'There, that is as good as a hat!' said Wasylya, as she laughingly passed the rest of the trail round her shoulders and down to her waist. 'It quite keeps the sun out of my eyes.'

Gregor's gaze had not left her yet, though he told himself that it could not be right to look at her as he was doing. Two of the broad pumpkin leaves seemed to spring from her shoulders like a pair of fluttering green wings, another lay upon her breast; he could see it moving, and the flash of the blue and yellow glass beads below it, and he could see other beads as well—the tiny, glistening drops of perspiration which shone upon her temples and upon her neck. As she sat thus before him, wreathed in the trails that made a sort of clumsy imitation of vine leaves, and laughing into his face with unabashed black eyes, he seemed to be looking upon a Bacchante fresh from the feast. and. for a moment. astonishment at himself overcame him. He knew that he had had his ideal of womanhood, and that this was not his ideal; but, through the golden haze which had hung about him all week, he could not recognise any of these things distinctly, and just now he was too busy watching the gleam of white from between her full lips, and wondering what life would be to the man who should feel upon his own mouth that 'second coral-red mouth.' As a child gazes on the ripe fruit that hangs too high for his hand, and in imagination tastes it, so did Gregor look on those tempting lips.

She put up her hand to pluck the faded aster from her hair, for she had found beside her in the grass a bright, blue gentian. He, not knowing what he did, stretched towards her and touched her fingers, tentatively at first, then, finding that they were not withdrawn, his own closed upon them.

'If Zenia saw this?' she said, with lowered eyes but no displeasure on her face.

'I am not betrothed to Zenia!' he said vehemently.

'But you are to be—to-morrow!'

'Yes, to-morrow!' he groaned, letting go her hand.

'Just in time,' she whispered, as at a little distance the Pope appeared, panting under a sackful of maize. 'Don't look so desperate,' she added very low; 'there is still the *toloka*!' And the glance of flame which struck him seemed to run through his blood like hot iron.

CHAPTER VIII

SUPPER was hurried over that evening, on account of the *toloka*, at which Father Nikodem was again to be the chaperon of his two younger daughters. The Popadia declared herself too tired to put in an appearance, and Zenobia, when questioned, answered very decidedly that she preferred going to bed. It was, therefore, the same company who had been to the maize-field who now went across to the barn.

'Hania has asked leave to go too,' said the Popadia to her husband, 'but mind you keep your eye upon her. I know it's only on account of Jurko she goes; so long as they peel maize in company I've no objection, but I fancy they have other objects in view, so if you see one of them disappear, keep your eye on the other; never let them both out of your sight at once. Nothing like a *toloka* for mischief to the girls,' she explained to Gregor. 'When every one is busy, and the corners all dark, nothing is easier than to slip out.'

'I'll look after her,' said the Pope, reassuringly, as they went out.

In the barn a large circle of men and women were

squatting around a small mountain of maize, their
deft fingers unwrapping each separate head from its
delicate, silk-like swaddlings.   Already the floor was
strewn with the sheathes, carpeting it more softly
than the thickest piled carpet could have done,
while head after head, relieved of its disguise, flew
through the air to increase the yellow pile in the
corner. The fiddles had tuned up, and the *wódki*
bottle made its first round.

'That's right, children!' the Pope said heartily, as
he wended his way to the seats of honour reserved
for the family—a couple of packing-cases and an
overturned tub. 'We're going to make the maize
fly, and the *wódki* too'—with a comprehensive wink
to the company. 'I swear not to dance a step of
Kolomeika (the Ruthenian national dance) until the
last head is peeled, and I swear not to breakfast
until I have danced a *Kolomeika*!'

A grin ran round the company, disclosing enough
sets of flashing teeth to make the envy of half the
society ladies in London, then hands as well as
tongues set off moving again.

Gregor found himself placed between Wasylya
and Paraska, on the same packing-case with the
former, but he could not make up his mind whether
to be glad of this vicinity or sorry that he was not
sitting on the other side of the circle, where he could
have let his eyes rest full upon her face. He felt
that to-morrow he could not look at her as he still
dared to look at her to-day, and he wanted not to
waste a minute of these last hours. Almost opposite

F

he could see Hania, the fair-haired, doll-faced, little servant-girl of the house, with her Jurko beside her—both peeling maize so demurely as to make the Popadia's apprehensions appear entirely unfounded.

Again that feeling of astonishment at himself overcame Gregor. It was so unlike what he knew of himself, to be making part of this noisy company, and to be listening to and even enjoying the lively airs that were being scraped out not far from his ear. Quite plainly he could feel how the infection which floated in the heavy and yet intangibly dissipated atmosphere began to gain upon him. It was as though he had discovered within his usually so austere self a second self, to whom all these things were congenial. The lanterns which dangled from the rafters lighted the big barn fitfully, but the very shadows in the corners seemed to add to the mysterious excitement of the scene.

Amid songs and stories and much passing of the *wódki* bottle, the pile of maize in the centre began to diminish in the same proportion as the pile in the corner began to grow. With terror Gregor noted the swelling of the one and the dwindling of the other; this meant that the time was passing—the last precious hours of this precious evening. Of private conversation there had been none between him and Wasylya, nor could there be under the circumstances; but out of every trivial word she spoke, out of each of her glances and her movements, Gregor read the conviction of some secret understanding between them, which existed as surely as though it had been put into words.

It was not very late yet—scarcely eleven—when, looking across by chance, he saw that Hania was gone from her place. The words of the Popadia came back to his mind : 'When every one is busy, and the corners all dark, nothing is easier than to slip out,' and he vaguely wondered whether Jurko would follow soon.

'A mouthful of *wódki*,' the Pope said to him at this moment, reaching him a glass across Paraska's head. 'But you had better take a bite of bread along with it, or you will find the stuff too strong for your head. Here, help yourself!' Gregor took the loaf, cut off a slice, and turned towards Wasylya to ask whether she would have one, and then only he noticed that the place beside him was empty. A minute ago Wasylya had said to him, 'It is suffocating in here, I must manage to get a breath of air,' but he had not then understood. Now he did understand. Having handed back the loaf, he waited until he saw the Pope turn the other way, and, quickly rising, escaped first into the shadows behind him—having now to wade his way through the litter of sheathes which reached half-way to his knees—and from there slipped easily out by the open door.

'Yes, it must have been suffocating in there'; he was aware of it only when he felt the night air upon his face. The moon was just rising above the trees, piercing the old orchard with its first shafts. It was towards the orchard that it seemed inevitable to turn; here, in the open yard, where everything was as clear as day, there was obviously nothing to seek. The first trees stood close beside the barn; the branches of one huge pear-tree even rested upon its roof, and sometimes dropped its fruit into the sky-lights. Gregor traversed the open space quickly, but in the shadow slackened his pace, peering about him with a heart that hammered on his ribs. The leaves on the branches were still thick enough to make a good stand against the moonlight; twice he thought that he had found what he was looking for, but once it was a crooked apple-tree which he had taken for a human figure; and once the whiteness of one of the old gravestones made him think that he saw her light dress. Then something breathed beside him, and he knew that she was there.

All this time he had not stopped to ask himself why he was looking for her, nor what he should do when he found her. The odd sensation he had been aware of lately of not being himself, as if some other force that was not his own will had taken over the government of his actions for the time, came over him again, as he more guessed than saw her beside him. Without a word, and without a thought, he put out his arms and took hold of that which met them. There was a little exclamation, half of fright, half of pain, for he had been more vehement than he knew, but there was no resistance.

'Once, Wasylya—Wasylya, only once!' he said, without knowing that he was speaking, and he felt

for her lips in the shadow. They were upon his
already, those 'coral-red lips' which he had dreamt
of all week in torment of spirit, and whose sweetness
he now drank of with closed eyes and brain that
began to swim.

They had not yet drawn apart when, with a shock
of panic, he felt a heavy hand on his shoulder.

'I've got you, you rogue, have I?' said Father
Nikodem's voice in his ear, 'and Hania, the demure
one too. No, no, my girl, you shall not escape me
so! I've promised the Popadia to bring you to
justice!'

With one hand still on Gregor's shoulder, the Pope
with the other took the girl by the arm and dragged
her out into the moonlight. 'You thought you
would catch me napping, did you? but——'

There he broke off short, for he had seen the face
of his daughter. From her he stared back perplexed at the second prisoner, bending towards him
and peering closely into his face. To Gregor it
seemed that the weight of his shame must press
him straight down into the earth. He could see
how the Pope's round eyes grew rounder and larger,
while the whites gleamed in the moonlight out of
the dark face, almost as though it were the face of a
negro; but at Wasylya he did not dare to look.
Then, just as he felt that he could bear this no
longer, Father Nikodem released him with a shove,
and burst into the most explosive laugh that Gregor
had ever heard from his lips.

'Ah, so that's it, is it? It's come to that, after

all?' he brought out in short sentences, between the fits of suffocating laughter, stamping up and down the while, and bending now to one side and now to the other, as though this were the only means of keeping himself from choking. 'I thought I was after two sparrows, and I've caught two doves, and just at the moment that they were crossing their bills, too! Oh, this beats everything!'

'I am a wretch,' said Gregor desperately. 'Do with me what you like.'

The Pope stood still beside Gregor, with a violent effort controlling his hilarity.

'Why, that is the tragic tone, my son! What is the need for that? I see quite a different way of looking at the matter, don't you, Wasia?' (It was the name by which he usually addressed his favourite daughter.)

Wasylya said nothing, but she crept a little nearer to her father, and half hid her face upon his sleeve. Her shoulders heaved slightly, though it was impossible to say whether she was laughing or crying.

'Are you astonished at my taking the thing so quietly? To be honest with you, I've seen it coming all week, nor could I see any reason why it should not come so. Don't you remember my telling you that when the four years were over you could come back and take your choice? Well, if you want my honest advice, I can only say, "Take the one you like best!"' and he laid his big hand on the dark head.

'But Zenobia?' said Gregor wildly.

'You are not bound to Zenia—unless you have said anything to her.'

'I have said nothing.'

'So much the better. Didn't I tell you from the first that the arrangement was only for us two?'

'But every one seems to think—it has been so understood; she herself——'

'Don't trouble your head about what has been understood; and don't imagine that Zenia will go a-begging for a husband because of your failing her. I'm ready to lay you a bet that she'll end by taking Hypolit Jarewicz.'

'If I knew it was right,' said Gregor, grasping at his head.

'If you think it is right to marry one sister after kissing the other one in the dark, then stick to your duty, by all means!' said the Pope, a trifle impatiently. 'But have you asked yourself what is to be said of Wasia, supposing it is not I alone who have seen you both in the orchard?'

Just then Wasylya softly lifted her head from her father's arm and gave Gregor one look—a look so full of reproach that he could not misread it even by moonlight, and with that same flame in it which had set his blood on fire that afternoon by the maize-field.

'What do you say?' asked Father Nikodem, looking from one face to the other. 'Shall I lay your hands in each other's or not?'

The Pope had got hold of his daughter's fingers, but Gregor abruptly drew back.

'Not until Zenobia has said that I am free,' he said obstinately.

'Have your way, you master in scruples!' laughed Father Nikodem, good-naturedly. 'We'll consult her at once; I dare say she has not gone to bed yet. For the sake of two people's night rest it would be as well to have the question settled without delay.'

Still holding his daughter by the hand, he turned straight towards the house, Gregor following in silence.

Zenobia was not in bed yet, but she was in her room, and when summoned by her father, appeared, looking scared and rather white, in a faded print dressing-gown, and with her black hair brushed out of her face and hanging in one heavy coil down her back.

'What is it?' she asked, standing still in the door-way, with one hand holding together the edges of the dressing-gown on her breast, where a button was wanting, while her dark eyes, more open than usual, passed questioningly over the three faces before her.

'It is this,' said the Pope, who had sunk heavily into his customary seat beside the big writing-table. 'Here are two young people who have found out that they are fond of each other, but who have taken it into their heads—at least one of them has—that they cannot be happy without your consent.'

There was no immediate answer, and in the light of the one low-burning candle which had been lit on

the table, it was difficult to read the expression of a
face that was almost out of the circle of light. In
that pause, full of anguish, the music of the fiddles
which could be heard from the barn seemed to
Gregor to be scraped out upon his own overstrained
nerves. Of Wasylya's face, still crushed against her
father, nothing could be seen.

'I don't know why you tell me this,' said Zenobia
at last, in a voice so cold that it touched Gregor's
heated fancy as though with a physical chill. 'I
have nothing to do with Gregor Petrow's happiness.
He is free to be happy with whomsoever he likes.'

'What did I say?' asked Father Nikodem, looking
at Gregor ; but Gregor himself stepped forward.
For him the release was not yet explicit enough.

'If by any word or look I have given you to understand——' he said earnestly, 'I am ready to fulfil
any obligations which you may consider me to have
incurred.'

Even through the shadow Zenobia could be seen
to smile, but through the shadow, too, the bitterness
of that smile could be read, while the hand upon her
breast was clenched more tightly.

'No, thank you, Gregor Petrow. I know you
don't mean to insult me, but even your proposal
shows me how little you know me, and how little
we could have suited each other.'

Just then something glided close past Gregor's
arm, and with a soft, kittenish movement, Wasylya
almost sprang at her sister.

'You give him to me, do you not?' she asked,

putting her cheek against Zenia's, but at the same moment she fell back, for Zenobia with an unexpected gesture had almost thrown her from her.

'How can I give to you what has never belonged to me?' she asked passionately. 'I have told you that I have nothing to do with him. Take him, if you will, and do with him what you like.'

Quickly turning she left the room, but not before Gregor had caught the glance she threw at her sister—a lowering glance of more than resentment—almost of hatred, and which, in after days, was often to return to his memory with a stab of pain.

The recognition of what had lain in that glance troubled him even now, but only for a moment, for in the next Father Nikodem had laid Wasylya's hand within his, and everything was swallowed up in the rapture of the present.

CHAPTER IX

DURING the golden weeks that followed, Gregor was no longer either the fervent aspirant to priesthood nor the humble recipient of the Pope's favours; he was simply a young man in love. In the sense that other men are young he had never been young before, but few had known the fervour of happiness that came now to his eager, stainless heart, where everything was new and untouched by the breath of previous passion. No spring had ever seemed to him more full of beauty and delight than was this autumn season. The fast fading marigolds — the flower most in favour for Sunday hats, and therefore occupying a corner of every peasant garden—now glowing among decaying leaves like the last embers of a great conflagration, appeared to him more full of charm than all the wealth of blossoms in May, their pungent odour more delicious than the perfume of violets and hawthorn. The miniature forest he had wandered in with Wasylya had been cut to the ground : but the brown stubble fields where the maize stalks stood stacked into sugar loaves, festively wreathed in the pumpkin trails which laced them into shape, and over whose surface the golden pumpkins themselves lay discovered, had to him a more intoxicating element than ever had green meadow in May. The red and yellow of the birch woods which formed the background of the village was far more grateful to his eye than their tenderest green in spring. For him it *was* spring—the spring of his hitherto so joyless life. Every day as he came from the village, following the cart-track which, with its rib of green seemed to be the backbone of the grassy common, he looked towards the mountains and the birch woods, and although he saw a sprinkling of snow on the one and a lessening of leaves on the other he felt none of the usual melancholy of autumn, for he knew that it was not winter that was coming for him, but that by the time those branches were bare, upon the spring of his happiness would have followed the summer.

In the Pope's house, too, everybody seemed satisfied. No doubt it was more customary to marry one's elder daughter before the younger one, but Father Nikodem, whose shrewd eyes had detected the evident sincerity of Hypolit Jarewicz's admiration of Zenobia, was quite at rest on that point. If Zenobia were a little spited by Gregor's change of sentiment, so much the better—it would drive her all the more surely into Hypolit's arms ; thus calculated Father Nikodem, whose knowledge of women was not quite on a par with that of his own sex—so that marrying Wasylya really meant marrying two daughters with one stroke, and there would only remain Paraska to provide for. And besides, what

clenched the question for him was that Wasia
evidently wanted it so; the pet child had never
asked for an apple or a cake without getting it, so
now that she evidently wanted Gregor, why should
she not get that too?

After the first moment of complete astonishment
—for of course she had seen nothing coming—the
Popadia made no objection to the change of programme. It was a bore certainly to have to alter
the clothes which had been prepared for Zenobia,
but fortunately Wasia was smaller, which would
providentially reduce the process to the taking in
of seams and deepening of hems; also there was
comfort in the thought that Zenobia would probably
not have left home before the next season's jam-
making. The prospect of having to manage without
her had already begun to exercise the poor Popadia's
mind. Zenobia herself, after that one burst of resentment, had sunk into what looked like indifference—
a rather too chilly indifference to be quite convincing,
but an attitude which at least helped to make the
situation possible. Her dark apathetic face was the
one blot on Gregor's happiness, a constant vague
accusation, and when he could avoid seeing it he did.
With especial pleasure he listened to every mention
which the Pope made of Hypolit Jarewicz; the mere
existence of that promising young man, whom already
in his schoolmaster days he had frequently met here
as a visitor, was just now an inexpressible comfort
to him. To hear of his cleverness, his good prospects,
and his obviously serious intentions, was to still the

uneasiness within him, by telling himself that instead of spoiling Zenobia's life, he was helping her to reach a far more brilliant future than she could have looked for as his wife. The fears, which that look of hatred, intercepted on the night of the *toloka*, had engendered within him, were dissipated by these soothing reflections. For a moment he had feared that she loved him in the way that he loved Wasylya, but she could not have been so quiet now if that were true—so he told himself. That look must have sprung from the natural resentment of the slighted woman, and would die its natural death when her own turn came to be asked in marriage. There were moments when, marking the apathy on the dark face, he almost doubted having seen that look at all.

But if he could have followed Zenobia to the far-off corners of the orchard, if he could have looked in by the window when she was alone in her bedroom, then he would no more have doubted, for there were times when he would have seen the woman, who appeared to him so apathetic, lying on the ground with her face pressed to the grass, or pacing the floor with nails that drew blood from her tightly-clenched hands, and wide open, flaming eyes that did not look like her own. Small blame to Gregor if he did not guess the truth, since no one of the family—not even Wasylya who shared the bedroom with her—had ever been witness of one of these fits of overflowing inner rebellion. Once only she was surprised in one of these unguarded moments, but it was only by Hania, the servant-girl, whom the Popadia had sent out one evening to give a final shake to a particular apple-tree from which she still expected a last dish of apples to roast for supper. It was getting on for supper-time already, and in her hurry and in the dusk Hania did not see the dark form on the ground, until she had stumbled over Zenia's foot.

Zenobia sat up abruptly, without having time to dry her eyes, and seeing the shine of her wet face Hania understood what had been that hollow, long-drawn sound which had puzzled her as she came along, and caused her to cross herself twice; for, in conjunction with the old gravestones, it had unavoidably made her think of the souls in purgatory. The state of things was too clear to leave room for dissimulation, and, recognising this, Zenobia attempted none.

'You must tell nobody,' was all she said, after a moment, still sitting on the ground, and almost savagely wiping her eyes with her cotton pocket-handkerchief.

'Not if you don't want,' said Hania, with a prodigious sigh, and then was silent out of pure fellow-feeling; for the little doll-faced servant-girl had a susceptible heart, and her acquaintance with Jurko had enlightened her regarding the pangs as well as the pleasures of love.

'If you love him so much, why do you give him up?' she asked, in genuine curiosity. 'I should never give up Jurko for all the sisters in the world.'

'He has given *me* up, Hania,' said Zenobia, not

loudly but with an intensity of accentuation which rather frightened Hania, 'and I had waited for him for four years!'

A minute ago Zenobia would not have believed that she could speak thus to Hania ; she could not have given away her secret with her own hand, but finding it thus stolen from her, so to say, she was wise enough or weak enough to make no effort to take it back. After those weeks of daily and hourly repression, the relief of showing herself unmasked, even to this foolish servant-girl, proved to be irresistible.

'But you could get him back again ; there is still time.'

Zenobia gave a low, hopeless laugh.

'How, I should like to know?'

'There are different ways ; I cannot tell you which is the best for you—but certainly there are ways.'

'I don't want him back if he does not love me.'

'But he will love you, he must love you,' said Hania, with the conviction of experience. 'He will have no choice. It was the same with Jurko and me ; for there was a time when Jurko nearly broke my heart by going after Teresa Pawluk. I prayed all day and I cried all night, and it did not help, and I put more beads round my neck, and a new headcloth on my head, and it did not help either. Nothing helped until I went to Ursula Adamicz, and after I had done what she told me he became mine again.'

'What did Ursula Adamicz tell you?' asked Zenia unwillingly. She knew that Ursula Adamicz, who lived on the other side of the birch wood, had the reputation of being able to do a great deal more than dry herbs or cure cattle. Personally she had never had any dealings with her, but being a Ruthenian, and consequently profoundly superstitious, she had never entirely doubted the truth of the powers attributed to her.

'What did she tell you to do?'

'Different things. One was to wash myself all over with spring water, and then to make a cup of tea with the water and give it to Jurko to drink; another was to sew a hair of my head into the hem of his coat. The cup of tea did not help, though it cost me a good shaking from the Popadia, for she came in just as Jurko was swallowing the last mouthful; but once my hair was in the hem of his coat he never looked at Teresa Pawluk again.'

Zenobia gave a half laugh, incredulous and yet not entirely contemptuous. She was still sitting on the ground, with her knees drawn up and her hands clasped around them. To any one who could not read and write—and, in truth, Zenobia had not learned very much more than this—what she had just heard must have sounded a little ridiculous, but not half so ridiculous as it would have sounded to any woman, not necessarily more intelligent but of more education, and living in different surroundings. She had not indeed heard of this recipe for a cup of tea, but she had seen sick calves incensed,

G

and dropsical hens made to swallow the tip of a blest palm.

'And he is true to you since then?' she asked, a little wistfully.

'He is like a dog at my heels.'

Zenobia sighed heavily and was silent again, staring with her tear-blinded eyes between the shadowy tree-stems.

'I have never seen Ursula Adamicz; what is she like?'

'Old and very wrinkled.'

'Would she betray any one who came to her?'

'Great God, no! It is her business to be as silent as the grave. She does not betray the girls who come to her for beauty powders—for she has powders for nearly everything—and' (Hania hushed her voice to an awestruck whisper) 'she did not betray Piotr Hadan when his wife died all in a minute, and though everybody knew quite well that the powder he put in her soup was that white stuff they kill rats with, and that he had got it from Ursula.'

'He killed her?' asked Zenobia, in a sharp, startled voice.

'Of course he did; don't you know the story? He wanted to marry Angjela Markew, so Zosia had to go. So he went and asked for a powder for the rats, and did it, and it was said that Zosia herself had gathered shirling by mistake instead of parsley for putting into the soup.'

'And they are married?' asked Zenobia, still listening intently.

'They are married, and seem to be happy despite their consciences, though I don't know how they manage it. No doubt Ursula Adamicz could hang him at any moment if she chose, but she won't choose, because she would be putting herself in prison for selling that white powder which they say only doctors ought to sell.'

'That must be a terrible powder,' said Zenobia below her breath. 'To think that it can do so much and so quickly! How could she dare to give it to Piotr?'

'It was for the rats, he said, and how could she know what he would do with it?'

'That is true.'

'Ursula Adamicz has never betrayed anybody, and she would not betray you if you went to her. I myself should advise the hair in the hem—one of your beautiful long black hairs—but Ursula may know something better, for she judges each case by itself. Go to her, Panna Zenia, and you will never have to cry any more!'

In Hania's voice there was a little tremor of earnestness. Her sympathy was quite sincere and her point of view perfectly simple. Zenobia was a far less exacting mistress than Wasylya, who never brushed her own clothes, and made scenes if her flounces were not faultlessly ironed; therefore, since it was obvious that only one of the young ladies could have Gregor Petrow, Hania naturally preferred to see Zenia successful.

'I don't know if I shall go,' said Zenobia wearily;

'perhaps; but is that not the *Matka* (mother) calling you?'

'The apples!' shrieked Hania, abruptly conjured back to the necessities of the moment, and to the acute terror of the Popadia in which she chronically lived. Nothing but her sincere interest in this so thrilling love-affair could have made her risk the scolding which would now infallibly be her lot.

It was dark by this time, but Zenobia did not rise yet. Still in her cowering attitude she sat on the damp grass, idly listening to the thud of the apples which Hania was shaking from the branches and then groping for on the ground. She was turning over in her head all that she had just heard.

CHAPTER X

WASYLYA stood before the glass re-arranging the folds of the white cashmere gown that was to be her wedding-dress. Like all the rest of the trousseau, it had originally been cut out for Zenobia, and the necessary alterations had still to be made, nor was there over much time to make them in, seeing that the wedding-day was not a week off.

'I told you that the skirt required more shortening,' said Wasylya to the assembled audience, which consisted of her mother, her sisters, and Hania, armed with pins, scissors, and threaded needles. 'Another pin, please, *Mamciu*, and I will show you what I mean. Any one can see that this dress was not made for me.'

'But you don't tread on it any longer,' objected the Popadia wearily, for the details of the toilet interested her far less than those of the prospective wedding-feast, at present absorbing all her energies.

'I don't tread on it, no—but it doesn't show my feet, either, and I should like to know why I should hide my feet, since I'm not in the least ashamed of them?'

She looked down coquettishly at the deliciously narrow little foot thrust out from beneath the white hem.

'If you think it such a pity to hide them, I wonder you don't get married barefooted,' remarked Paraska, in true younger-sister fashion.

'I shouldn't mind it a bit if the weather were warmer. I know that Zenia is not so particular about showing her feet, and that is why she had the dress cut so long; but since it is I who am to wear it——'

She laughed, looking mischievously towards Zenobia's foot, which, though well-moulded and in perfect proportion to her figure, was not by any means so delicate an object as was Wasylya's.

'Shall I cut a strip off the bottom?' asked Zenobia stolidly. 'If you want it so short as that, there will be enough over for the hem, at any rate.'

'No, no! No cutting! Only a mark with a pin. How do I know what I may need the dress for, later? And who knows whether, when I am married, I may not want to hide my toes. I mean to be tremendously sedate as Gregor's wife.'

She squeezed together her short, thick, black eye-lashes as she said it, and looked at her sister from between them. She usually looked at Zenobia when naïvely parading her triumph, but whether out of mere delight in her victory, or from that unthinking and almost irresponsible cruelty which causes a child to pull off the wings of a fly, it would have been hard to say. Curiosity, most likely, had the chief share in these experiments, for every woman is a riddle to every other woman, and the interest of finding out exactly how much Zenobia felt, and to what degree her experiments hurt, were, in great part, the cause of their being tried.

'Give me the orange blossoms, will you?' she now said. 'I want to see whether they will look best at the neck or on the front of the dress.' Then, as Zenobia, without moving a muscle of her face, handed her the white cotton flowers, which went by the name of orange blossoms, Wasylya held them to her breast and apparently forgot to take them away again, gazing in a sort of ecstasy at her own reflection. Suddenly she uttered an exclamation, leaning sharply forward towards the glass.

'Great heavens! What do I see?'

'What?' asked four voices in one breath.

'A pimple on my forehead! Another! Several pimples! Why, it is a regular rash, there, under my hair. Oh, fancy being married with a rash! And I wanted to look my best!'

'It will be gone again by this day week,' said the Popadia soothingly.

'How do I know it will be gone? It may be worse by this day week. It's the same sort of rash that I got in summer when I was heated and put my face into cold water, and that lasted a fortnight. I suppose I must have got another chill—perhaps the other day after that walk. Orange blossoms and pimples! It's impossible! Oh, what shall I do, what shall I do?'

She was almost in tears as she examined her face in the glass, and, despite the soothing assurances of her mother and Hania, and even of the now sympathising Paraska, was not to be entirely comforted.

'Why do you say nothing, Zenia?' she asked fretfully, stung by her elder sister's somewhat contemptuous silence. 'Do you too think it will be gone?'

'I think it no great matter whether it is gone or not.'

Wasylya shot a resentful glance towards her sister.

'Perhaps it does not matter; Gregor will not find me ugly, even with the rash,' she said, in the irresistible desire of venting her grievance upon somebody.

'Perhaps not,' answered Zenobia, as stolidly as ever; but Hania, watching curiously, saw a quick contraction about lips and eyelids, and, with a woman's instinct, knew that the blow had struck.

That evening Zenobia came in late for supper, which was all the more astonishing, as the day had been wet throughout.

'Where have you been?' asked her mother querulously. 'I wanted you to help me with the *pirogi*.'

'Lying down on my bed. My head was aching; probably you did not see me in the dark.'

'But your hair is quite wet!' cried Paraska. 'You can't have been on your bed all the time.'

Zenobia put up her hand and felt her hair, on which the big raindrops flashed in the lamplight.

'No, not all the time,' she said slowly. 'I was also out in the orchard; I wanted to see if the air would help my head.'

'And it did help it, I suppose,' remarked Wasylya. 'You have got quite a colour now.'

Zenobia's cheeks were indeed glowing as though from the contact with the air; she appeared to be at once excited and confused, and breathed rather more quickly than usual, after the manner of a person who has been walking fast.

'Yes, it may have helped,' she said very seriously, as she applied herself to her supper.

Outside in the passage, meanwhile, Hania was nodding her head approvingly over a pair of excessively muddy boots.

'She has not told me, but I know where she has been,' she murmured under her breath. 'She has borne a good deal, but the wedding-dress was too much for her this morning.'

And in haste Hania caused the muddy boots to disappear behind the kitchen cupboard, in case they should meet the Popadia's eagle eye, for their state made it quite evident that they had been outside the orchard.

The few remaining days of Wasylya's betrothal were as full of furbelows that were being sewed as of

tarts and pies that were being baked. The chronic
state of trying-on, on which she had entered, was a
phase of her existence during which Wasylya ought
by rights to have been perfectly happy, and yet she
could not be perfectly happy because of the fear of
not looking her best. That rash on the forehead
was not disappearing quickly enough for her taste,
and this despite the miscellaneous advice collected
from every available person. Every one in the house,
beginning from Gregor himself and down to the
servants, was earnestly consulted as to the best
means of recovering the flawlessness of her complexion in time, but few of the advisers would take
the matter seriously enough.

'I should recommend starvation,' said the Pope,
with a jocularity that was maddening under the
circumstances. 'You've probably eaten something
that has disagreed with you ; but if you live on
water and dry bread for three days your complexion
will come round.'

The Popadia advised cooling drinks, and uncorked
more than one bottle of her famous raspberry juice,
which Wasylya—finding it far more to her taste than
her father's recipe—drank of copiously, reclining on
the sofa the while, partly because to play the invalid
was to be exempted from all necessity of helping her
mother in the kitchen, and partly because the position was favourable to the display of her feet and
ankles, of which she was so proud. Lotions and
ointments, too, were called into requisition, with the
effect that, on the day before the wedding, the rash,

although still visible, could no longer be considered as a serious blemish.

'It won't be noticed from a distance, I think,' said Wasylya, with a sigh of resignation, as she settled herself among the cushions of the sofa; 'and then there is the veil. But I shall have to put it up at dinner, and those Jarewicz girls have such horribly sharp eyes! Perhaps it will be paler still by to-morrow. Zenia, another glass of raspberry juice, please; it cools me more than anything.'

'Presently,' said Zenobia, who had entered the room with a tray of freshly-baked cakes.

'They look good,' remarked Wasylya, watching Zenia as she ranged them on the piano, 'but I daren't eat one now for fear of my complexion. What a good thing it is to have a complexion like yours, Zenia! Always the same colour. Heat and cold seem to make no difference to it.' She gave the peculiar little laugh she had got into the habit of uttering when she was going to try one of her experiments.

'It's almost a pity, is it not, that it's not you who are going to be married to-morrow? There's nothing wrong with *your* complexion, nothing different from usual, I mean, for I suppose nothing could ever make it white.'

Ranging the cakes with her back turned, Zenobia made no answer.

'Tell me, Zenia,' began Wasylya again, while the chronic curiosity within her became suddenly acute, 'do you really feel nothing at all, or are you only pretending? You don't hate me, do you, for taking him away? I should not like to be hated. There would still be time to change places, you know—if *he* consents!' she added, with a little self-satisfied chuckle. 'Say, do you want him back again? I dare say I can get another husband.'

Zenobia turned round suddenly, with a livid face, and with those wide-open eyes whose size always took one by surprise in the rare moments when they were fully revealed.

'If you don't like to be hated, then never speak again like that! Would you give him up if I asked you to? No, you would cling to him all the tighter. You are playing with me like a cat with a mouse ; but I am not a mouse, and you had better not make me desperate.'

There seemed to be more words on her lips, but she forced them back abruptly, for Gregor was entering by the opposite door. He had heard no more than the last sentence, and that but indistinctly, but the tone in which it had been spoken was enough to make him look from the face of one sister to the other, trying to guess what had passed. That something had passed was evident from Zenobia's pallor, as well as from the look of astonishment—almost of consternation—in Wasylya's face. A momentary disturbance came over him but vanished again as his betrothed stretched her hand towards him, calling him to her as though in need of protection. Without a further word Zenobia took up her tray and went out, to return a few minutes later with a glass in her hand.

'Here is the juice,' she said, and, though she spoke quite steadily, Gregor noticed that her hand was shaking and her colour had not yet returned.

'And you really think I shall be able to stand the orange blossoms to-morrow?' asked Wasylya for the fiftieth time, when they were again alone.

He echoed only the last word, probably he had not heard the others.

'To-morrow!' he mused, looking past her at the little square window which a gorgeous sunset was turning into a sheet of reddish gold. 'How often have I longed to be able to say "to-morrow," and now it has come! Look, Wasia, the sun is going down already! Only one more night—the last that holds us apart.'

To-morrow! He went home with the word hammering in his head, beating about his heart, and seeming to career through the very blood in his veins, with the speed of a messenger of good tidings. Oh, the darkness, the sealed-up mystery of those to-morrows, which so long as they remain to-morrows are so full of delight, but which turn into such different to-days!—like a figure which seems a veiled beauty so long as we do not see its face, but which, abruptly unmasking, strikes terror into the heart by the hideousness of its countenance. To-morrow! Had Gregor been able, not to guess, but only to conceive what that to-morrow was to give him, most certainly he would rather have held back the hours which now seemed to him to drag so slowly ; to spin out that one short night, which he now regarded as the last obstacle to his happiness, into something indefinite and never-ending.

There are such things as apprehensions of coming evil, nameless terrors of the mind which come from no one knows where, but none of these touched Gregor. No cloud of doubt lay upon his expectations, as early, very early, next morning he set his face along the cart-track which had been his path to happiness for so many days now. The humble huts he had passed by were gorgeous just now with the gold of their pumpkins piled in mounds against their walls, and of their maize hanging in bunches beneath the broad eaves and sometimes fringing the whole length of a roof. The sun was not yet up, but the assurance of its coming was written on the pale, pure sky and on the lightly frosted grass. The best setting to a wedding-morn which the season could afford—the newly fallen snow-wreaths on the distant mountains—seemed perfectly in keeping with the scene, as did the white of the birch stems, now almost bare of leaves and seeming like a vista of marble columns leading to some distant sanctuary.

It was not till he was quite near the house that Gregor began to wonder at its silence. True, it was very early still, but yet he had expected more signs of bustle. Had he not left the Popadia moaning over the many jobs still to do, and, although the wedding was not to take place till midday, was he not coming thus early himself in hopes of being able to lend a helping hand at any point were it might be required?—being prepared to lay a table, or even to scour a saucepan, if necessary.

At the gate, still no movement, and not a window open on this side of the house! Could he have made a mistake about the hour? But no, there was the first sunbeam striking sparks from the white mountain tops. Fancy oversleeping oneself on such a day, thought Gregor, as he went in by the gate, which he had never found closed either by day or by night. The front door was still locked, but the back door—to which he went round—stood open. Nobody yet, either in the entrance or in the wide open kitchen, where unwashed pots and pans, speaking of yesterday's activity, stood about. His first impression was that the house was still asleep, but, having stood still for a moment, he became aware of an inexplicable sound which seemed at first like the hum of flies, with now and then a gentle hiss, as of water spilled. He listened again, and the hum resolved itself into a murmur of voices, and the hiss into the nervously accentuated *ss* of whispered words. Then, for the first time, fear sprang upon him, like some animal that has been lying in wait. At the end of a passage a door stood open, and towards it Gregor walked straight, though he knew it was the door of the bedroom where both Zenobia and Wasylya slept, and which he had never entered before. It was not a large room, and it seemed to him full of people, some of whom he knew and some who were strange to him. He recognised one

or two of the farm servants and felt momentarily
shocked at their presence, for there were men among
them. Not thinking anything nor surmising anything, but only more frightened than he had ever
been in his life, he pushed his way through the small
crowd, which paid no attention to him, but kept its
eyes all turned in one direction. Then he became
aware of the Pope sunk on to his heels at the foot
of a wooden bedstead and sobbing like a child, with
his head among the bedclothes, while beside him
Paraska sat on the floor, rocking her thin body from
side to side. On a chair sat the Popadia, not crying,
but very stiff and yellow in her soiled night-cap, from
under whose edges the grey hairs strayed over her
eyes in long dry wisps. Zenobia he did not see.
Wasylya? What was that old woman doing to her?
With a sudden movement of anger Gregor pushed
aside the peasant who bent over the pillow with her
ear held downwards, as though she were listening
for something.

Wasylya was lying on her back, with her mouth
a little open, and with both arms stretched rigidly
before her on the bedclothes. Against the black of
her disordered hair her face looked of an almost
bluish pallor, and her closed eyes appeared to be
sunk rather deeply in her head. Gregor told himself
this, even while unconsciously noting each small
detail, such as the frayed edging of her night-gown,
or the empty glass with the spoon in it which stood
beside the bed, and in which the flies were collecting
around the last drops of sugary juice. Without

speaking he bent down and touched her hand, then started upright and looked first towards the mother. There was vacancy in the glance which met his, but the grey head began to nod slowly as though it were saying, 'Yes, yes, it is so!'—and, having begun, apparently could not stop, but went on mechanically and regularly nodding, after the manner of certain china figures.   Then Gregor looked at the next face —it was that of the old woman whom he had pushed aside—and he read there the same thing.   Behind him, from different points of the room, there came loudly-breathed, noisy sighs; on the floor Paraska was snivelling audibly, while in one corner Hania, with her apron thrown over her head, was uttering a species of suffocated howl.   Gregor looked at them all—from one face to the other—it was easier to read the truth reflected there than to spell it out for himself upon that other face against the pillow, and every face, both the seen ones and the unseen ones, gave him back the same answer, 'Yes, it is so!   Yes, it is so!'

H

CHAPTER XI

FOUR days after the one that was to have been
his wedding-day, Gregor was back again in
his uncle's house. The process of getting there, as
well as the resolve which had led to his departure
from Hlobaki, was marked in his memory by a great
blank. Of what happened after he had got that
dumb answer to his dumb question he could never
afterwards, even by the most careful reflection, give
himself an account. He supposed that he must have
eaten during those days, since his strength had not
failed him, and he had a confused recollection of
being dragged back from the bed on which the dead
girl had been laid out in state; but, even her image
in the white dress that showed her ankles so plainly,
and with the cotton orange blossoms on her breast,
was faint and blurred, like something seen at a distance. In all these featureless days there was one
moment only which was perfectly and painfully
clear—the moment after the funeral, when all the
mourners were gone and he found himself alone in
the little wooden church which still reeked of the
incense used during the ceremony, and where stood
the wooden platform on which the coffin had been

placed. Outside, the workmen were still busy with
the grave; through the open door he could hear the
clink of their spades and the ring of their careless
voices. But even had they been gone it was not
beside that freshly-dug grave that he would have
thrown himself on his knees, it was before those
golden gates through whose lattice-work he could
indistinctly see the altar. To the altar he felt himself drawn strongly, irresistibly. Kneeling before it,
with eyes desperately turned towards it, it was now
that he began to come to his senses, to recover that
individuality which he seemed to have laid from him
on the day when, stepping off the cart which had
brought him to Hlobaki, he had met the gaze of
those black eyes, whose gaze had transformed the
world for him, and himself in the world. On that
day he had lost himself out of his own sight, as it
were, and painfully now—amid a convulsion of the
soul that with its long-drawn plaints and breathless
sobs came near to being a convulsion of the body—
he was finding himself again.

'God's scourge! God's scourge!' he groaned, as,
with forehead that touched the floor, he lay before
those golden gates which to his excited fancy seemed
to have closed themselves for ever in his face. 'It is
His judgment, and I have deserved it—oh, tenfold!'

The boards were smeared with fresh mud off the
boots of the coffin-bearers who had stood there a
minute ago, but he did not heed it, as, regardless of
the long *soutane* and black sash he had always
watched over so reverently, he prostrated himself

after the manner of peasants. If the detail could have
pierced to his notice it would only have added to the
bitter satisfaction of the moment, so great was the need
he felt of debasing himself, of humbling himself under
the weight of the almighty hand which he thought to
be aware of upon him, even with his bodily senses.

'His scourge! His scourge!' he repeated, dragging
himself on his knees a little nearer to the sanctuary.
'His scourge for the faithless man!'

There were two distinct acts of faithlessness
weighing upon his soul, but his want of fidelity
to Zenobia was the one that pressed most acutely
just now. That sense of guilt in her presence which
his personal happiness had always succeeded in
suffocating, had flared up into blazing self-accusation,
now that that happiness had ceased. He had aban-
doned her for Wasylya, and God had punished him
by taking Wasylya from him. To the childlike
cast of his mind, as well as to that natural sense of
piety which could never die within him, the matter
appeared quite simple. But it was not to Zenobia
alone that he had been faithless, it had been to himself as well. Whither had flown that zeal which had
been born in his heart during the night that he had
watched upon the village common? Whither that
yearning towards the fulfilment of his vocation,
which had never left him for one hour in all the four
years at the seminary? All the impatience which he
had felt in himself lately had not been for the day
of his ordination, but for his wedding-day. His
thoughts and visions had been the thoughts and

visions of any gross-minded peasant, of any frivolous worldling who hopes to possess the woman that
pleases him. Ah! Father Spiridion had been right
when he had spoken of spiritual pride. Others had
looked upon him as a saint, he himself had made
comparisons between his own conduct and that of
his comrades, and now, after four years of rigid self-
discipline, he had in one minute become weaker
than the weakest of them could have been. Oh, he
deserved to lose her, he deserved it! But even as
he told himself so, he knew, with that certainty that
cannot deceive, that the wound in his heart would
never heal; that, pour what floods of resignation he
would upon his soul, the pain of losing her would
remain as sharp as ever, base and earthly being
as he was, incapable of that higher resignation
wherein God's creatures should find peace—never
having felt baser and smaller than now, as, cowering
under the chastening hand, he pressed his face
against the mud-stained boards in a very passion of
humiliation. In this alone there was relief: to feel
that hand almost tangibly upon him, since this was
a blow which only from that hand and from no
other, could be endured. He had heard of people
who did not believe in that hand, and in the midst
of his anguish he asked himself wonderingly what
those sort of people do when stricken as he was
stricken. It was a speculation which surpassed his
rather limited imagination.

When, half an hour later, he left the church, the
workmen had done with the grave. He looked

towards the fresh mound and hesitated ; the craving
to throw himself upon it, and to weep out what
remained of his strength, was for a moment almost
irresistible.   Then he remembered that he had just
been weeping before another sanctuary ; would not
the tears of resignation and of penance be defiled by
those of pure regret which he felt now rising to his
eyes?   With a hurried movement he passed on, as
though flying from a temptation.

Before night he was in his uncle's house, without
having looked further into the future.   He had not
got so far as that yet.   The necessity of leaving
Hlobaki had alone been clear to him, and on that
necessity he had acted, almost without reflection.
After that burst of mental energy in the church,
exhaustion had come over him—a certain stiffness
of mind which made consecutive thought an almost
unbearable fatigue.   It was the interval which
Nature required to collect her scattered forces before
taking up the further battle of life.   If it were
possible to live without thinking, it might be said
that Gregor thought nothing in these days, least of
all did it occur to him to think over the circumstances attending Wasylya's death.   To look for an
explanation of the catastrophe could not come near
a mind which accepts everything as coming straight
from heaven.

Gregor's uncle, far more astonished than pleased
at his abrupt appearance, watched his guest per-
plexedly, and wondered how long he was going to
have him on his hands.   Nothing could have been

easier than to turn him out of the house, only that this small government official, being a prudent man, thought it a pity to quarrel with Gregor, until it was known for certain that he was going to be a failure. The collapse of the marriage was distinctly disappointing, and the circumstances tragical enough to impress even the narrowest and driest nature; but time was known to do wonders, and accordingly Filip Petrow waited with as good a grace as he could command.

When he had waited for several weeks, and become disagreeably aware that Gregor was showing no signs of departure, but continued to divide his time between long hours in the church and solitary wandering about the country, Filip Petrow thought that the moment for speaking had come.

'I see that the bishop is to ordain on the 30th,' he observed one evening at supper, pointing to a paragraph in the Lemberg paper, which the evening post had brought.

'Is he?' asked Gregor indifferently, as he took the sheet which his uncle pushed towards him across the table. When he had read the paragraph he raised his sad eyes.

'Why do you tell me this? It has nothing to do with me—*now*!'

'It could have a great deal to do with you if you chose. There is still time to prepare; you always intended to be ordained together with Prokup and Franek.'

'That was before——' said Gregor, beginning to tremble.

'I know it was, but everything need not come to an end because of one misfortune. Look here, Gregor, I think it is time for you to tell me your plans.'

Gregor stared with his empty blue eyes at his uncle.

'Plans! I have no plans.'

'But you will have to make some. You know quite well that I cannot have you here eternally, and you know quite well that you will have to live. Have you considered how you mean to live? You don't want to go back to the schoolmaster business, I suppose?'

Gregor sat looking at his uncle, still without speaking.

'You have studied for the priesthood and for nothing else; therefore nothing seems clearer than that you must become a priest, and the sooner the better. Who knows when the next ordination may take place? Certainly not before the end of the winter; and have you thought of where you are to spend this winter?'

Gregor put his hand to his forehead; he had not even thought of that.

'You should be ready for this ordination, and you can be if you choose.'

'But I have no wife,' said Gregor, in a deeply moved voice.

'You can get one in plenty of time still. The

Pope Mostewicz has other daughters besides the one who died. I always understood that it was the elder one whom you had first thought of? Well then, why not think of her again? After having studied at Mostewicz's expense it would scarcely do for you to look for your wife outside his house. But there is no time to lose, and no reason why you should not go to Hlobaki to-morrow.'

'Impossible! It is impossible!' cried Gregor, overturning a glass in the vehemence with which he started from the table, and without another word he left the room.

He had been tramping about for hours among the wintry fields that afternoon, and, having lain down, fell fast asleep from sheer physical fatigue. But when, after two hours, he woke up, he knew immediately that he would not sleep again that night. The body rested, it was the mind that regained the ascendency. Those few phrases that had been exchanged at supper stood ranged before his inner vision, as in former days his scholars used to stand drawn up in order, waiting to be examined, and they had been waiting thus all the time he was asleep, as he now became aware.

Impossible! But why was his uncle's suggestion impossible? Was there anything else that was more possible? Filip Petrow had said nothing that was not strictly true; he would have to live, not only in the sense of feeding and clothing himself, but also in the sense of having some object which would make existence seem worth while. Out of the wreck of the past there was nothing but that hope of priesthood which remained to him ; could he throw that away ? Not that he was worthy of it—ah, far more unworthy surely than when he had kept his vigil on the village common !—but that nothing else could suffice to give him back the power of living. And to be a priest he must have a wife, and what other wife could he possibly choose than the one woman to whom he owed a reparation ? Was it not towards this that Providence had been leading him along so rough a path ? Lying back on his pillow, with his face turned up to the ceiling, on which the street lantern opposite threw a pale reflection, Gregor tried to realise to himself what exactly was his position with regard to Zenobia. What was she to him ? A woman whom he had once thought to love until he had found out what really was the thing which men called by that name. A woman whom he had cruelly slighted, while never ceasing to esteem, and who perhaps loved him. Doubtless she would be the right helpmate to have at his side in the life of serious work, which was what he began to see before him, bare of all those dallyings and soft pleasures of which he had dreamed, but oh, so briefly ! For him the recreations of life had ceased, and there remained only the work—and Zenobia could work, he was sure of that—better, no doubt, than——! no, he could not speak the name even in thought, without the wound beginning to ache.

And that, too, was true what his uncle had said about the impossibility of looking for his wife elsewhere, since it was Father Nikodem's money which had made priesthood possible to him. How strange that he should not have thought of this before! It could only be because he had thought of absolutely nothing. Having remembered it now, the urgency of the reason began to grow so rapidly in his mind, and the necessity of action to press upon him so heavily, that he found it difficult to lie still in his bed. Yes, he would go to her without delay; but would she listen to him now? If not, he would accept his rejection as part of his punishment—one more reason for humbling himself to the dust.

On the next day, without further hesitation, but also without joy, with the calmness of one who fulfils a self-evident duty, Gregor started for Hlobaki.

CHAPTER XII

THE snow was dropping slowly from a low, grey sky as Gregor stopped before the familiar gate. In the mist of flakes which veiled the irregular circle of crouching huts, the village common might have been a plain stretching into immeasurable distance. From the outside the house looked very still, just as it had looked on that frightful morning, thought Gregor, with a shudder; but in the entrance, and while he was shaking the snow from his shoulders, he could hear the voice of the Popadia, high and strident as ever, disputing with somebody behind a closed door. Hania, having peeped out of the kitchen, seemed, on seeing him, to become suddenly transfixed with astonishment, her open-mouthed, goggle-eyed face remaining immovable in the chink.

'Is the Pope at home?' asked Gregor, at which, to his consternation, she burst into tears.

'Has anything new happened?' he asked, but without emotion.

'No, no, only the old thing; but it is so dreadful, so dreadful! I cannot sleep for thinking of it.'

She had come out of the kitchen by this time, and was fumbling for his hand, which, while pressing

on it the obligatory kiss, she managed to cover
with tears.

'The Popadia is engaged?'

'Yes, in the dining-room, bargaining with Sylvester
Robak about the price of his marriage.'   Suddenly
she looked up straight at him.   'What have you
come for?   Not to woo Panna Zenia?'

Upon her round face, that was so like the face of a
wax doll, and on which all strong emotions sat so
incongruously, something like terror was grotesquely
painted.   Gregor gazed at her in astonishment.
'She must have been fond of her mistress,' was the
thought which crossed his mind, unconsciously
inclining him more indulgently towards the foolish
little servant.   He had not answered her when the
Popadia came along, in a dressing-jacket he knew of
old, not looking very different from what Gregor had
always seen her.   Just now, in fact, there was an
unusual shade of satisfaction on her face, for the
bargain with Sylvester Robak had been distinctly
favourable.   In the crises of life it is a great thing
to have a quantity of small habits to fall back upon,
and which to our petty natures often do better
service than any more exalted source of consolation;
and the necessity of keeping the storeroom in order,
and of seeing that the apples did not freeze, nor the
preserved plums grow mouldy, had been so soothing
an occupation as to avert anything like a breakdown
of the nerves.   Instead of beginning to cry, as
Hania had done at sight of Gregor, her face showed
as much pleasure as it was capable of.

'Gregor Petrow! Well, it is time you should think of us! I saw you getting out of the sledge, but I was not quite done with Sylvester Robak. The Pope leaves everything to me now. You have not seen him yet? You will find him very much changed.'

Looking closely at her Gregor saw that she too was rather changed, after all; the wrinkles on her brown leather face had deepened, and also there was an additional touch of acidity in the tone of her voice, even though she obviously meant to be amiable.

'I have not seen him yet, but I want to speak to him urgently.'

'Then come this way.' She led him a few steps down the passage, and then stood still again.

'What do people say about Wasia's death?' she asked, looking at him keenly.

He gave a start, almost as though the word had been a bodily stab.

'I have heard nothing. I have been at Bolotyn all the time.'

'Ah, yes, and that is too far away for them to talk; they do not know us there. But here, you cannot imagine what nonsense has been chattered, and yet it is all so plain. The doctor himself attested an inflammation of the intestines. That rash that we thought so little of meant mischief from the first, and it evidently was driven back too abruptly. Ah, my poor Wasia! She always was over anxious about her face!'

'Will you take me to the Pope, please?' said Gregor, feeling that he could 'bear no more of this.

'Of course, of course. Come this way.' She led the way through the dining-room to the Pope's private room, then stopped again with her fingers on the door-handle.

'You will find him changed—changed!' she repeated, as she stood back to let him pass; evidently he was to go in alone.

The falling snowflakes wrapped the room in a sort of white twilight. The Pope was sitting where Gregor had always found him sitting—in front of the ink-spotted table; but, though there was paper before him and a pipe beside him, he was neither writing nor smoking; the paper was blank, and the pipe empty and cold, as Gregor could see, as he drew nearer. He sat with his back to the door, and even before he turned, Gregor was struck by the silver shine upon his black head. For a moment he took it to be the reflection of the snow outside, but soon he convinced himself that the effect was solely due to an almost incredible increase of white hairs within these last few weeks.

'Father Nikodem,' began Gregor, wondering at the immobility of the massive figure. Then Father Nikodem turned, and Gregor could see the change more plainly. It was not only that he had aged, but that his cheeks had grown baggier, his mouth looser than it used to be, and that the clear brown pallor of his dark face had taken on a tinge of

yellow. The round black eyes that had been wont
to gaze so merrily into the world, looked now dully
at the entering figure, presently to kindle into
undisguised astonishment.

'Gregor Petrow!' he said, almost incredulously.
'Is that you? What can you be looking for here?'

He was staring at Gregor now, his big eyes
opened to their full, the black shadows about them,
that were like smears of charcoal, startlingly conspicuous—and without any signs of welcoming the
guest.

'Do you not know,' he added fretfully, as Gregor
—too painfully moved to speak at once—remained
silent, 'that the best kindness you can do me is to
leave me alone?'

'I would not disturb you if it were not urgent, and
I will not detain you long. I have come with a
serious purpose.'

Then, in a set and prim little speech, which he had
arranged in his head as he came along in the sledge,
Gregor made his request for Zenobia's hand. The
tremors which had assailed him, when four years ago
in this same room he had made this same request,
were not with him to-day. To-day, as then, he was
prepared for a rejection, but what he was doing
to-day was a duty, and whether rejected or not the
duty would be fulfilled.

At the first words Father Nikodem had begun
visibly to tremble. His eyes grew wider, left
Gregor's face, and swerved uncertainly round the
room, while his big hands, which were like the hands

of an overgrown child, played with the papers before him, nervously and restlessly bending them into dogs' ears.

'You are sure,' he said, breathing heavily as Gregor ceased, 'you would take her? Have you considered everything?'

'If she will take me, she will do more to me than I deserve.'

The Pope looked at him almost wildly for a moment, and his lips twitched as though he were beginning to speak, but instead of saying anything he noisily pushed back his chair, and began pacing about over the well-worn strips of carpet that crossed and re-crossed the painted floor.

As he watched him Gregor felt the astonishment growing within him. This was something more than the change which the Popadia had prepared him for. He had not looked for so complete a breakdown as this, and, despite his own immense grief, he wondered at it; for it was not only grief that he read on the face of the sorrowing father, it was something beyond grief, and apart from grief, an unquietness of movement that was yet not vivacity, and an uncertainty of the gaze which was wont to be so aggressively open. The alteration was one to shock him even in his religious feelings, for had not Father Nikodem the same sources of consolation that stood open to himself, and could he not dip into them more deeply, since he was able to stand at the altar? How he could fail so entirely in that Christian resignation, which he

I

had heard him so often commend, was a riddle to
Gregor.

'Do you give your consent?' he asked, after a
minute, thinking that in some new paroxysm of
grief the Pope had forgotten the subject in hand.
But Father Nikodem only ran his hand through his
thick hair, giving him another doubtful look the
while, and obviously hesitating.   This too astonished
Gregor.   However doubtful he might feel as to the
daughter's decision, he had not expected any resistance on the part of the father.

'Am I to go away?' he asked, after another long
silence.

'You have not considered—you have not considered,' was the Pope's agitated answer.   'You have
not thought of how people will talk of this!'

'I suppose they will talk,' said Gregor resignedly.
'When a man goes backwards and forwards between
two sisters he must expect to be mocked at, but so
long as Zenobia can bear it, I know that I can.   She
must decide.'

'Yes, you are right, she must decide,' said the
Pope, standing abruptly still.   'She alone can say
whether this is to be ; I will bring her to you.'

He had stopped close beside the door, and now,
without looking again at Gregor, he went out.

Gregor walked to the window and stared out into
the snow, trying—without quite knowing his own
intention—to pierce the falling veil, and catch the
outline of the little humpbacked brown church under
whose shadow he knew that Wasylya lay.   Although

he was waiting for Zenobia, it was of Wasylya alone that he thought.

When the door opened again he had to rouse himself with an effort to the recollection of what he was here for.

Zenobia, in her black mourning dress, came in behind her father. By the start she gave Gregor could see that she had not been prepared for his presence.

'Here is Gregor Petrow,' said the Pope, speaking more firmly than a minute ago, and keeping his eyes upon his daughter. 'He has come to ask you whether —after all that has happened—you can still consent to become his wife? Answer him yourself, Zenia; you must know whether you can say yes.'

The blood rushed suddenly to Zenobia's face, as with one hand she took hold of the back of the chair beside her, putting out the other before her as though to push something invisible from her.

'His wife?' she said quickly. 'No, no, I cannot be that; that could never be!'

'You mean that you cannot forgive me for my want of faith?' asked Gregor, without excitement.

'There was no want of faith. I am not speaking of you.' She put up her hand to her forehead and pressed it as though it hurt her. Her father's eyes were still upon her face, closely watching, with a strain of anxiety which Gregor vaguely noticed, without understanding. All that struck him was that that scrutinising gaze might well confuse Zenobia at such a moment.

'Would you let me speak to her alone?' he asked,

looking at Father Nikodem, and without a word the Pope turned and left the room.

'Zenobia,' said Gregor, and for the first time to-day his voice shook a little. 'Think again before you send me away. You have every reason to spurn me, but think again! I am a very unhappy man; my life is in ruins, and you can help me to build it up again.'

'Are you sure that *I* can help you?' asked Zenobia, looking at him steadily now. 'Is it true that you really believe in me so far? Are you afraid—are you afraid of—nothing?'

Her gaze seemed to be boring into his, intent on piercing to the truth.

'Afraid only of not deserving your generosity,' he said, openly returning her look.

She withdrew her eyes, apparently satisfied with what she had read in his. The next moment a change came over her face.

'But you do not love me, Gregor Petrow,' she said bitterly. 'You want to marry me only because you owe my father money.'

His sense of guilt towards her was too great to let him dare denial.

'I have loved once,' he answered wearily, 'and I do not know whether one can love twice. I have told you why I want to marry you; because my life is broken, and because, if you have ever loved me a little, you may help me to mend it.'

Over her face there came a second change, far more swift. far more intense than the first.

'A little! Oh, Gregor, I have never loved you a little! I have loved you much. Oh, God knows, how far too much! Yes, I will help you to mend your life. Take me, Gregor, for I am yours—I have always been yours!'

And, making two steps forward, to Gregor's amazement and consternation she fell at his feet, with hands that clutched at the hem of his *soutane,* and a face on which tenderness and passion were fighting for the upper hand, turned up to his.

CHAPTER XIII

LITTLE by little after his marriage—or, more properly speaking, after his ordination — a certain measure of quiet came back to Gregor. Piece by piece he found again those reasons of attraction towards his vocation, which for a time he had so completely lost sight of that he had thought them swept away from him for ever. His first Mass, the first confession he heard, the first dying man to whom he carried the viaticum, the first child on whose head he poured the baptismal water—each of these brought to him not only a moment of supreme solemnity, but dazzling revelations of the sublimity of his office. Some of the same naïve astonishment which the schoolmaster had felt on seeing himself obeyed now came over the priest, on realising that his word was actually able to bring comfort and to absolve sin.

Together with this feeling of wonder came that of gratitude towards the God who had made him His instrument, and the renewed resolve to be worthy of his trust. He would keep his sacerdotal robe as unspotted as it was humanly possible to keep it ; he would not spare himself, nor count fatigues, but

would—with the help of Heaven—become such a
priest as there had never been before. A holy hunger
for all these souls under his charge had come over
him, on the very first occasion when he stood on the
steps of the altar and overlooked the tightly packed
village church, in which he saw old faces and young
faces, the sunken eyes of old men, and the limpid
eyes of little children all turned expectantly towards
him. Why should even one of these be lost? And
with this new zeal upon him he threw himself into
his work, glad of the enthusiasm which had come
back to life, and careful not to analyse his own senti-
ments too closely, lest perhaps he should discover
that the zeal was not zeal alone, but that inextricably
mixed with it was the desire to kill thought. In
these early times he committed the usual fault of
zealots by losing sight of the fact that man has
a body as well as a soul. If he did not break down
physically in the first months after his ordination, it
was only because Zenobia was there to persuade him
to eat at the necessary times, and to relieve him of
the fatigue of many of his self-imposed sick visits.
So entirely did she fit into his new scheme of life,
that after a few weeks he already seemed to himself
to have been married for years, for Zenobia had none
of the exactions or obtrusiveness of a young wife,
while her eminently domestic habits saved him all
petty household troubles. Independent though he
was of material comforts, it was impossible not to
recognise the advantage of having his meals served
punctually, and of finding his linen duly mended.

Also, although not given to much talking, there came moments when to speak of his hopes, his plans, his disappointments—and they were not few—became almost a necessity, and Zenobia was above all a good listener. Not that she could entirely grasp his aspirations, nor even pretended to do so. Brought up as she had been, in the peculiarly exclusive atmosphere of a Pope's household, the popular standard for a priest had been too intimately intertwined with early habit to be easily loosened. Nor was her imagination readily fired, nor her spirit quick to take new impressions. That slight suggestion of heaviness which prevented her regular face from being beautiful was to be found, not only in her bodily movements but also in her mental ones. If she listened patiently and even sympathetically to Gregor's talk about the good he meant to do in his parish, it was not so much because she appreciated these dreams as because she loved the man who dreamed them. If she took his place beside a sick-bed it was in order to spare the health which was to her more precious than her own, rather than because she quite acknowledged the necessity of the action. All these things seemed to her not so much good in themselves, as good because it was Gregor who did them. Where comprehension failed, her blind faith stepped in, as is almost always the case with women in whom instinct preponderates over intellect. Sometimes this very instinct put her on the track of an idea which had escaped him.

'I think you frighten them,' she said once, when

Gregor had been deeply vexed at discovering that one of his parishioners, on the eve of his wedding, had preferred to make the obligatory confession in a neighbouring parish.

'*I* frighten them?' echoed Gregor, wide-eyed with astonishment, for he could not conceive himself as inspiring the sentiment of fear. 'Have I done them any harm?'

'No, but you do them so much good that they don't know how to explain it. They think there must be something else behind. They tell each other—I heard it from Jusia—that you look so like a saint that they are afraid to shock you with their confessions.'

'Strange!' said Gregor, sinking into deep thought.

These calm talks with Zenobia, the almost maternal solicitude with which he felt himself surrounded, all tended to give him back his hold on life. The one disturbing element in his intercourse with her was the thing which to most men would have been most welcome—the consciousness of her love for him, or rather of its depth and passion. At the moment when, in her father's room, she had fallen at his feet and stretched yearning hands towards him, he had got his first startled glimpse of that depth, and had recoiled as a man recoils before an abyss, hitherto unsuspected, which he suddenly discovers at his feet, and which merely to look into entails giddiness—for if she *now* loved him thus it meant that she had loved him thus all these four years, and if she rejoiced now so unboundedly it meant that she had mourned—more than mourned, that she had despaired—within these last weeks. 'My God, what she must have suffered!' was the thought which had come to him disturbingly in that moment, and which returned to him each time that he caught another glimpse of the abyss. Not only did the discovery heighten his sense of guilt towards her, but he did not want to be loved in this way, in this purely human manner,—it did not fit into his plan of life. What he wanted in her was not the passionately adoring wife, but a helpmeet in his work. Probably it was again Zenobia's instinct which turned her so rapidly into the outwardly sober and even placid wife. Yet, despite herself, there came moments when the truth looked out of her eyes and stabbed Gregor's conscience, as happened on the January day on which the 'Jordan' feast was celebrated, and on which Gregor had, for the first time, gone through the ceremony of blessing the water. Though the winter was mild there had been a sharp frost lately which had yielded splendid blocks of ice, wherewith to build up the cross which stood on the river bank. All the village, armed with pots and jugs wherewith to bring home some of the blest water, had crowded down to assist at the ceremony. Gregor was rather vexed with Zenobia because she declined to be of the congregation.

'Are you afraid of the cold?' he asked. 'You have got your new fur.'

'No, it is not the cold, but the people. The whole village will be there.'

'And why not you?'

'I do not like to go where there are so many people,' said Zenobia, with something like ill-humour in her voice.

It had struck him more than once that she shrank from going anywhere in public, and avoided even their neighbours in a way that almost smacked of misanthropy, but he had never thought of looking for causes, and to-day he had no time for argument.

It was on this occasion that—the water having been blessed—and while men and women were crowding to the edge of the ice to dip in their pots, that Gregor, in his haste to make way for them, slipped on the smooth surface and fell heavily upon one side. There was no bone broken, as the subsequent examination proved, but the pain in his knee was so great that he could not put his foot to the ground, and never would he forget Zenobia's face when they stopped before the door with the primitive stretcher on which he lay. It was one of those rare moments when her eyes, opened to their full, revealed their whole size, and the whole of their dark depth; and, reading the expression of anguish about her drawn mouth, he once again said to himself, 'What she must have suffered! My God, what she must have suffered!'

Against his will he was forced to imagine the different phases of torment through which she must inevitably have passed, and against his will—by a mere logical deduction—came the question of what must have been her feelings towards her sister who had supplanted her : but that way he did not dare to look, for fear of imperilling this so painfully acquired peace.

It was not long after the 'Jordan' feast that Zenobia told Gregor of a new hope in her life, and that he felt his heart leap up on an impulse for which he immediately rebuked himself as being too purely human. But, chasten his nature as he would, a warm, infinitely soft satisfaction remained. A child to complete the family circle, and to lead up in the right way, seemed indeed more blessing than he deserved. Life had obviously become possible again. A new bond drew him to his companion ; more than hitherto did it become possible to share his thoughts with her. Soon everything was open between them —everything with one exception, for there was one name which neither of them had pronounced since the events of last autumn, one locked chamber in the far back of each of their hearts which each felt must not be unlocked at the price of their present happiness,—or what bore the appearance of happiness.

CHAPTER XIV

IN this way, and without other incident than Gregor's slip on the ice, the winter passed. It had been a snowless, and only at moments a severe winter, so that a belated snowfall, when already the buds were swelling, moved every one with an almost indignant surprise. Gregor's newly built sledge which had stood idle all winter, was brought out for the first—and presumably also for the last—time on the latest Sunday of March. On the Saturday evening he had said to Zenobia, 'I have just heard that Father Nikodem is at Lussyatyn, and will be there to-morrow. I do not understand why he has not sent us word, but if we drive in to-morrow, directly after the service, we are sure still to find him, and of course you will want to see your father.'

To his astonishment Zenobia hesitated in her reply.

'I do not know whether that would do well,' she said uncertainly.

'But do you not want to see him?'

'How do I know whether he wants to see me?' she said, with a shade of sullenness on her face.

'There can be no doubt of that,' Gregor was be-

141

ginning, when it struck him that if Father Nikodem
had been very anxious to see his daughter, and even
if his time had been too short for the drive out here,
he might easily have sent word of his presence in
the neighbouring town.   The look of puzzlement on
his face was so great that it evidently struck Zenobia,
who hastened to say, in answer to his thoughts—

'Probably he was in a hurry—some ecclesiastical
business, no doubt.   Yes, it will be best if we drive
in to-morrow.'

It was for this that the sledge had been brought
out.

Certainly it felt far more like Christmas than
Palm Sunday—the Roman Catholic Palm Sunday—
as they were reminded of by the string of church-
goers on the outskirts of the town, with the strangely
unseasonable-looking palms in their hands, wading
up to their knees in snow, or standing aside to make
way for the sledge.   The more economical had put
their handkerchiefs over their Sunday head-coverings,
for it was still snowing evenly and noiselessly ; the
flakes clung to their moustaches, their eyelashes, and
to the blest palms in their hands.   The effects of
this long, windless fall were fantastically visible on
all sides, having filled the forty minutes' drive with
all sorts of amusing surprises.   The pollard willows
in the hedgerows had their round heads padded with
smooth white cushions which, in conjunction with
the naked twigs bristling through the surface, gave
them something of the appearance of monstrous
pincushions.   The branches of the wayside bushes

weighed down by round, square, and three-cornered patches of snow, made one think at first sight that to-day had been chosen as a huge, universal washing day. Every hole in the paling had been patched up with snow, every horizontal bar had a second bar of snow upon it, every perpendicular one a beautifully pointed cap, which grew higher and sharper every minute. Upon every tree branch that was only a little aslant there was a second branch of snow,—even the tiniest twig had its white duplicate. All the more precious are these wonderful pranks of the departing winter that he who sees them knows that they are but for a day, or at most two. If it were Christmas in reality, and not only in appearance, then the pincushions might endure for weeks, and the snow handkerchiefs hang out for as long, but in March all these wintry glories can but turn to slush: to decorate the world thus profusely is but a useless piece of extravagance,—the last wild revel which the Winter King is holding before quitting the field.

Although not exactly knowing where to look for Father Nikodem, it seemed to Gregor most obvious to inquire for him at the house of the parish priest, Father Urban Jarewicz, where he was probably lodging. When Gregor remarked this to Zenobia, she agreed as to the probability, but added immediately, as though having thought over the matter—

'While you go there I can be seeing about these new pots for the kitchen ; they are very urgent.'

'But will it not appear strange if you do not come with me? You have not met them since our marriage, and yet they are old acquaintances.'

Over Zenobia's face there came again the sullen look which he had seen there yesterday when she had spoken of her father.

'I do not care to pay visits now,' she said shortly. 'I would rather not go, and it may be that my father is not lodging there.'

'We shall hear that immediately,' answered Gregor, who at that moment had caught sight of two tall, angular young women approaching upon the strip of humpbacked pavement, and deeply occupied in keeping their fashionable Sunday frocks out of the slush to which here, in the town, the snow was already turning. 'There are the Jarewicz young ladies!' and, pulling up the sledge, he handed the reins to Zenobia, and quickly descended, in order to intercept the two daughters of Father Urban—the same young persons whose musical accomplishments had so fired poor Wasylya's ambition.

Zenobia had made a gesture, as though to detain him, but it had been too late; and, without a word, she took the reins and sat upright and rather rigid, looking straight in front of her.

Melanya and Agata Jarewicz had come within half a dozen paces of the sledge without appearing to perceive it; then Melanya looked up, checked her pace for a moment, and saying something to her sister, they unexpectedly entered the shop of a tinsmith, alongside.

Gregor turned towards Zenobia in almost naïve surprise.

'I felt so certain that they had seen us,' he said, and then only caught sight of the rigid set of her features.

'They *did* see us,' said Zenobia, who spoke as though she were choking.

'It can't be,' he asserted, in all sincerity, for such an incident lay out of the circle, not only of his experience, but also of his comprehension. 'I shall go and speak to them.'

Again she made a movement as though to check him, and again failed, and within the same minute Gregor was entering the tinsmith's shop, where Melanya and Agata were looking round them in an extremely leisurely manner. He had known these angular young ladies slightly in his school-master days, and had renewed acquaintance with them since becoming a clerical neighbour of their father's. From the first, the feeling which their fashionable clothes, their assurance of manner, as well as their accomplishments inspired him, had been one of awe. Distinctly they represented a new departure in those clerical manners which, until quite recent years, were universally recognised as rustic to the point of boorishness—'he eats like a Pope,' being almost synonymous with saying 'like a peasant'; while to say of a woman, 'she dresses like a Pope's wife,' was equivalent to stigmatising the unhappy creature for ever as a dowd. But Melanya and Agata Jarewicz meant to change all that, for it

K

was to them that the family owed its present reputation. Father Urban, a mild and conciliatory old man, whose one desire was to be at peace with the world, had no revolutionary yearnings of his own, but had long ago yielded himself up into the hands of the enterprising Melanya. To be modern and up to the latest dodges of civilisation was the object in life which the two sisters had set before themselves, and although they made some funny mistakes—such as eating with their gloves on, and having their calling cards printed with an ornamental border— on the whole they represented a welcome sign of progress, in the social sense of the word. Their assurance, far more than their charms, confirmed their success; for, to speak truthfully, both these progressive sisters were about as plain as it is possible to be at nineteen and twenty. An almost grotesque formation of features was common to both; a hanging jaw, which sloped so sharply downwards as to give to the profile something horselike; add to this, protuberant lips, and long, prominent teeth; and all this with absolutely nothing but a moderately fresh complexion to redeem it. For imaginative people it was painful to think of what these two faces would become after the departure of that ephemeral freshness, and from the merely æsthetic point of view both Melanya and Agata would undoubtedly be wiser to depart this life before being reduced to depend on their features alone.

As Gregor entered the tinsmith's shop he could see a glance exchanged, and it seemed to him to be a glance of mutual consultation, which apparently resulted in his favour, for immediately Melanya's teeth appeared in a friendly smile, while a carefully gloved hand was held towards him at the latest fashionable angle.

'Who would expect you here in such weather, Panie Petrow?' she murmured in the best social style.

'I am not here alone,' said Gregor, lifting his snow-covered hat. 'Zenia is with me; she is in the sledge outside.'

'Is she indeed?' said both sisters, with such an absence of surprise as to make it clear that they had seen her in the street.

'I wonder she does not find it cold,' added Agata, after a reflective pause.

'We came in to inquire after Father Nikodem; we heard he was here. Can you tell us where to find him?'

'He was here, but he went home this morning.'

'Without sending us word!' said Gregor unthinkingly, and with astonishment plainly depicted on his face.

Melanya said nothing but began examining a tin pot beside her, as though deeply interested in its construction.

'Then we have come for nothing!' he added, in a tone of almost childish disappointment, in which was also mixed a little anxiety on Zenobia's behalf. Would not the drive home again, without rest and without refreshment, be too much for her in her present state of health? But it could not come to that. All that he knew of the rules of hospitality forbade him to believe in such a contingency.

'My wife would be very glad to salute you,' he said, rather helplessly, getting no answer.

'We also shall be pleased to see her,' said Melanya, becoming all at once immensely polite, and after exchanging another glance, and apparently after a moment of hesitation, the two sisters stepped gingerly out on to the slushy pavement.

Zenobia was still sitting very upright in the sledge, with the reins in her hands, and the snowflakes falling now more thinly about her.

'Good day,' said Melanya, standing still on the edge of the pavement, but keeping her hands in her muff—indeed it would have been rather far to stretch across to the sledge. 'You have missed Father Nikodem by only a few hours; he went home this morning.'

'I thought we should not see him,' said Zenobia, returning the sisters' salutation, rather haughtily, as it seemed to Gregor. And then for a moment nobody said anything, while he stood uncomfortably beside the sledge, and wondered whether there really was nothing for it but to resume his place beside Zenobia. Presently Melanya began talking again, but it was only about the extraordinarily unseasonable weather. Glancing furtively from one sister to the other Gregor could see that both pairs of eyes remained fixed on Zenobia's face with evident interest, but which did not strike him as a friendly

interest, and above all with a sort of eager curiosity
which he could not explain, as one looks at a person
who is remarkable in some especial way.   Quite
suddenly he recognised this expression as one which
he had seen on the faces of his own parishioners, and
that too when they were looking at Zenobia,—and
yet, what was there about her that was remarkable,
or that made her worth looking at with this sort of
half-fearful interest?   He himself could see nothing.
A newly married woman is generally more stared at
than another, but this seemed to him to pass the
bounds of mere idle curiosity.   He was saying this
to himself, when on the pavement, at a few paces
off, he caught sight of a knot of people likewise
looking at the sledge, while at the open door of a
Jewish shop a bunch of hook-nosed, ringleted faces
struck his eyes—and these too were looking at
Zenobia.   All at once it seemed to him that the
whole street had its eyes turned in their direction.
So irksome was the sensation becoming, that without
any further remark he mounted quickly to his place,
and took the reins from Zenobia.

'If they want us they will stop us now.'   The
thought went through his mind as he settled the fur
cover, but all that Melanya said as she stepped back
to save her dress from being splashed was:

'It must be charming to spin over the snow to-
day.   I shall certainly have the sledge out this
afternoon.'

And in the next moment already the bells were
jingling, and the horse's head turned homewards.

'Are you not hungry?' asked Gregor, turning to his wife.

Into Zenobia's eyes there came a spark, and on her dark face a flame, as she answered :

'No, I am not hungry ; do not trouble about me, Gregor.'

'I thought for certain that they would ask us to stay.'

'I did not,' said Zenobia, scarcely unclosing her lips, and keeping her teeth together.

He looked at her inquiringly. There seemed to be something here which he did not understand, though she apparently did.

CHAPTER XV

EXACTLY four weeks after the sledge drive to Lussyatyn, Gregor and Zenobia were again on the same road; this time not in a sledge but in the little light cart which represented their summer equipage. It was again Palm Sunday—the Palm Sunday of the Greek Church, and consequently their own—a flower-decked and sun-gilded Palm Sunday, in contradistinction to that other one on which the world had seemed to lie dead, smothered under its counterpanes of snow. Of all that wealth of decoration, not a trace; the same branches that had been white with flakes were now white again with blossoms; the pollard willows were wearing green veils; the roadside ditch, then blotted out of existence, had got a new green lining; not even on the mountain heights, which made a background to the town, was a gleam of snow to be seen.

On the previous evening, when a message had come from Father Urban Jarewicz, there had been between Gregor and Zenobia an exchange of words which almost amounted to a dispute. Father Urban, whom a bad chill prevented officiating on Palm Sunday, had called upon Gregor to replace

him ; and Gregor, reflecting that the smaller parish
had better remain unserved rather than the larger,
had acquiesced. The message likewise comprised an
invitation to the midday meal, as was indeed unavoidable under the circumstances.

'They hope to see you too,' he said to Zenobia,
after reading the note.

'Let them hope,' replied Zenobia drily.

'Have you taken offence at their coldness last
time? As for that, I think I have found the explanation.'

'Have you?' she asked quickly, glancing up from
the sewing she was busy with, and seeming to hold
her breath.

'Yes; do you know who I think is the cause of it?
I think it is Hypolit.'

'Hypolit?'

'Probably they are angry with you for not having
married him.'

Zenobia's sewing dropped into her lap, as she
burst out laughing more heartily than Gregor had
ever heard her.

'Oh, Gregor, what a child you are sometimes!'
was all she said.

'But is it not true that he wanted to marry
you?'

'Quite true,' she said, without a shade of embarrassment; 'but it was *he* who wanted it, not his
sisters. *Their* dream is to see him return from
Vienna with a fashionable Viennese wife; somebody
from whom they could get hints for their dresses

and their manners. I was always far too dowdy and
old-fashioned for their taste.'

'Oh, well then, I was mistaken,' said Gregor,
rather crest-fallen; 'and probably their coldness
dates from the days when they were still afraid that
you would marry him.'

'It is indifferent to me what their coldness dates
from.'

'Zenia, this is not quite Christianlike. They may
have failed in charity, but this message proves that
they are ready to make amends.'

'This message proves nothing,' said Zenobia
obstinately; 'or at most it proves that Father Urban
thinks that his daughters have overdone the rude-
ness. He is always for keeping on the safe side with
everybody; besides, since he was asking a service
from you he couldn't help throwing in the invitation.'

'All this is no reason to refuse it. Zenia, tell me,
what is it that makes you shrink so from meeting
people? What makes you hide from the world, as
though you were afraid of it?'

'Ah!' said Zenobia, having pricked her finger at
that moment, perhaps because she had started.
Looking up she saw Gregor in front of her, his blue
eyes fixed inquiringly on her face.

'My health,' she murmured, staring at the drop of
blood which had fallen on the piece of baby-linen she
was busy with.

'That is not a sufficient reason. Do you not see
that you make yourself peculiar by withdrawing

from your neighbours in this way? That it will make people talk?'

'Of what?' asked Zenobia, rather faintly.

'Of different things; for instance, of the other marriage that was projected for you. If you do not go to the Jarewiczs' house the Jarewiczs themselves may think that it is because you are afraid of meeting Hypolit.'

For several moments Zenobia went on stitching so assiduously that Gregor could see nothing but the top of her black head, with the smooth, thick hair which, though somewhat coarse in texture, was yet beautiful of its kind. Then she glanced up.

'Very well,' she said, more quietly; 'perhaps it is better if I go. There is no necessity for people talking nonsense.'

The Jarewiczs lived in a new house which obviously aspired to the name of 'villa,' and stood on the outskirts of the town, but Gregor drove straight to the church, so that the meeting with Melanya and Agata did not take place until after the termination of the long service. The expression on the faces of the young ladies with the horse-like profiles (glorious to-day in brand-new spring costumes), was of necessity more amiable than it had been four Sundays back; but even to-day cordiality was less conspicuous than that sort of chilly curiosity which had disturbed Gregor on that occasion.

'Papa is so very much obliged to your husband for replacing him,' said Melanya to Zenobia, as—palms in hand—they picked their way along the

short piece of road which divided the church from
the priestly dwelling. The Roman Catholic palms,
or rather the willow twigs which represented them,
had been decorated only with woolly buds, but
those of the Greek Church this year were already
green.

'It is so very kind of you to accompany him ; we
scarcely hoped that you would.'

'They why did you ask me?' said Zenobia
bluntly.

'Oh, because of course we hoped. But we had
heard that you don't care to go about much.'

'It is wonderful how fond people are of talking
of each other,' said Zenobia, with a scornful tremor
in her voice. 'What reason should I have for not
going about? I am quite well.' She looked at
Melanya as though demanding a reply, and so hard
and straight that, despite her assurance, the other
preferred to turn away her eyes.

'Of course there is no reason,' said Melanya,
rather lamely, and the rest of the way was passed
in silence.

The ambitious-looking verandah, with the white-
washed pillars and the plaster stucco-work over the
windows, was deserted, but in the would-be modern
drawing-room—where the tables were so laden with
knick-knacks that it was scarcely possible to find a
place for putting down a hat, where photographs
were stuck about in every conceivable and incon-
ceivable place, and where modern magazines, with
paper-cutters left in them as marks, lay about osten-

tatiously—Father Urban (his lean throat wrapped in two or three comforters) awaited his guests. He was a frail and sickly looking old gentleman, whose frailty gave him an air of refinement which he might possibly not have possessed if in robust health, with lanky white hair, small features, ravaged by ill-health, deep shadows under his pale eyes, and a slight lisp in his voice, caused probably by missing teeth. About his wistful amiability there was nothing to be discovered of the veiled hostility in his daughters' bearing, as he smilingly welcomed the arrivals, inclining himself profoundly before Zenobia, and exchanging the usual kiss of brotherhood with Gregor. It would seem even as though he were anxious, by a double dose of hospitality, to make up for any remissness on their part.

'Again, nothing but a gain to my parishioners!' he laughed mildly, in reply to Gregor's condolences on the state of his throat. 'Your voice would have been at all times a good exchange for mine; and if I had been able to sing at High Mass to-day the preface would not have been quite the same thing, would it, my son? But what have you done with Hypolit?' he asked, looking forlornly about him with his washed-out blue eyes.

'Is Hypolit here?' put in Gregor quickly, glancing towards Zenobia's impassive face.

'Yes, on his Easter holidays. But why have you not brought him home with you?'

'We have not even seen him,' said Melanya, carefully pulling off her Suède gloves.

'He was not in church?'

'No.'

Father Urban sighed, mournfully settling his comforters.

'Ah, those young men, those young men!' he said, looking almost apologetically at Gregor. 'Nowadays one would require to lead them to church with a string.'

'Sunday Mass does not seem to be the fashion in Vienna,' put in Melanya, likewise with a touch of apology in her tone, yet not with complete displeasure, for it was pleasant to be able to talk of Vienna so familiarly. 'Men of science are so very —inquiring, you know, and it is difficult not to be influenced by the ideas around one.'

'Very liberal ideas!' sighed the Pope.

'Very advanced ones,' corrected his daughter, smiling uncertainly, for these 'advanced' ideas of Hypolit had long been both the pride and the terror of his family, round which, despite all efforts, the web of tradition and of the clerical habit of thought still clung.

'Well, we can't keep Pan Petrow waiting for his dinner because of Hypolit's ideas, whatever they are,' said Father Urban, with his wistful smile. 'I know how hungry the long gospel used to make me in my young days. Is the soup ready, Melanya?'

They were seated at table, and the *wódki* glass had just passed between the two men, when steps were again heard on the verandah, and Agata said —'There he is!'

As Hypolit entered the room, Gregor saw at a glance that, despite the townish cut of his clothes, and despite the growth of hair upon his face, he was scarcely changed from the small, dark, keen-eyed youth whom he had known in his schoolmaster days. Insignificant in height as well as in feature, Hypolit might have stood as a type of his race better than either of his lanky sisters. His was an essentially Slav face, which, like all Slav faces, had to be looked at full, having no profile to speak of—a low, broad forehead, wide nostrils, flat eyebrows, narrowly slit and intensely black eyes, the lower part of the face running sharply to a point, and this almost triangular shape of countenance as though purposely accentuated by the close-cropped, black whiskers which outlined the cheek and terminated in an aggressive-looking little beard, as sharply pointed as a dagger that has been dipped in ink instead of in blood. The most provoking thing about Hypolit was a habit of never speaking seriously, or at least of avoiding the appearance of doing so, and an almost melodramatically mocking smile which he always had ready to hand, and which was used both on suitable and unsuitable occasions. His cleverness was written on his face, but he was one of those irritating clever people who seem to think that cleverness consists solely in saying startling things, and in saying them as sarcastically as possible. This chronic sarcasm, in conjunction with the pointed beard and the smallness of his stature, suggested a sort of immature evil

spirit, ' a pocket Mephistopheles,' as one of the wits
of Lussyatyn had once remarked. But despite the
shape of his beard, those who knew Hypolit best
knew that he was not quite so Mephistophelian as
he wished to appear. To his own eminent displeasure, and notwithstanding the hardening process
of a scientific education, his innermost feelings still
remained of the violently emotional order that is
common to his nation, nor could any one who had
seen this cynical talker turn pale at the news that
his father had caught another chill, or that one of
his plain-faced sisters had fallen ill, believe that he
had succeeded in shaking himself free of the trammels
of family affection.

The only vacant place at the table was beside
Zenobia's chair, and although Gregor was the least
curious of human beings, he could not forbear to
look on with a certain interest while the miniature
Mephisto went through the customary salutations
and took his seat. Not that jealousy of the man
who had wished to supplant him had any part in
his feelings, for Gregor was not in love with his wife,
and he knew that his wife was in love with him,
two excellent reasons for not being jealous, but that
for the sake of his future peaceful relations with the
Jarewicz family, it would be a distinct advantage if
Hypolit's sentiment had died a natural death. And
what Gregor saw seemed entirely reassuring. Watch
as he would, no symptom of smouldering passion
was to be detected, or at any rate not by Gregor's
perspicacity. The habitual mocking smile on the

thin lips remained unimpaired, as Hypolit seated himself beside Zenobia, and the black eyes—button-like in their smallness, and yet keen as knives—even while passing over her face, showed no sign of emotion. His conversation, too, could not, from Gregor's point of view, be considered suspicious, consisting of a lightly dished-up hash of the latest news of the capital—fashionable, political, and scientific—flavoured with necessary cynicisms and sauced with the unavoidable suggestion of mockery, without which Hypolit did not seem able to open his mouth, for this young man had a way—even while saying such harmless things as that the sun was shining—of giving the impression that he was laughing at somebody or other in the process.

' No, it is not possible that he can feel deeply,' said the naïve Gregor to himself, as he listened to the somewhat gruesome description which Hypolit was giving of his experiences in a Vienna hospital. A minute before, Father Urban had been struggling with a particularly obdurate roast chicken, which he was vainly endeavouring to carve in the correct fashion.

' Hand it to me,' said Hypolit laughingly. ' It's too painfully evident that you have not studied anatomy.'

' Nothing so useful as anatomy,' he discoursed, while with his small, nervous hands he deftly severed the appetising-looking joints ; ' and nothing so en-joyable either. Whoever has not stood before an operating-table with a knife in his hand and a nice, clean corpse before him, does not know what real happiness means.'

'For goodness sake, you are not going to talk of corpses now?' ejaculated Melanya, with a little gesture of deprecation.

'Why not? Is not this a corpse that we are about to feast on now? and is it not insulting to the human race that human corpses should be considered a less agreeable subject of conversation than animal ones?'

'Human corpses are corpses of people who have died of illness, while this hen has been struck down in the very flower of its health.'

'Every one does not die of illness; there is such a thing as violent death,' smiled Hypolit, carving away lustily at the chicken. 'Now, I remember a man who was brought to the hospital last winter under suspicion of having been poisoned with arsenic. There were two parties among the students —for and against the supposition; and if you had the imagination of a Puschkin and a Victor Hugo rolled into one, you could not conceive the intoxicating triumph of the moment which proved my party to be right. When the intestines——'

There was an elegant little scream simultaneously from Melanya and Agata.

'Oh, Hypolit! At dinner! How can you?'

Hypolit, his white teeth still gleaming under his black moustache, looked slowly round the table, into one face after the other.

'Is the subject unpleasant?' he asked, with

L

well-feigned surprise. 'Shall we leave it till after dinner?'

'Leave it altogether, rather,' said Melanya, passing her napkin before her face as though to flick away something disturbing; '*we* are not studying anatomy, you know.'

'As this mangled animal testifies only too plainly. Can I dare to offer you this mutilated object which was once a wing?' and Hypolit turned laughingly to Zenobia, whose passive face neither responded to the pleasantry, nor seemed to indicate that she had even heard the remarks which had just been made.

CHAPTER XVI

WHEN everything, down to the finger-glasses (which were the latest innovation in the household), had been done justice to, and the afternoon being so mild that, with an additional comforter, Father Urban thought he could risk sitting outside, the black coffee was ordered on to the verandah. The little garden which divided the house from the road, although necessarily devoted in part to the needs of the kitchen, and not absolutely safe from the invasion of domestic animals, showed desperate efforts towards modernity in the form of various star-shaped and oblong beds, destined to enlighten Lussyatyn in the mysteries of carpet-gardening, as well as in an eruption of red, yellow and blue glass balls, crowning the supports of the standard roses. The buds were swelling on all sides, and the newly turned earth smelt good ; a peasant cart rattled past with a foal scampering at its mother's heels, and on the mountain side opposite the solitary birches made tender green patches among the sombreness of the pine forests. Gregor, leaning back in his basket-chair, listened in agreeable indolence to Father Urban's plans for

pulling down the wooden church, which he had been
taught to consider a blot upon his parish, and building a brick one in its place. Presently he heard
himself addressed by Melanya, whose conversation
with Zenobia did not seem to be getting into proper
flow.

'You are musical, I know, Pan Petrow. Shall I
sing you something?'

'If you will be so kind.'

'One of our new duets,' added Agata, rising with
alacrity. False diffidence was not among the sisters'
defects.

'You will hear perfectly out here,' said Father
Urban, who wanted to go on talking about his
church; and Gregor, who had made a movement as
though to rise, sat down again.

On the other side of the verandah Zenobia still
reclined in her basket-chair, her fine and somewhat
severe profile plainly outlined against the pale green
of the garden bushes, the black of her hair and of
the mourning dress she still wore, broken boldly by
the orange stripe on the shawl which she had thrown
around her shoulders. At two paces from her stood
Hypolit, leaning against one of the white pillars and
blowing his cigarette smoke out into the garden.
As the first chord sounded on the piano, Zenobia
rose leisurely.

'I think that, after all, I shall hear better inside,'
she said, as she passed in through the open door.

Melanya and Agata had vigorous voices, moderately well trained, and Gregor would have preferred

to listen to the duets undisturbed by the necessity of
saying 'Yes' and 'No' to Father Urban's rhapsodies
on his future church; it was therefore a distinct
relief when somewhere about the middle of the
third duet the old priest rose hastily, saying—

'I am quite forgetting myself; it is time for me to
be gargling my throat.'

Gregor put his head back against the seat with
something like a sigh of relief. The duet came
presently to an end; there was the sound of a discussion at the piano, and then Melanya's voice was
heard alone. What was that? At the very first
note Gregor felt himself shaken from head to foot,
while his hands tightened nervously on the arms of
the chair—for this was the song of the 'Black Eyes'
which he had not heard since last autumn, and which
he had then heard sung in *her* voice :

> 'I walk on the earth,
> I sail on the water,
> But whether sunshine glitters,
> Whether thunder groans and lightnings flash,
> Whether the stars burn in the sky,
> Whether day, whether night surrounds me,
> Whether in the dark, whether in the light,
> Always with me and before me
> Those black eyes shine.'

With one hand laid over his face, Gregor listened.
He felt as though it were impossible not to groan
aloud, and yet feared by that groan to lose one note
of the exquisite agony of the song. It was as
though a hand had been unexpectedly laid upon
the wound that was not yet healed, that only had

not smarted too sensibly because it had not been touched.

'Is it *her* black eyes you are thinking of, or the other one's?'

The words were spoken at a few paces from him, low and yet painfully distinct. Gregor looked up with a start; he had quite forgotten that he was not alone. Over there, Hypolit Jarewicz still leaned against the pillar, and the cigarette smoke still floated about him; from out of the bluish clouds the dark face, with its fatiguingly brilliant smile, watched keenly, giving to Gregor the impression that it had watched thus for several minutes past.

'What do you mean?' asked Gregor, in sudden confusion, like a culprit detected.

'I mean that they both had black eyes—Zenia and Wasia—and I am wondering now whether it was the eyes of your wife you were thinking of just now when you covered your face with your hands?'

With a few leisurely steps Hypolit had crossed the verandah, and now put his shoulder against another pillar—one that stood straight opposite to Gregor's chair. He closed his lips, letting the cigarette smoke issue through his wide-slit nostrils, and with his eyes fixed on Gregor's face. The look seemed to Gregor so aggressive that he glanced aside.

'No answer?' laughed Hypolit lightly; 'that is as good an answer as any, for if it had been your wife's eyes that you were thinking of you would have told me so at once. But seriously, Gregor, this sinks you in my estimation considerably ; I thought better of your taste than that. The idea of comparing the two ! Do you remember the days when I used to astonish Hlobaki with my bicycle ?—the days when you still hammered A B C's into infantile heads. Well, as long ago as that I was jealous of you already, so what do you suppose I am now ?

Said differently, the remark would have been something different, but with these gleaming teeth so smilingly displayed, it could easily pass muster as a rather audacious pleasantry. Yet something in the expression of the eyes fixed upon him disturbed Gregor and quite confused his ideas as to how the remark was meant to be regarded. Always awkward in anything like a bandying of words, he sat helpless before his interlocutor, handicapped by the impossibility of even feigning to treat lightly a subject which seemed to himself so desperately serious.

'If she could have loved you, I would have left her to you,' he said at last, with an earnestness which made an almost comical contrast to the other's flippancy.

'Would you really ? ' Crushing the stump of his cigarette against the pillar, Hypolit hurled it out into the garden with an almost vicious gesture. 'But how could she, while she had *your* blue eyes to dream of ? There are songs about blue eyes too, are there not ? More, I think, than about black ones. Does she sing them, I wonder ? '

'She does not sing,' answered Gregor, at which Hypolit uttered a fragment of an exceedingly un-

musical laugh, and began to roll a fresh cigarette
between his fingers.

'If you were vain you would teach her. But I
suppose the elements of vanity do not exist in your
nature ; if they did, you ought to have grown at
least six inches since last autumn. I 've seen something of the world, my friend, and I can tell you
that it isn't every husband who is purchased at such
a price.'

Gregor was again losing the thread of the idea.

'A price ? You are speaking of the money which
Father Nikodem advanced me ? '

'I wonder if you are as simple as you look ? No,
I am not speaking of the money.'

'Of what, then ? '

'To buy a husband with money is nothing so very
new, but to be thought worthy of a crime——— ! '

'I understand nothing,' said Gregor, opening his
blue eyes to their full.

'Then you are the only person who does not.
Tell me—' and Hypolit bent suddenly forward
towards Gregor—'can you seriously believe that
Wasia died a natural death ? '

Hypolit's small, intense eyes were boring into
Gregor's as he spoke, and for a moment the smile
was extinguished.

Immovably, and almost unblinkingly, Gregor stared
back into the face above him, without feeling the
power of looking away. He had heard the words
quite plainly, without having yet begun to follow
out the idea they suggested, or even quite grasped

their meaning. If he felt a slight shiver pass over the skin of his head it was because of the significance of the look bent upon him, rather than because of the words he had heard. With his upright fair hair, his wide, mild-looking blue eyes and his rigid, shaven face, he was, at this moment, almost alarming to look at.

It was only when Hypolit changed his position that he felt able to remove his own eyes, and then also, the momentary mental paralysis being passed, something which could only be comprehension flashed through his brain. All he was conscious of in that first moment was a wave of frank indignation, sweeping aside even all feeling of pain.

'It is *that* you accuse her of?' he cried, rising almost threateningly to his feet.

'Ah, no,' said Hypolit, who was smiling again, 'not I—alone.'

Gregor could not be sure whether he had heard the last word aright, and before he could speak again he saw Hypolit's eyes move towards the open door, at which Father Urban had just reappeared.

CHAPTER XVII

DURING the drive home, Gregor, though rather silent, was more than usually attentive to his wife, for he belonged in general to the order of husbands who have more talent for being waited upon than for paying the usual little attentions. It had not been possible to have another word alone with Hypolit, nor to express the honest indignation with which the base insinuation, uttered so flippantly, had filled him ; and the only way of easing his feelings in this direction was by settling the rug about Zenobia's feet, and by asking her from time to time whether he were not driving too fast ? Zenobia herself, agreeably surprised at this assiduity, could not forbear remarking upon it.

'Really, Gregor, you should pay less attention to me and more to the horse,' she said, with a happy side glance, 'or else we might end by finding ourselves in a ditch.'

The hot sense of indignation was still upon Gregor when he drew up before their little rustic dwelling at Rubience, and so full were his thoughts of all the things that he ought to have said to Hypolit, of all the refutations of the odious calumny which already

had occurred to him, that it became difficult either
to keep up conversation, or to settle to anything
definite ; and that, with Zenobia's chronic taciturnity,
threatened to make the evening drag interminably·
It was almost a deliverance when, declaring herself
tired by the day's outing, she withdrew early, for
now, at least, he could think his own thoughts, undisturbed by her questioning gaze, which, merely to
meet, made him feel vaguely guilty, as though only
to have listened to those words of accusation were
a disloyalty towards her.

With a deep breath he rose, as the door closed
behind her, and began to pace about the small, low-
ceilinged room, where everything—from the modest
furniture and white lace window-curtains, down to
the two or three glass vases and the five or six
photograph frames, which was all that adorned the
bare walls—was still of a painful newness, without a
stain or a speck of dust, but also without the conse-
cration which long habit gives. He had been much
in the open air to-day, yet he felt no trace of sleepi-
ness, but, on the contrary, so wide awake that he
could not just now imagine what that sense of
drowsiness must feel like which he had seen a
minute ago in Zenobia's dark eyes. Until now he
had not had leisure to examine those dreadful words
which Hypolit had spoken. If he had heard aright,
and he was certain that he had heard aright—they
could only mean that Zenobia was suspected of
having killed her sister, and popularly suspected, it
would seem, to judge of Hypolit's last words: ' Not

I alone.' Well, considering the blackness of the human heart, and the peculiar circumstances of the case, it was not so very surprising that the calumny should have arisen. The coincidence of the death, happening on the eve of the wedding, had been most unfortunate, certainly; but the Popadia had said expressly that the doctor had attested an inflammation of the intestines, and it was to be supposed that doctors do not make mistakes. If only it had not been for that unfortunate coincidence! No, it was not only natural, it was almost unavoidable that the rumour should have arisen. Poor Zenia! Did she know herself suspected? he wondered, and at the same moment stood still in his walk about the room. He had just remembered her marked dislike to appearing in public, and the scene in the street of Lussyatyn, when so many eyes had looked at her so curiously. Of course she knew, and probably had suffered acutely. Why had the poor girl not spoken to him frankly? Perhaps because she had not wanted to touch his wound by even so much as the name of Wasia. But it was he himself who would speak first; it was not right that she should suffer thus unjustly! He would assure her of his absolute faith in her, even at the cost of an inner pain!

He was but one step from the little window, and having reached it, leaned there with his forehead against the pane, gazing out with fevered eyes into the starlit night. Before him lay the plain which separated the village from Lussyatyn, and across which they had driven to-day; beyond the mountains—the same mountains he had loved to gaze on from the common at Hlobaki, but so much nearer here — masses of transparent shadow against the transparent night sky. But, though Gregor's eyes were wide open, he did not see those things now; what he saw was only Hypolit's face, and the faces of his sisters, as they had appeared that day in the street. No more need now to look for an explanation of their coldness—that and many other things were explained now. And these calumniators called themselves Christian people! Oh, monsters of uncharity!

For a moment longer Gregor remained immoveable, with his hot forehead against the glass, whose coolness was grateful, then straightened himself quickly, and, going to the table, took up the petroleum lamp which stood there, and opened the door into the bedroom. Would Zenia be already asleep? Evidently she was, or else she would have moved at his entrance. Treading softly, he walked up close to the bed. Zenobia, her long black plait hanging over the edge of the bed, and almost on to the floor, her face pressed into the pillow, lay there breathing softly. With his left hand shading the light, Gregor gazed down long and intently. He was aware of feeling provoked by her position, which prevented his seeing her face clearly; a cheek he could see, and the strongly moulded jaw, and the sweep of one black eyebrow, and, for the first time, it struck him how full of individuality the face was—of a strong and almost violent individuality, under its mask of apathy. Such a woman ought to be capable of great actions, of unusual actions even.

All at once it struck him as strange that he should be standing thus here, and doing what he was doing. In a flash he seemed to catch sight of his own image and action as seen from an outsider's point of view, and could find no explanation for it but one, the one which the outsider would probably have put upon it.

He set down the lamp hastily, almost angrily, on the table at the foot of the bed, and for a moment he thought of waking up Zenobia in order to assure her in that very instant, without any delay at all, of his full belief in her innocence. But that impulse he quickly recognised as foolish. It would be better to wait until to-morrow, when he could speak to her quietly, and when the unpleasant excitement produced by his talk with Hypolit was vanished.

'It will be gone to-morrow!' he said to himself, as he hastily undressed.

But, although he put out the light, he could not for long get rid of that terrible sensation of wide-awakeness.

It was nearly midnight when he ceased to be aware of Zenobia's breathing beside him, and that for the last time he said to himself: 'It will be gone to-morrow!'

But when he opened his eyes in broad daylight, it was not gone; and, together with his consciousness, there came to him a thought which seemed to have watched beside his bed, ready to pounce upon his imagination with the agility of some animal of prey.

'Can it be that her father himself thinks her guilty?'

That was the thought, and, scarcely born, it seemed to grow with the rapidity of some monster of fable. With unpleasant vividness he remembered Father Nikodem's so strangely broken look on the day when, for the second time, he had proffered his request for Zenia's hand. He recalled the shock he had felt at the Pope's changed appearance, and how it had seemed to him even then that this breakdown, both physical and moral, seemed not quite explained by his fresh grief. But if the unhappy father had had that other thought, and had harboured it, then any change could be explained. Yet, was it conceivable that he should have harboured it? Her own father! —a priest of God!—knowing his own child intimately, and able to judge of events at a close view?

Gregor turned uneasily in his bed and became aware that Zenobia was no longer beside him. She was up and busy in the house according to her thrifty habit. Time for him, surely, to be busy as well! With a hasty movement he arose and began to dress. It was long since he had been so remiss, and neither had he the sensation of having been refreshed by his sleep, but was aware of a smarting about the eyes, as of a man who has passed his night out of bed.

As he passed out through the sitting-room, on his way to hear confessions in the church, Zenobia, with an unbleached linen apron covering her dress, was busy dusting the slender collection of knick-knacks—all of them wedding-presents—which she never trusted to the servant girl's hands. The colourless apron was not particularly becoming, and the chill morning air, coming in by the open window, gave a pinched look to her sallow face, round which the hair still hung uncombed.

'It is strange what Hypolit can see in her!' was the thought which crossed his mind, as, unknown to himself, he went through a swift mental comparison between this face and another which he would never see again and which he had always seen to the fullest advantage.

'Why did you not wake me as usual?' he asked reproachfully.'

'You looked so tired, and it seemed to me that you slept restlessly.'

'What? Did I speak?' asked Gregor quickly.

'No, but you groaned several times. I rather think that pudding yesterday was underdone,' added Zenobia, in a matter-of-fact tone.

The remark was so much of a relief that Gregor nearly laughed. There was no servant within hearing, and it would have been easy to take her hand and to give her the assurance that he had wanted to give her last night. For a moment Gregor thought that he was going to do it, but when he opened his mouth it was only to say—

'Don't expect me back until one o'clock at earliest.'

'Very well,' said Zenobia resignedly, 'but don't forget to eat the sandwich which I put into the pocket of your coat ; you will always find a moment between the confessions.'

This being the time of the Easter confessions, the primitive confessional in the church was already beleaguered by a crowd of men and women with work-worn faces, which the long, rigorous fast-time —now approaching its end—had rendered often haggard and sometimes ghastly ; for neither age nor sickness is regarded as a sufficient excuse for shirking this severe discipline. Many sat upon their heels, some had sunk down squatting on the floor, and the eyes of old and young strayed towards the door, even while the lips kept moving incessantly ; but on all these waiting faces not one sign of impatience or irritation. In such improvident eyes as those of the Ruthenian peasant time has no value, while weariness to him exists not within the four walls of his little wooden church, where the gilt background of bright pictures, where huge, rudely carved candlesticks and enormous flower-decked candles of solid bees'-wax rejoice his childlike heart and flatter his colour-loving eyes, and which, above all, is the only place in which he ceases to be a beast of burden. A hard-worked and pleasureless life these people lead, yet possess a treasure which many of the prosperous of the earth would gladly lay down their riches to possess—the gift of a simple, unswerving faith, the happy consciousness that this is not the end of all, and that however bitterly the

M

tears may flow beside a deathbed, they will infallibly be dried some day ; for them there is no parting that is final.　Though their tired backs may be bent over the spade, and their weary faces bathed in sweat ; though the maize may fail and the potatoes rot, it can only happen with the will of One whom they feel able to submit to, and who can another time give as much good as it now pleases Him to dispense evil ; and if the worst comes to the worst, there is always the *cerkwie* (church) to go to—the *cerkwie*, which, after all, is only the first landing-stage of that country where the maize will grow of itself, and will require neither to be hoed nor peeled.　Take the little wooden building from the heart of each group of straw-thatched huts, and you take from the dwellers under those roofs the one golden spot in their life, whose brightness suffices to gild all the rest of their existence.

There was a pulling together of limbs and a raising of heads as Gregor took his seat in the confessional, to which an old man hastily tottered. This poor old sinner spoke so indistinctly that it was all Gregor could do to gain a clear view of the state of his soul.　A young woman followed him, then an old one, then another and another ; to Gregor the stream seemed interminable.　The functions of a confessor were those which, as a rule, he fulfilled with most enthusiasm, finding in them the greatest scope for personal influence ; but to-day he quickly became conscious of a want of interest, an inner dryness and indifference, for which he rebuked himself at every minute. At moments he caught himself not listening at all, but going over the details of his conversation with Hypolit. Each time he pronounced the words of absolution he inwardly resolved to give his whole mind to the next confession, and again, while listening to the monotonous list of offences which he knew by heart already, his thoughts would stray, and always to the same point. At intervals, sometimes right in the middle of a confession, something new would occur to him ; as, for instance, when with an inner start he remembered how on the day of his betrothal to Zenobia the Pope had said to him : ' You know how people will talk.' And how Zenobia herself had asked : ' Are you afraid of nothing ? ' He understood now, though he had not understood then.

Scarcely had he detected himself on this train of thought when he again pulled himself together, and began, almost with asperity, to lecture the penitent in the confessional on the duties of charity and the wickedness of harbouring thoughts of evil against one's neighbour.

During a pause in the long and weary ceremony Gregor went out to breathe the air on the grassy space behind the church. His neck was stiff with the cramped position, and in his head there seemed to hum all the hushed and tremulous voices that had just been pouring their secrets into his ear. Mean and commonplace secrets they were, for the most part, yet stained more than once with the real black of sin, and smirched with its mud. These childlike-looking peasants were neither so inoffensive as they looked nor so saintly as their faith would have made them had they but lived up to it, but were given to the commonplace failings of men and women all over the world. The disgust of much that he had heard to-day surged over Gregor now, bringing with it that disgust of his fellow-creatures in general, from which he had always slightly suffered. Human nature was after all a worse, not a better, thing than he had taken it for, and full of alarming possibilities.

All the rest of that day partook of the character of weary length which had marked the previous evening. Towards night, having forced himself to analyse the restlessness within him, he found it to consist of an impatient desire to speak to Hypolit again, not only in order to express his indignation more explicitly, but also to put some questions. He wanted to know what were the particular circumstances which had chiefly given rise to this awful idea. Hypolit was no farther off than Lussyatyn, but nothing but urgent business could explain his leaving his parish at so busy a time as Holy Week. Gregor shrank from the invention of a pretext, not because of others, but because of himself. To go to Lussyatyn now would be to acknowledge to himself that the odious suspicion had troubled him far more deeply than he was yet prepared to acknowledge. The Easter days must absolutely be waited for, and meanwhile Zenobia must not, on any account, guess that he had even heard of the calumny which was afloat. With this thought in his mind, he put so careful a guard upon his demeanour that all that Zenobia noticed was an increase of assiduity which almost amounted to tenderness, and which she, inwardly rejoicing, attributed to the solicitude awakened by her state of health, and gratefully and humbly acknowledged by a passing pressure of the hand or an occasional glance of deep affection. But these glances were the one thing that came near to breaking down Gregor's self-control, for he did not want just now to be reminded of her love. If in the early days of his marriage he had often remorsefully asked himself what she must have suffered, the thought came back to him now with a new importunity, suggesting reflections, the consideration of which, he felt, would definitely destroy his peace.

The Easter visit to Lussyatyn proved a failure. Although all the notabilities of the place were elbowing each other in the Jarewiczs' dining-room, where Melanya and Agata had done their best, by various little elegances of decoration, to temper the too patriarchal character of the time-honoured *swiezone* (Easter repast), Hypolit was nowhere to be seen. 'The Chrobaks *would* have him at their *swiezone*,' Melanya explained. But a new hope sprang up in Gregor's breast as she added: 'He is not going back to Vienna before the end of the week.'

During that week, Gregor, now regardless of

appearances, made several efforts to meet Hypolit, always without success; for at this Easter season there was much gaiety going on.

'He is sure to be staying over the Sunday,' said Gregor to himself, as alone in his little cart he took the road to Lussyatyn on the following Sunday afternoon.

From the street he caught sight of Agata walking in the garden. Abruptly he drew up, too impatient to drive round to the house, and leaping to the ground, approached the paling.

'Good afternoon, Pani Agata! I have caught Hypolit this time, have I not?' he asked, in a tone of artificial jocularity that contrasted unpleasantly with his usual grave address.

Agata stood still on the gravel walk, turning an early pansy between the tips of her fingers.

'Hypolit! Really, Pan Petrow, you have no luck! Hypolit went off last night to catch the express.'

'To Vienna?' asked Gregor, his jaw dropping slowly.

'Of course. He is gone back to his studies.'

'And he returns?'

'In July, for the summer holidays, like every other year,' said Agata, evidently astonished at this warm interest in Hypolit's movements. She had never been aware of any particularly intimate friendship between her brother and Gregor Petrow.

'Then it is all over for the present,' said Gregor, turning his back upon Agata, principally because he feared that there might be something to astonish her in his eyes, and gazing along the road which wound away down the valley, and white already with the first dust of the season. As he stared along its blinding length he seemed to himself to be gazing upon the chain of weeks which he would have to pass before he could again speak to Hypolit, and therefore before seeing any clearer in his present perplexity. Until the middle of July! And this was scarcely May yet! More than two whole months to live with the secret locked up within him—in company with that doubt which he now recognised as something alive within him, and which would feed on his very heart if it could find no other food.

He stood so long gazing down the valley that Agata asked—

'Will you not come in and have a cup of tea? Papa will be glad to see you.'

Then he turned round.

'No, thank you; my wife expects me home. Pray give my respects to your father.'

And without stopping to ask himself how his somewhat erratic conduct might strike her, he mounted to his seat and turned the horse round.

CHAPTER XVIII

THAT moment when he had stood upon the road looking up the valley, with his back to the Jarewiczs' garden, had been to Gregor a turning-point in the history of his inner life. Whereas until now he had shrunk from any close examination of the facts of the case, he now began to investigate them with an impatient eagerness. It was from Hypolit that he had hoped for an appeasing of the horrified curiosity within him ; but now that Hypolit was lost to him for two whole months, there was nothing for it but to try and appease this curiosity in other ways, which could only be by a close investigation of every detail of the case. Certainty was what he wanted ; the mere belief in Zenobia's innocence no longer sufficed—it must be made into certainty.

And now that he gave them audience, the memories, each of them of sinister significance, crowded in upon his mind, like petitioners that have long beleaguered a closed door. But not one among them spoke for that innocence which he so earnestly desired to prove to himself, in order to be rid of the horror of the thought which had never left his side since Palm Sunday, which walked with him in the street, sat with him at table, lay down with him to rest, was watching by his bedside when he opened his eyes—yea, which even accompanied him up the very steps of the altar. To the large-minded, the fundamentally easy-going and primitively constructed Slav there exists but one supreme, one unforgivable crime, and it is that of bloodshed. Every other sin, be it as black and as base as human nature allows of, can be forgiven, and even excused; but the taking of life, never!—for that right belongs to the Almighty alone, and no penance can condone it when done by human hand. The mere thought that a person standing so near to himself was accused, even though unjustly, of the one crime that *counts*, was enough almost mentally to paralyse Gregor, who, despite all individual qualities, was a true representative of his nation.

One memory showed him the glance of repulsion, almost of hatred—yes, he recognised now that it had been hatred—which Zenobia had hurled at her sister on the evening of the betrothal, while the scraping of the fiddles had sounded across the yard, through the open door of the barn. He had seen that same look again on the very eve of the catastrophe, when, entering the room abruptly, he had surprised the sisters evidently in dispute. Zenobia's tone and look then had been the tone and the look of a woman capable of an unusual action—but of a crime? No, surely not; and yet she herself had said: 'I have loved you too well!' What could she have meant?

With his head in his hands, Gregor, while Zenobia supposed him busy with his entries in the parish books, would pass hours in trying to imagine what had probably passed in her mind during the days that preceded Wasylya's death. From time to time a shiver of mental terror would run over him. *Why*, after all, had he at first put aside the supposition as impossible? Was anything impossible where human passion entered? Had not such crimes been committed thousands of times since men and women were created? And were not all the usual premises for a crime present here? It was at least most conceivable that Zenobia had wished to see her sister removed, since that sister was the one obstacle to her happiness ; and had not even his short experience in the confessional already taught him that from the thought to the deed there is only one step?

Then, in the midst of this train of thought, would arise another memory-picture: the face of the servant-girl Hania, when he had come back to the house, and her frightened, almost horrified question: 'Surely you are not going to woo Panna Zenia?' That, too, fitted in to the story in which Hypolit Jarewicz pretended to believe.

Gregor himself did not believe ; but, forced on by that deep-seated mistrust which is the bane of the Ruthenian mind, and which already in the seminary had rendered him evil service, he turned and re-turned each of these circumstances in his thoughts—finding, indeed, no certainty of any sort, but feeling how, in the process, that vainly found peace, which he had been at so much pains to acquire, gradually withered away. If he did not in these days betray himself to Zenobia, it was only because of the almost savage restraint which he put upon himself, and because the Slav's inherent talent for secrecy did him good service at this time.

But Hypolit's coming was too far off. Soon Gregor began to feel that he could not remain inactive until July. It was towards the end of May that, with a certain embarrassment of manner, he announced to Zenobia his intention of driving over to Hlobaki, in order to ask Father Nikodem's advice regarding a difficulty with a parishioner. Zenia looked surprised, but made no objection beyond saying—

'Could you not ask Father Urban's advice just as well? If you go to Hlobaki you cannot be back the same day.'

'I know, but I can be spared for a day at this season; and I have a far greater regard for your father's knowledge of the people than for Father Urban's.'

The pretext sounded plausible enough, and yet Gregor knew quite well that it was only a pretext, and did not breathe freely until it became clear that Zenobia was not going to offer to accompany him.

Hlobaki lay between its birchwoods, with cloud shadows driving over its roofs and across the grass-spotted common, when Gregor saw it again for the first time since his marriage. At the sight his heart swelled painfully, big with acute recollections.

He was following the well-known track when the

tiny tinkle of a bell fell upon his ear. From out of
one of the side lanes that ran between the huts,
a group of men and women were issuing with bent
heads and clasped hands, and at their head he marked
a broad figure in priestly robes. Quickly he pulled
up his horse in the middle of the common. Father
Nikodem, with the *viaticum* in his hands, was evidently
on his way back from the bedside of a dying person.
He would follow the little procession, and thus gain
a few minutes with the Pope outside the walls of his
house, which was what he preferred. Confiding the
horse to the nearest of the goose-herds, Gregor crossed
the common to where the string of peasants were
heading for the church. He could not see Father
Nikodem's face, but looked sorrowfully at the bent
figure which a year ago had still been upright and
sturdy. Up to the gate of the cemetery he followed
with the peasants, who respectfully saluted him, and
then stood still on the road to wait for his father-
in-law. He knew that on the other side of that
wooden wall, at only a few dozen paces, there was
a spot towards which he had often yearned in his
dreams, but a sense of unfitness kept him from putting
his foot on that ground.

One by one the peasants dispersed. He was alone
when Father Nikodem, dragging his feet a little,
came back through the gate; and now Gregor could
note how the black shadows that had always marked
the Pope's swarthy face had grown deeper and
blacker within the last months. At sight of Gregor
he brightened momentarily—it was evident that he

had not noticed him until then—but on the brightness followed swiftly a look of anxiety.

'What is it, my son? Nothing has happened with you?'

'Nothing,' said Gregor, with an uncertain smile of reassurance.

'Zenia is not with you?'

As he said 'No,' Gregor, watching closely, seemed to see a relief of the tension on the father's face.

'I have come to ask you about a difficulty I have in the village—and also to see how you have all passed the winter,' he added a little lamely, suddenly conscious that the other pretext was not strong enough to stand alone.

'Oh, well enough — well enough,' said Father Nikodem hastily; 'but, of course, one grows older every year.'

'Yes, but one ought to grow only one year older every year,' said Gregor, looking hard into the Pope's face, 'and you seem to have grown ten years older. How is that, Father Nikodem?'

The old priest gave an uneasy laugh, and began to walk down the lane, as though to escape from the gaze fixed upon him.

'One year is not like another, my son. You yourself have changed. Are you content with Zenia?' he asked suddenly, darting a quick side-glance towards his companion.

'How should I not be content? She is all a wife should be.'

It was said readily, but without enthusiasm, and

the Pope's black eyes still sought Gregor's face uneasily.

'If you have confidence in your wife, all will go well,' he said, after a moment, with a certain solemnity; 'for if one thing is certain, it is that she loves you.'

Gregor said nothing, and for a minute they walked on in silence, and each of the men had the very vivid sensation of being closely watched by the other.

'Father Nikodem,' began Gregor abruptly, just as they emerged on to the common, 'to harbour suspicion without proof is sinful, is it not?'

'Of course it is,' replied the Pope, with an asperity that Gregor had not known in him. 'We should never think evil of our neighbour, not even when he is evil; how much less when the evil, maybe, exists in our evil thoughts alone!'

Their eyes met for a moment as he said it, and although this remained the most explicit word spoken between them, each knew that the other had understood. In that glance Gregor recognised that Father Nikodem suffered from the same disease as himself, and a sensation almost of pain began to settle down upon him. Her father! Her father himself! in whom he had hoped to find a confidence which might support his own! Where was he to look for that confidence now? It was this, then, which had extinguished the genial smile and bent the sturdy shoulders? this same thing that was boring into his own thoughts like a worm?

What more was said before the house was reached

belonged to the commonplace order of remarks, and did not always hang well together, as commonplace remarks should; and once within the walls of the parsonage, the presence of the Popadia put a natural end to the *tête-à-tête*. Nothing more had been said about the difficulty with the parishioner, and Gregor, as he sipped the tea set before him, began to make plans in his own mind for starting home that same night; there was no use in staying on here further, since he had already found out what he had come to ascertain. So little was he aware of his surroundings, that he did not notice how it came about that he presently found himself alone with Justina Mostewicz. It required her rasping voice to rouse him to the fact.

'Tell me the truth, Gregor Petrow, how is Zenia?'

Gregor looked up, collecting his thoughts with difficulty, and found the haggard eyes of Zenia's mother fixed inquiringly upon his face.

'She is well in health.'

'Yes—but in mind? I did not want to question you before Father Nikodem; he himself is ill in mind, as you can see for yourself. Does she not allow these wicked rumours to prey upon her? You know, of course, of what they accuse her?'

Gregor nodded, not finding enough voice to say, 'I know.'

'It is dreadful how people's imaginations run wild, said the Popadia with a deep sigh. 'As if any daughter of mine could ever forget herself so far! I have never even known anybody who could have thought of killing another person, and now they want to make my own daughter into an assassin! I myself don't believe that these things are ever done in cold blood. That a man may put a knife into another in a quarrel is possible enough, but all these stories of poisoning are taken out of books,—that is my conviction. Is it not yours, Gregor Petrow?'

'Of course,' said Gregor, pressing his hands so tightly together that the knuckles whitened under the skin.

'My poor Zenia! How worried she must feel with this false shadow upon her! You can't imagine how I miss her in the kitchen and the storeroom now,—but I don't grudge her to you, Gregor Petrow; you know how to appreciate her, and to believe in her too!'

To Gregor it was a relief when an interruption cut short these confidences. Somehow there was no more comfort for him to be found in the Popadia's belief in her daughter, a belief which struck him too obviously as narrow-minded, than in the Pope's evident mistrust.

Early in the evening, despite the Popadia's hospitable speeches, Gregor had his horse led out again. He meant to drive through the night, if necessary. As he crossed the common, over which the sun rays still slanted brilliantly, his eye was caught by the brown cupolas of the little church standing out against the sunset sky, and although his road did not lead him past it, he jerked the horse's head round in that direction. The desire to see again that mound behind the wall had suddenly become paramount, and at the same time he became aware that the restraining influence of a little while ago was gone. He attributed to himself a right to go there which he had not felt before his talk with Father Nikodem.

The cemetery of Hlobaki, as is the way of the country, was as much orchard as cemetery, Ruthenian priests being as a rule too thrifty to allow a good piece of ground to lie waste and useless, merely from a sentimental scruple. The first apple- and plum-trees are put into the ground together with the first corpses, and never fail to flourish upon so congenial a soil, so that long before the space is full the Pope can gather rich harvests of fruit, and can continue to gather them for years after the ground has been officially closed as a cemetery, and has reached its ultimate destination of an orchard, as was the case with the one at the back of Father Nikodem's house, in which the *Matka Boska* presided over the harvests.

In the enclosed space where he now stood, Gregor had often seen the plums dangling on to the rude monuments, or some mound covered by a shower of unripe apples, shaken down by the last gust; to-day there was only the snow of over-blown blossoms upon the graves, or drifted into the narrow passages —a snow that at places was turning brown already, at others still tinged with a doubtful pink. Though the sun was still shining outside, the air had here the feeling of confinement, damp and close as in a cellar;

N

for, doubtless out of motives of economy, the trees
had been so closely planted as to allow but little
light to reach the ground ; mildew and moss had
eaten into the wooden crosses, rust into the iron ones.
It was an iron one that stood on Wasylya's grave,
but the rust had not had time to touch it yet.
Gregor had to wander for several minutes among the
mounds to find the one he sought for. The name in
gaudily gilt letters was too plain to be mistaken, and
yet he stared for a moment incredulously, as though
it were not possible to believe that this—*this* was all
that remained of Wasia. A slight convulsion passed
over his features as he stood immovable before the
terribly distinct inscription ; then, falling on his
knees, he stretched his two arms over the damp
mound, and, with his face upon them, burst into
tears. A storm of pity, almost more than of pain,
was sweeping over his soul. To think of Wasia—
Wasia, of all people in the world—sleeping in this
dark, cold place ! Wasia, who had said to him that
all she wanted of life was warmth and movement
and noise,—and now to have to lie so still and so
alone, with the snow over her in winter, and scarcely
a sunbeam that could reach her, even in summer,
and with nothing to listen to but the wind among
the leaves overhead, or the thud of an apple upon
the earth ! Even as he sobbed out the compassion
which seemed to be tearing his heart in two, in a
swift turn of memory he saw her as he had seen her
in the maize-field,—with the sun in her eyes and the
beads flashing on her neck, and the trail of pumpkin

leaves wreathed about her shoulders ; and as he looked back at that picture, and thought of what now lay beneath this clammy earth, a shudder, which was as much yearning as horror, ran over him. Oh that he could take her out of that narrow bed, and speak into her ear words that would bring back the smile to those lips of clay !

It was many minutes before, exhausted by his paroxysm of grief, the first he had indulged in unrestrainedly since his loss, Gregor wearily rose and slowly moved down the path. It was not the path he had come by ; but tears had so blinded him, that he did not see that, instead of regaining the gate, he was following the track which led to a back entrance, arranged for the convenience of those parishioners who came from the side of the plain—no more than a stile in the high wooden planking which enclosed the space. Here the trees ceased, and the hill sloped away suddenly, so that Gregor, emerging from the dark track he had been mechanically following, found himself unexpectedly in the sunshine once more, with the free air of heaven about him, and the smiling country, chequered with its sprouting cornfields and its freshly green copses, and with the flash of the river over the plain, all stretched before him. It was like the opening of a prison door, like a return from death to life. The dead lay behind him, the living before him. To which would his loyalty belong?

CHAPTER XIX

DAWN was scarcely yet whitening the sky when Gregor drew up before his door, in which the key was peacefully sticking, for housebreakers have not yet spread to this corner of the earth. Having taken the horse to the stables and unharnessed it, without any one having been awakened in the process, he introduced himself quietly into the house, and, weary with the long drive, felt his way to the bedroom. The grey light, just beginning to look in at the windows, was enough to show him Zenobia sound asleep, and not moving at his entrance. The second bed, with its snowy pillow and temptingly turned-down sheet, looked singularly inviting to a traveller whose joints had almost been shaken out of their sockets on the cross-country roads. Gregor began unbuttoning his coat, and then, suddenly desisting, turned away and began pacing the room. He had taken off his boots in the entrance, so that there seemed little danger of awakening the sleeper. There had come over him a sort of horror at the idea of lying down beside this woman. 'Have confidence in her!' Father Nikodem had said; but the look he had said it with had not tallied with the words: he had no confidence in her himself.

Before he had taken his second turn there was a sound in the bed. Softly though he walked, Zenobia had heard his steps in her dreams, and now opened her drowsy eyes to see the shadowy figure of her husband moving about the room.

'Gregor! You back already? You did not spend the night at Hlobaki?'

'No; my business was done quicker than I expected.'

'And you found my father well?' she asked, almost timidly.

'As well as he has been since last year; he will never get over your sister's death.'

For a minute Zenobia said nothing, tongue-tied with astonishment. It was the first time since their marriage that Gregor had even indirectly referred to the tragedy, and she could not immediately know what construction to put on this symptom. After a moment only she asked in a changed voice—

'But are you not very tired? What keeps you from lying down?'

'I do not know what keeps me. I was tired, but it seems to be gone. Zenia,' said Gregor, standing still beside the bed, and acting on an impulse whose approach he had not observed, and which unexpectedly mastered him, 'what is your own opinion of your sister's death? The truth ought to be clearer to you than to anybody.'

In the doubtful light he could not quite dis-

tinguish her features, but he saw the mass of black
hair against the pillow, and from out of the immovable face two big black patches—unnaturally big
and unnaturally black they looked—which could
only be her eyes, fixed on him in horrified consternation.

'Why to me?' she asked at last, almost inaudibly.

'Because you slept in the same room with her.
Can you not explain at all what made her die so
suddenly?'

'The doctor said——'

'I know what the doctor said; but there was no
examination, and doctors sometimes make mistakes.
Do *you* believe he was right in what he said? Think
again of that day, and tell me!'

Zenobia sat up quickly in bed, and grasped at
Gregor's hand.

'Do not ask me to think again of that day!' she
said, in a voice which shook to its depth. 'It was
the most terrible day of my life; I cannot think
again of it—no, I cannot!'

With a wrench Gregor released the hand she held,
and turned from the bed without speaking. Zenobia
sat upright for a moment longer, then sank back on
the pillow, also in silence. Her tremulous lips had
closed and hardened in their lines, but Gregor would
not have noted this, even had it been broad daylight.

It was not only the conviction that Zenobia's
father believed her guilty, which Gregor had brought
back with him from Hlobaki, it was also the newly

awakened grief for his own loss, which those few
minutes passed beside the grave-mound with the new
iron cross upon it had abruptly and vehemently
brought back to life. Hitherto, almost instinctively,
he had refrained from thinking too much of the dead
Wasylya. Even while examining the evidence
against Zenobia he had conscientiously striven to
keep his personal feelings out of the matter. Now
at last he allowed himself to think of the dead girl,
and he thought of her as he had never thought of
her before—in the light of a victim who had been
wrongfully robbed of her portion of life. In this
light the loss became far more difficult to bear ; for
now it did not show so clearly the character of a
direct intervention of Providence. In these days he
began to see Wasylya's face beside Zenobia's, looking at him with imploring eyes, as though she were
asking to be revenged, and piercing his heart with
the pain of regret. Had Wasylya lived longer, it is
possible, and even probable, that Gregor would have
found out in time, and no very long time either, that
she was, after all, but a shallow and commonplace
girl, with little education and no higher qualities
either of heart or mind—a sparkling little heathen,
at most ; but he had never really seen her except
through that golden haze which hangs about most
men's lives for at least a few weeks ; and before the
haze had time to disperse, Death had come, and by
putting her quite out of sight, had made her memory
safe for ever, and ensured for her over the rest of
Gregor's life an influence which, living, she never

would have been able to retain. It was this influence that now made him shrink from Zenobia with a
beginning of aversion. The man in him turned from
her as well as the priest—the man, because he suspected in her the person who had robbed him of his
happiness ; the priest, because he felt the shadow of
that sin (which as yet was only a possible sin) upon
himself, and because that spiritual pride, which he
had once been warned against, and which since then
had shown signs of degenerating into spiritual
vanity—just as though his spirit had not been strong
enough to bear the weight of his vocation—made him
recoil from contact with the sinner.

Yet all this was but in his blacker moments, for
hope was by no means dead within him ; at times it
seemed even to be coming back to life. To see
Zenobia moving so quietly about her household
duties, looking so like what another woman looked
like who had never hurt a fly, seemed to be a constant
refutation of the calumny. Certainly the thing was
too horrible to be believed in without much stronger
proofs. It was as though before committing itself to
the final belief, and just because he felt it so near, his
spirit, still fighting for its liberty, recoiled, before
irrevocably binding itself. There still at this time
came moments, although his guard over himself had
greatly relaxed, at which Zenobia was astonished by
some little attention on his part ; these were the
moments in which the gnawing mistrust was cried
down by the voice of charity. At these moments
the realisation of the immensity of the wrong he

might be doing her would overwhelm him suddenly, and he would wish passionately to hear her protest her innocence, no matter with what vehemence of reproach, and yet he refrained from putting the direct question, for fear of hearing no such protest, and of seeing his last hope vanish. And Zenobia herself was evidently not going to speak unasked. By the reserve of the attitude she had maintained ever since his return from Hlobaki, it was evident that she knew herself suspected, and much time did Gregor spend torturing his brain in the hope of fathoming its significance; for it might well be the natural reserve of an innocent creature, deeply wounded by an unjust suspicion, but almost equally well might it proceed from the consciousness of guilt which has nothing to say for itself.

Exactly these alternations between suspicion and hope were the worst part of Gregor's torture, growing at moments so acute that it seemed as though to obtain the certainty of Zenobia's guilt would be easier to bear than to live between this eternal horror of the one supreme crime, and the terror of wronging a fellow-creature, the woman who loved him, and who was to be the mother of his child. His child! Even this thought was poisoned for him now, for it would be Zenobia's child as well, and he would think to see upon its forehead the same mark that in his blackest moments he thought to read upon its mother's brow. Not *his* child, but the child of Sin it would be, the direct fruit of an awful deed, if that deed had ever been done—oh, confusion and perplexity! He was back again at the old point of absolute uncertainty.

In this long-drawn-out agony of spirit the weeks of the early summer passed, without bringing any explanation between husband and wife. If it had not been for the certainty that Hypolit would return, and for the hope of the light which he might be able to throw on the matter, it is hard to imagine how Gregor would have lived through the time, for even the joy in his priesthood had failed him,—as dead again, seemingly, as it had appeared to be after Wasylya's death. Perhaps other people could have told him as much as Hypolit could tell him, but to initiate a third person into his thoughts seemed to him impossible. It was upon Hypolit's arrival that he kept his mental gaze fixed, as upon a hope of salvation.

CHAPTER XX

'TICKETS for Kolomea!'

Hypolit Jarewicz was among the second-
class travellers who, one dusty July afternoon, responded to the call. Rousing himself from the half
slumber into which the monotonous rattle of the
wheels, together with the almost tangible suffoca-
tion which seemed to rise from the dirty drab
cushions, had cast him, he smoothed down his thin
black hair, and looked about him. Kolomea was
his station for Lussyatyn, and the landscape he
looked at now already bore a familiar face. The
broad-bladed fields on each side told him that he
was back in the maize country, while the long-drawn
blue wave that lapped along the horizon spoke of
the welcome coolness that even on this torrid day
reigned in the deep Carpathian valleys. Thirty-six
hours ago Hypolit had lounged along the *Karnthner
Strasse*, and feeling as much in his element there as
any of the soldiers or civilians he brushed shoulders
with. The atmosphere of the capital, intense, keen,
restlessly on the move, was inherently congenial to
him—the only one in which his own keen and intense

nature could exist with enjoyment for any length of time ; and yet the sight of those maize-fields and of that blue mountain-line never failed to move him, in a way for which this *fin de siècle* philosopher scorned himself intensely. There were many other things for which Hypolit Jarewicz scorned himself, without being able to get rid of their influence, and as he now gazed out at the home landscape, one of these things, the one for which he scorned himself most and was least able to escape from, seemed to be suddenly standing quite close to him.

What there was in Zenobia Mostewicz—now Zenobia Petrow and lost to him for ever—to make her image live through the crowd of more brilliant or more engaging faces which peopled the streets of the capital, not even Hypolit's abnormal sharpness of wit had ever been able to account to itself satisfactorily. There was something almost illogical in the attraction, whatever it was, which this half-educated and distinctly dowdy country-girl exercised upon the man for whom fashion and progress and modernity, whether in scientific discovery or in clothes, were the very breath he lived on. And here there was no golden haze to dim his sight ; clearly he recognised her as both half-educated and dowdy ; but even the laughing comparisons which he made between her and the faultlessly dressed Viennese beauties, altered nothing about the fact that these did no more than tickle his fancy for a moment, fading away again into the crowd they came from, while this one dark, somewhat ponderous image, with its heavy-

lidded glance, never moved from its place. Was it
because the laws of contrast have to be followed,
and because he himself was small and physically
slight, that the almost monumental lines about this
large, reposeful woman, who never seemed to be
more than half awake, had taken such a hold of his
capricious fancy? Or was it simply because he had
not succeeded, and that the thought was particularly
galling to the almost universally successful lady-killer,
whose original style of ugliness had proved a pitfall
to far more frail female hearts than the straightest
noses and broadest shoulders among his fellow-
students?

There never is any answer to these questions, and
there was no answer here. Fling what bitter taunts
at himself he might, the fact remained that for this
cynical despiser, this light-hearted betrayer of women,
there really existed but one woman, and that was
Zenobia Petrow. Even in his own thoughts it was
odious to him to have to call her by that name. For
many years past he had hated Gregor. During all
the time that the walls of the seminary had hidden
him, he had seen in him the rival who, even though
invisible, still remained triumphant. But it was since
his marriage, or, more truly speaking, since Wasylya's
death, that this hate had become perfect. That
Zenobia loved Gregor he had known for long, but
that she had thought him worth a crime had shaken
him through and through,—for that remark dropped
at Easter had been no invention of jealous spite;
for him the crime existed as certainly as though

proved in a court of justice, and by its existence, instead of darkening Zenobia's image, gave it a more dominant force. A woman who could love to the point of murder, here was something to still the cravings of his excitable imagination, to satisfy his love of the vehement, the extraordinary, of anything that went against that ancient code of morals long since recognised by him as a worn-out garment, which human society, under the guidance of such leaders as Nietsche, was making ready to cast off. If his envy for Gregor had been a thorn till now, it now became a dagger. To have been the cause of this magnificent crime! How did this boyish, blue-eyed priest come by this honour? Oh, to stand in his place, and know himself bought at such a price! Was it possible that this miracle of *naïveté* did not know himself to have been thus bought? As Hypolit, with his luggage ready beside him, sat upright on his seat, staring out at the window, he vaguely wondered whether that consternation betrayed at Easter had been genuine or not. Certainly it had *looked* genuine, and yet so complete an ignorance of that which was being cried aloud on the house-tops was difficult to believe in. During the next few months he would probably have an opportunity of judging of this. He drew down his black-beetle brows rather low at the thought, for the prospect of spending the rest of the summer in Zenobia's vicinity had about it something that was as disturbing as it was exciting. As matters stood now, he had no intention of approaching her, principally, let it be said, because he could see no hope of success ; but occasional meetings would probably be unavoidable, and he knew that each of these would bring him that sense of enraged humiliation which he had always been conscious of in her presence.

'Kolomea!' shouted the guard, tearing open the door; and from a thought-engrossed individual Hypolit became transformed into a particle of a jostling and hurrying crowd, guiltless of all thought except that which regarded the safety of his luggage.

When after sunset that night, Hypolit, having washed off the dust of the four hours' drive, sat at the paternal supper-table, the very name he did not want to hear—that of Gregor Petrow—was one of the first to mix itself in the conversation.

'He has been inquiring after you constantly lately,' said Melanya, as she poured out the tea. 'Only yesterday he was here, and so disappointed not to find you yet. I had no notion you were such friends. He said he would come back to-morrow.'

'Extremely flattered, I am sure,' said Hypolit, with a rather one-sided grin ; 'but I doubt whether it is friendship so much as burning curiosity; he probably wants to know what is the last fashion in altar-cloths in the capital. I always said that he is an inquiring young man.'

'Hypolit!' remonstrated his father, doing his best to purse his feeble lips.

When next afternoon came, Hypolit, having drunk his coffee in a more silent mood than usual. turned to his father with an abrupt question as to whether he could have the dog-cart?

'In this heat?' asked Father Urban, starting from the gentle doze into which he had just glided. 'Surely this verandah is a much pleasanter place than the dog-cart on such a day as this?'

'And then Gregor Petrow is coming,' remarked Melanya. 'If you go he will miss you again.'

'I want to miss him,' said Hypolit, with his pleasantest smile.

'Does he bore you? Certainly he is not very amusing.'

'Yes, he bores me. At any rate I find the society of Martin Chrobak more entertaining; and as I have a packet to deliver to him from his brother in Vienna, I mean to deliver it to-day. Can I have the dog-cart, father? I shall drive myself.'

The dog-cart was of course forthcoming, as everything always was that Hypolit desired, and, with a certain hurry, he mounted it. His wish to miss Gregor had been no figure of speech. The thought of opening relations so quickly in that quarter did not suit the plans he had formed of keeping as clear of the Petrows as circumstances permitted. If already on the morrow of his arrival he was to meet Gregor, he knew that the detestation which the sight of that fair, boyish face awoke within him would have too much time to grow big before the end of the vacation.

At this hour and under this beating sun the road was almost deserted. The dust-powdered leaves on

the trees which stood on either side hung so still
that they might have been made of cast-iron. The
short grass in the ditches almost disappeared under
the layers of dust that smothered it. The cattle in
the fields were lying down, and the small boys and
girls who herded them were mostly fast asleep under
linen umbrellas.

It was unfortunate, certainly, that the road to
Martin Chrobak led close enough past the village of
Rubience to let Hypolit catch a glimpse of the roof
of the Petrows' dwelling, which distinguished itself
by being the only tin roof among a mass of wooden
ones ; but this was a sight which he would have to
grow used to during the next few months. As,
despite the blinding light, he strained his eyes in that
direction, asking himself angrily what the dwellers
under that roof might be doing at that moment, he
failed to notice the cloud of dust rolling towards
him, from which there first emerged a horse's head
and then a vehicle not unsimilar to his own. It was
not until he heard himself sharply apostrophised by
name that he turned to see Gregor Petrow, only a
few yards distant, sharply pulling up the horse which
he had been urging on in a contrary direction.
Though not given to looking stupid, Hypolit looked
rather stupid now. He had not foreseen this danger,
never having supposed that Gregor would start so
early, in the very heat of the afternoon. For a
moment he thought of driving straight on, unheedful
of the interruption, but something in Gregor's face
made him give up the idea. Even his first glance

o

had showed him an expression there which required explanation, and his ever lively curiosity meant to have that explanation.

'Good-afternoon,' he said quite agreeably, pulling up his horse while they were still abreast. 'A hot afternoon for driving, isn't it? Funny that we should both hit upon it!'

'You were coming to see me?' asked Gregor, leaning eagerly over the side of the cart.

Hypolit looked him over quickly, and then his eyes turned towards that roof in the distance.

'Yes,' he said, with a deliberation which would have surprised himself had he been given to surprises, 'I was coming to see you. We are close to the turn, are we not?'

'And I was on my way to you. Yes, that is the turn. I suppose'—Gregor looked backwards and hesitated—'that we are much nearer to Rubience than to Lussyatyn?'

The opportunity of speaking to Hypolit had come at last, that was clear; but rather than his own house he would have chosen any place for the interview, and yet there was no help for it.

'We shall be glad to welcome you,' he said a little stiffly, as he turned his horse's head.

CHAPTER XXI

THE drive that remained was but a short one, and, owing to the necessity of keeping single file on the narrow track that led to the village, no consecutive conversation could be kept up, of which Gregor was secretly glad. Now that the moment for which he had been waiting for two and a half months had come, he felt suddenly overwhelmed by the difficulties of putting that question which yet would have to be put.

If the road had seemed to be asleep, so did the village. Most likely the grown-up inhabitants were anything but asleep, but out in the fields hoeing their maize; but the effect to the passer-by was the same. Behind the high screens of their wattled palings the huts stood like houses of the dead, with no face either at door or window, without the bark of a dog or the laugh of a child, and with only here and there the dimly seen tail of a cow whisking in the darkness of an open byre-door. The pigs, the natural scavengers of the lanes, lay stretched in the shadow of the palings, too lazy to grunt, and even the sunflowers that nodded over the wattled tops seemed to be taking their afternoon siesta.

211

It was in one of these narrow lanes that Gregor's dwelling stood, also behind a paling, but of freshly painted white wood. The white curtains were drawn down over the small square windows, and nothing moved on the tiny verandah, round whose wooden pillars the vine had scarcely begun to grow, and which was now flooded with the merciless sunshine. Only a yellow cat lay upon one of the steps, stretched out to a seemingly unnatural length.

'I declare it's like a fairy-tale,' said Hypolit, as he laughingly alighted. 'Everything seems asleep except the flies.'

The rooms inside were empty, and comparatively cool.

'Shall we sit down here?' asked Gregor nervously, feeling the approach of the moment he dreaded and longed for.

Hypolit looked out through the door, which stood open, on to the long strip of garden at the back.

'I think I ought to pay my respects to your wife first.'

'She is in her room, I think, resting,' said Gregor quickly.

'Ah! Then let us go out. It looks nice under that nut-tree.'

The nut-tree was the one remarkable thing belonging to the clerical dwelling, about which everything else was painfully new and painfully commonplace. The house, which had been built barely a year ago, still smelt of mortar and paint; the half-dozen shrubs, planted anyhow in front of the windows, had scarcely had time to take root; the long, narrow kitchen-garden at the back, pressed thin between two walls of wattled paling, was barely emerging from its former condition, which had been that of a maize-patch; everything was still uncertain and unformed; the nut-tree alone, soaring far above the low roof, and stretching gnarled giant arms far around it — far too far for the wellbeing of the cabbages and beetroots—was absolutely sure of its position in life. It even seemed that if the nut-tree had not been there the house would not have been there either—that it had been chiefly for the sake of including it in the garden that this particular spot had been selected for its site. Under its myriads of glossy leaves it was good to sit as in a tent, inhaling their pungent odour, and resting tired eyes upon their cool green. A couple of garden chairs always stood there; but so low did the sides of the tent fall, that it was not until the two men reached the spot, that one of the chairs was seen to be occupied. Zenobia, in a loosely flowing, cream-coloured gown, whose stately folds veiled her figure, her head thrown back against the crimson cushion which she had pushed under her neck, slept there, with the green light from the nut-leaves playing upon her forehead.

Hypolit and Gregor stood still abruptly.

'The sleeping princess!' whispered Hypolit, smiling more brilliantly, and perhaps a little more nervously, than usual. 'I told you it was a fairy-tale.'

'I thought she was in her room,' said Gregor,

frowning, and at that moment Zenobia moved her head. Her eyes, still full of sleep, went from Gregor to Hypolit, then back again to Gregor.

'I thought you were gone to Lussyatyn,' she said, colouring faintly as she sat up. Something touched her hand as she spoke, she lifted it towards her head, but too late to arrest the uncoiling of her magnificent hair, which now fell heavily over her shoulder and in a coal-black flood across her breast. With a more vivid colour in her face, aware of Hypolit's eyes upon her, she attempted to fasten it up, but the mass was too heavy and too slippery; pushing it back impatiently, she slowly stood up.

'I must put myself in order,' she said, smiling in momentary embarrassment. 'And I shall bring you something to drink, something cooling after your hot drive. Do you like raspberry or currant juice best, Pan Jarewicz?'

'Currant,' said Hypolit, as he stood aside to let her pass. As she moved down the straight path her black hair hung about her like a mantle; and Hypolit, who had never seen her hair down to its full length, though often tormented by the desire to do so, stood without moving and without turning his head, until he heard Gregor's voice saying beside him—

'It is impossible!'

Turning sharply round he saw that Gregor had sunk into the second chair, and sat there with burning eyes raised to his face.

'What is impossible?'

'What you told me in spring. It is a wretched calumny. Could a woman who has done the thing they accuse her of have enough peace of mind to care whether a visitor prefers raspberry to currant juice?'

Hypolit passed the flat of his hand across his eyes, and mechanically sat down on the chair beside him, the one which Zenobia had just left. On the crimson cushion, which was slung over the back, he could still feel the warmth of the head which had reposed there. Though Gregor's tone had been pressing to the point of urgency, he did not speak at once. The very urgency had been to him a revelation. In that one moment in which he had laid his hand across his eyes he had seemed to catch a lightning-like view of the situation: of the husband's ignorance; of his suspicions, which might be either confirmed or not; of the many startling possibilities that were here entailed—and all this mixed with the vision of the wife's hair, that dense black hair which held his fancy as though with ropes. It was what there was of honest in him which kept him silent for so long; but with the vision of that hair there came an impulse which he recognised as wicked, and yet welcomed as the solution of his momentary doubt.

'Then you were not acting in spring?' he observed at last, with the customary smile come back to his face, and with almost the customary lightness of tone. 'I thought I had never seen a man feign surprise so well.'

'Acting! No, I cannot act. Hypolit, you don't

know what you did to me that day, nor what I have suffered since. The only way you can make it good is to speak plainly now. In common mercy be honest, and tell me what grounds there exist for suspecting my unhappy wife—what grounds beyond the vulgar surmises of the crowd.'

'Don't ask me!' said Hypolit, darkening for an instant, and fighting what would probably be his last battle. 'Don't expect honesty from *me*! I am not an unprejudiced witness. Have you forgotten that I meant to marry your wife myself? How do you know that I might not be speaking out of mere spite and jealousy?'

'I don't care what makes you speak, I only ask you to speak; I only want to see the facts of the case plainly. I don't know whether you care for Zenia still; but even if you do, I am not afraid of you, because I know—oh, I know it only too well!— that she loves me, and not you.'

Stretching out a nervous hand, Hypolit tore off a piece of nut-leaf beside him, and held it crushed together before his widening nostrils, drinking in the pungent odour with a fierce and almost furious delight.

'Well, if ever a man had a proof of affection given him, you are that fortunate individual,' he drawled with elaborate affection, his small eyes squeezed almost out of sight.

'So you assume, or pretend to assume, I don't know which. I suppose you hate me, Hypolit; but even if you hate me, you might give me the plain answer, which is all I ask for. Once for all, are you playing with me or not? Is your belief an honest one, or has it been invented in order to torture me?'

'You insist upon my answering truly?'

'I insist,—I implore!'

'Well then,' and sitting up straight in his chair, Hypolit gave Gregor the first entirely square look he had given him that day, his own lips growing a little white under his thin moustache as he spoke, 'it is my honest belief that Wasylya died by poison. Indeed, the facts of the case seem so plain that I find it difficult to believe in the complete ignorance you affect.'

For a moment longer Gregor remained in his attitude of eager listener, his body bent forward, his haggard eyes jealously reading Hypolit's expression, then slowly his face sank into his hands. It was upon these hands that Hypolit's gaze remained fixed during the pause that followed,—jealously and intently fixed. How he hated them, those white, womanishly delicate hands, that were his rival's only real beauty, and which probably were more guilty of his own defeat than even the clear blue eyes.

'But what proofs are there?' Gregor began, speaking very quickly after that pause. 'People often die suddenly; and if this were really believed, why should there have been no public accusation, no inquiry? And where could she have got the poison from? And how could there have been no traces?' All the questions, which for two months past had been pursuing him, now poured pell-mell from his lips.

Hypolit, quite cool now, answered each one quietly and clearly, without any more sign of either hesitation or excitement, and with an obvious sincerity which was more deadly to hope than could have been the most pointed insinuations.

'Proofs? I did not speak of proofs, but of surmises, which to any one but a student of medicine will probably remain surmises, though for me they are conclusive. Why was there no inquiry? That, surely, is obvious enough. In another family there would have been an inquiry, but Father Nikodem is too much respected by people in general, and by old Doctor Robowski in particular, to let a scandal grow beyond the unavoidable whisperings in the ear.'

'You mean that he gave a false certificate?'

'He has not told me so—indeed he denied it when I taxed him with it to his face, but in a manner which could leave no doubt in my mind.'

'And now he is gone from this district,' said Gregor reflectively. 'But the poison? Where could she have got the poison from?'

'From Ursula Adamicz, who has once before been punished for selling arsenic indiscriminately.'

'Who is Ursula Adamicz?'

'An old woman who aims at the reputation of a witch, and has succeeded so well as to have made acquaintance with the police.'

'I never heard of her before; I don't believe Zenia even knows her.'

'It is almost certain that she visited her about a week before her sister's death. She was seen on the road to Ursula's hut one rainy evening in October. Perhaps you remember her coming to supper late one night, and with her hair wet?'

Gregor remembered that evening. At the time he had not even been aware of paying any especial attention to the incident, but now, with a swift pang, there came back to his recollection even the rain-drops that had glistened on her hair, and the tone of obvious embarrassment in which she had answered her mother's questions. Getting up from his chair he made one step towards the trunk of the nut-tree, and stood leaning there with fast-beating heart. He had felt it necessary to make a movement of some sort. The network of proof seemed to be joining its meshes around him, and the mere fact of sitting still increased the dreadful sense of helplessness. He took out his handkerchief and passed it across his forehead; there was a dampness there which had nothing to do with the abnormal heat of the day, which was not hot, but lay coldly clammy about his temples. Suddenly he heard Hypolit's dry laugh beside him.

'Really, Gregor, allow me to use the privilege of an old acquaintance to say that you are the greatest simpleton I have the pleasure of knowing. Are you aware that you have grown as white as that butter-fly on the cabbage-leaf?'

'Then you *are* making fun of me?'

'Indeed I am not; but I am observing you with the greatest interest, and, let me say so, the sincerest pity. Do you know what you are for me at this moment ?   Not Gregor Petrow at all, but the embodiment of the old theories which *we* are making ready to throw overboard.'

'We ?'

'Yes ; Fredrich Nietsche, and those who follow the new light.   Every man for himself, and away with the weakling Pity, which has only been invented to be pushed into the place of Force, by men who had no force.   No obligation towards anything or anybody, except, of course, towards the police authorities, so long as rotten institutions continue to exist.   No obligation ?   What do I say ?   Rather the obligation to tread down everything and everybody that stands in your way.   It is only by every man doing the best he can for himself, physically and intellectually, that he can become a true benefactor of his race.   These are the new truths, my friend ; those which in a few years will have upset the old world.'

With wide-open, blue eyes, Gregor, still leaning against the tree, listened speechless ; and as in all moments of consternation, his reddish fair hair seemed to be standing almost upright above his forehead.

'I don't understand what you mean by *new* truths,' he said at last simply.   'Truth cannot be new ; I only know of one truth, and that is older than the world.'

But Hypolit had got too deep into his subject to heed him.

'And just look at the disadvantages of your point

of view!' he pursued, with eyes which now sparkled with eagerness. 'There is a man ready to faint with horror because I tell him that his wife loves him well enough to commit what your school calls a crime, but what *my* school calls the one obvious thing she had to do, so long as she felt that she could not live without you, always supposing that she had a reasonable chance of escaping the arm of what has idiotically been dubbed justice. Yes, I pity you, Gregor, I pity you; you are suffering from the disease called "morality," which our Master designated as the most fatal kind of ignorance. Put me in your place, and catch me cankering my mind by scruples! Catch me doing anything but drinking full-throated from the cup of enjoyment offered me!'

'These words are not for me,' said Gregor, in deep perplexity. 'I understand them only enough to understand that they are blasphemous. Let us not begin these discussions—it is certain that we can never agree; but tell me only what I want to hear, and leave me to bear it in my own way.'

'But what *do* you want to hear exactly?'

'One thing or the other; that she is innocent, or that she is guilty. Certainty, I can bear—certainty of any sort; it is doubt that is killing me. Help me to find that certainty.'

'And when you have found it?'

'I shall push her from me; I shall denounce her!' cried Gregor, with suddenly flaming eyes.

'Then you should denounce yourself with her;

since you were the primary cause of what it pleases you to call a crime.'

With a groan Gregor turned his face towards the rough tree-trunk. This was a truth which had formed part of his torture of the last weeks.

'That is true; I am more guilty than she is; no, I cannot denounce her; perhaps I cannot even send her from my house; but she shall become a stranger to me,—if she has done it. But it may yet be that she has not done it. Ah, my God, how get away from that doubt? Hypolit, help me to *know*—not to guess, but to know!'

Hypolit's eyes were upon the path, at the end of which Zenobia had just become visible, with a tray of glasses carefully balanced in her hands.

'I will help you,' he said, without looking at Gregor.

CHAPTER XXII

IF on that hot July afternoon when he had called out aloud for the deliverance of certainty, any one had told Gregor that at the end of two months he would not yet have attained that certainty, and yet would neither have lost his reason nor his life, he would have denied the possibility; but so it was. As in July he had eaten and slept, and risen and lain down, automatically fulfilling his duties the while, without knowing whether the woman at his side were a criminal or a martyr to calumny, so it was in September. Hypolit had not broken his promise, but apparently it lay beyond his power to keep it to the letter. The grounds for suspicion, indeed, were accumulating—brought to him one by one by the medical student. From the servant-girl Hania he had found out that Zenobia undoubtedly knew not only Ursula Adamicz's address, but also that she sold poison. It was Hania herself who had given her the information one evening in the orchard, as she distinctly remembered.

'Then the simplest thing would be to ask Ursula Adamicz herself,' Gregor had suggested, on hearing this. ' There might be ways of inducing her to say whether she sold arsenic to Zenia or not.'

' If she were in the country there might be ways, but she left the country immediately after Wasylya's death.'

Gregor groaned aloud ; a new proof this !

' The girl is a goose, of course,' added Hypolit, ' but she is quite positive about her conversation with Zenobia. She told me that she had burned six candles in church since Wasylya's death, in order to atone for her own responsibility in the matter. She thinks that if she had not mentioned the poison Zenobia might not have had the idea. And I had to swear not to betray her ; she is evidently haunted by the terror of being beaten to death by the Popadia if it comes out that she has had any dealings with Ursula Adamicz.'

In the course of these two months Gregor had the opportunity of convincing himself that the narrow-minded mother was the only member of the family who even pretended to believe in Zenobia's innocence. This was on an occasion when the Popadia, with her youngest daughter, had come over to spend the day at Rubience. In Paraska's eyes Gregor immediately noticed that same look of terrified curiosity that he had seen so plainly in the streets of Lussyatyn, only that here it was mingled with a certain sense of personal importance, for, after all, it is not everybody who has a sister accused of so imposing a crime. But the most painful moment to Gregor was when, refreshments having been brought out under the nut-tree, the girl hastily, and in evident embarrassment, declined the glass of raspberry juice prepared by Zenobia.

'Why did you not drink the juice?' he asked, with unwonted sharpness, the first moment that he found himself alone with her.

'I don't like it—no, I mean it reminds me too much,' stammered Paraska, turning scarlet.

'Of what?'

'Of—of the way Wasia died. You know,' she whispered, raising her awe-stricken eyes to his face, 'they say she did it with raspberry juice.'

Gregor almost glared at the girl, as he flung away from her side. So this child, too, found it possible to believe! And he remembered the glass quite well which Zenobia had brought into the room on the eve of the catastrophe. Had that been the deadly potion?—no wonder, then, that her hand had trembled so as she handed it to her sister; or had it been in that other glass which he had seen standing empty by the bedside on the morning of the catastrophe, and whose image, with the sticky rim and the flies crawling in and out of it, had been photographed on his memory with all the intensity that belongs to moments of strong emotion?

Yes, the proofs were standing thick by this time, and all on one side, while on the other there remained nothing, absolutely nothing but the difficulty of belief engendered by the sheer horror of the thing. Yet with all the horror there was one side of Gregor's consciousness that was not only prepared, that

P

wanted to be convinced of Zenobia's guilt, and this in order to be able to wreak its own pain on somebody—the pain which had never left him since his visit to the churchyard; while the other, healthier, more natural side, yearned for deliverance from these wearing emotions, and towards the final recovery of his whole plan of life. But it was the morbid side which held the upper hand. The dead Wasylya, who had seemed to follow him out of the churchyard gate, now stood for ever between his wife and himself; and in her phantom presence the personal aversion, born of suspicion, grew large. Together with the sullen reserve of Zenobia's attitude, it made the hope of a frank understanding between husband and wife more hopeless day by day, as Hypolit, who imperceptibly had become a frequent visitor, carefully marked. The part Hypolit had had to play so far had come to him easily enough : there had in reality been little else to do but to answer Gregor's questions; nor any need to do more, since Gregor's peasant mistrustfulness, once set agoing, worked on by itself, boring and boring for proofs, and having grown so enamoured of the hole it was boring as to put its eyes and its whole soul into it, and to forget to look up and around it, wrapped up in one idea, as is the way with natures that are both narrow and deep.

The summer having passed without outward events, the autumn brought a blow, the news of Father Nikodem's death,—sudden, yet not quite unexpected, for his health had obviously been failing since spring. It was in the village street that Gregor met the messenger from Hlobaki, and remained for a while rooted to the spot with the open letter in his hand.

'It is her guilt that has killed him,' he said to himself when the first consternation was passed. 'He has died of his suspicions—no, of his convictions; they must have been convictions to kill him so quickly.'

And in a sudden paroxysm of reproachful indignation, he almost ran back to the house, and searched breathlessly for Zenobia, until he found her under the nut-tree, whose breadth almost blocked the narrow garden, with a large basket beside her, collecting the nuts which a high wind had shaken down in the night. Bursting from their green husks, they scattered the earth, with here and there a yellowing leaf among them.

Gregor's first impulse, one of almost brutal spite, had been to say: 'Your father is dead'; but at sight of her, and at the remembrance of her state of health, he controlled himself sufficiently to remark.

'There is bad news from Hlobaki.'

She straightened herself out of her stooping posture to ask quickly—

'My father?'

'Yes, your father.'

'Not dead?' she asked, her eyes growing large with apprehension.

Gregor nodded. He knew that if he spoke at

once the feeling of spite, which was his chief sensation at the moment, would appear too plainly.

Zenobia sat down quickly on the chair beside her, covering her face with her hands.

'That it should have come so quickly!' she said, in a stifled voice.

'Grief kills quickly, and he has been unhappy since last autumn.'

She remained for a moment longer quite still, then her hands dropped.

'You are cruel, Gregor,' she said, in deep agitation. 'God is not so cruel as you. If I have been wicked, I have suffered for it.'

She had risen as she spoke, and, with the last word, stretched out her hand almost timidly to lay it upon his arm; but it did not touch it, for Gregor had stepped back, gazing at her with horror-stricken eyes. Was that not a confession which he had heard from her lips? And this woman wanted to touch him!

'Leave me—leave me!' he said incoherently, as he turned away and began walking rapidly towards the house. Within the first dozen paces he brushed against something, and only with difficulty, in such tumult had his thoughts been thrown, recognised Hypolit Jarewicz. He murmured some excuse and passed him quickly, having only vaguely wondered why Hypolit was looking so yellow, and why he threw aside his cigarette with so vehement a gesture.

Zenobia was still standing under the nut-tree, beside the basket half filled with nuts, when Hypolit reached her, and she was still obviously struggling

for composure. At a glance Hypolit saw the opportunity which for two months he had waited for.
He had not always felt quite certain that when the
opportunity came he would avail himself of it. It
is one thing to proclaim Nietsche's principles, and
quite another thing to act up to them in real life;
and loudly though he might cry to himself with
Zarathustra to 'Become hard! become hard!' and
to throw all feeling of moral obligation to the winds,
there yet were moments when he would feel himself
clogged by the traditions of that old morality in
which he had been brought up, entangled, as it were,
in that worn-out garment so supremely scorned, but
which still hung together sufficiently to seriously
hamper his movements. Enthusiastically though he
approved the Master's preaching, it required the
impetus of passion to carry him quite up to its
height.

To-day the impetus was there; neither doubt nor
scruple disturbed his mind as he stood before Zenobia,
with twitching mouth and burning eyes.

'Don't,' he said, in a voice that was uneven with
excitement. 'Don't do what you are going to do!
Don't try and put on your everyday face; don't tell
me that nothing has happened—I wouldn't believe
you. I did not hear what he said to you, but I saw
his gesture—that was enough. Zenia, Zenia, is it
possible that you should still love this man who
pushes you from him? who has no understanding
for you? who prefers the laws of a stupid morality to
such a love as you are able to give?'

Zenobia had instinctively moved a little away, gathering about her the grey shawl which hung upon her shoulders. Her great black eyes, still open to their fullest, were fixed upon Hypolit's face in a mixture of astonishment and perplexity.

'I don't understand,' she said, still obviously agitated.

'Is it possible that you fail to see that your husband is turning from you? He will never forgive you for the past,—never, Zenia, never! To him you are a criminal, a sinner, while to me you are a heroine!'

He would have moved nearer to her, but something in her eyes stopped him.

'Now I understand,' she said, while the agitation on her face sank suddenly into a cold, an awful severity, just as the heavy eyelids sank down to half conceal the eyes. 'You are making love to me; is that not it?'

'You know that I have always loved you, Zenia,' murmured Hypolit, half choked; before the coldness on her face, even his supreme audacity stood aghast.

'And you dare to tell me this to-day, *to-day*? My father died yesterday, my child may be born to-morrow, and this is the moment you choose for talking to me of sinful passion? Oh, go away! Go! But no, stop a minute longer until I explain. You must not think that if you come back another day my answer will be different. Whatever day you choose it would always be the same, and it is, that I never loved any man but my husband, and could never love any other. I would rather be his servant than another man's cherished mistress; I would sooner hear hard words from his mouth than soft ones from yours, or any other man's!'

'But he does not love you, and I do!' cried Hypolit, in a voice which rang with real despair.

'I did not say that he loved me, only that I loved him. As for you, you have never been anything to me but an acquaintance, a former playmate; but you shall not be even that from to-day. I do not want to see you ever again—ever! Go away, I tell you, and do not come back again!'

Hypolit, white to the lips with the rage of humiliation, raised his head. He thought he was going to retort, passionately, vehemently; but before he had brought out a word, something made him look towards the paling, and there, peering over the top, with puffed-out cheeks, and eyes round with astonishment, was a chubby child's face—a witness too young to be inconvenient, and yet sufficient to remind Hypolit that this was scarcely the place, sandwiched as they were between two gardens, to make love to one's neighbour's wife. Without another word he turned and went, furious with himself for obeying, and yet intimately convinced that there was nothing else to be done, for by the helpless twitching of the muscles of his cheek he knew that he had lost control, not only over his thoughts but also over his nerves. There could be no object in exposing this pitiable spectacle any longer, either to Zenobia or to that inquisitive brat over there; it was best to retreat before the moral rout became too apparent, and he

therefore went, leaving Zenobia alone under the nut-
tree in the midst of the devastated garden, in which
the cabbages had already been cut from their stalks,
and where the paths had been strewn with fading
nut-leaves by last night's storm.

CHAPTER XXIII

WHEN, two days later, Gregor, returning from his father-in-law's funeral, alighted at his own door, he was met by an elderly woman, whose face he did not recognise.

'The Lord God has been merciful,' this stranger said to him, with an unmistakable air of personal importance ; 'she is doing well.'

'Who is doing well?' asked Gregor, extricating himself with difficulty from the lugubrious train of thought into which he had fallen during his drive.

'Your wife, Father Gregor. It is my good fortune to announce to you that you have a son,—a little before the time, it is true. No doubt it was the bad news that did it ; but, with God's help, all is going as it should.'

Gregor looked at her with vacant eyes, into which gradually there came first understanding and then something like excitement.

'I have a son?' he repeated, with as blank an astonishment as though the idea of such a possibility were not more than a minute old.

'And as fine a one as ever rejoiced father's heart. Come and see him, Father Gregor ; why are you still sitting there? The Pani has been waiting for you this last hour.'

Leaving the reins on the horse's back, Gregor descended precipitately from the vehicle, and, without another question, followed his petticoated guide. Without her guidance it is even possible that he would not have found his way to the bedroom, for his gait was that of a man who has received a blow on the head.

In the room, flooded with autumn sunshine, Zenobia lay, her eyes fixed impatiently on the door ; and beside her lay something carefully sheltered from the sunshine by a muslin curtain, which was flung over it. Gregor walked close up to the bed without seeing anything but that muslin curtain, without even properly seeing Zenobia, until he felt fingers closing over his hand.

'Gregor—oh, I am so happy—he is just like you!' she said, in a voice which he had never heard before.

Then he also saw her face as he had never seen it—radiant, with a mildness about the mouth, a subdued, yet penetrating light in the eyes which wonderfully transformed it. She had never appeared to him so young as at this moment, and for the first time it occurred to him that perhaps after all she was beautiful.

'You must not touch him, he is asleep. Don't bend too low, your breath might awake him.'

As she cautiously lifted a corner of the muslin cover, Gregor with difficulty restrained an exclamation which was not one of admiration. Instead of

rapture his first sensation was far more like consternation. Exactly like him? How little we know
ourselves, to be sure! Never would he have supposed
that any likeness could exist between his own
countenance and this small, deep-red face, of which
it seemed so much more probable that it was made
of india-rubber than of human flesh and blood, like
one of those toy faces that children love to squeeze
into innumerable wrinkles. But while he stared at
it stupidly, the tiny eyelids opened and he met his
own clear blue eyes, unmistakably his, only in a
miniature edition, staring back into his face with an
astonishment obviously as great as his own.

'Oh, he is awake ; now you can see what he really
is like,' and Zenobia shifted her position. 'What do
you say to him, Gregor?'

Gregor said nothing. A series of sensations that
were quite new, and consequently not recognisable,
were chasing each other through his soul. Back
through many years, back to the days when he used
to sit alone in his mud-paved room, listening to the
cries of the peasant children outside, and wondering
whether he would ever attain a domesticity of his
own, that little red face on the pillow had carried
him, and if he did not speak now, it was principally
because he was not sure of what might happen to his
voice.

'Are you happy, Gregor?' he heard Zenobia asking, right through the memory-trance into which he
had fallen. Just then the door closed behind the
woman, who had gone out to fetch water, and at the

same moment Zenobia put out her hand again and pulled him down beside her.

'Gregor,' she said, in a voice that trembled through and through; 'there must be no more cloud between us! We have *this* to hold us together now, and nothing else must come between. I know what you believe of me, but it is not true. I did not do it; things look bad against me, but I did not do it. Do not believe what they say!'

Gregor had started upright at the first word.

'Why did you not tell me this long ago?' he asked, having struggled for breath for a moment.

'I should have, but I was angry, too angry to speak; even as a child I used to be obstinate, but I have been punished enough. I did not mean to speak unless you asked me, but now I am too happy to be silent. I am innocent, Gregor; you believe me, do you not?'

'Yes, I believe you!' said Gregor, as, sinking to his knees, he hid his face in the coverlet. The joy of the deliverance was so great as to be almost a pain, and, pressed against the coverlet, he felt how his face was growing wet and hot. The burden which he had carried with him since that awful Palm Sunday was taken from him at last, so quickly, so easily and definitely, as, in this moment of nervous exaltation, he did not doubt. The natural instincts of the natural man within him had, with one leap, taken the upper hand. That life of quiet domesticity, which had once been his ideal, seemed again within his reach. In one instant all the cankering doubts seemed gone, withered away under the new radiancy of Zenobia's eyes. What was it that had tormented him for so long, and which yet a few words could take from him?

'Oh, thank you for having spoken!' he whispered, pressing his trembling lips upon Zenobia's hand. 'But this is enough. We shall never speak of it again—never!'

'Never, unless you want it!' said Zenobia, smiling a little faintly, for to her, too, the last few minutes had been mentally exhausting.

The two weeks which followed upon his return from Father Nikodem's funeral were for Gregor a time of almost perfect happiness, mixed perhaps with a little too much mental excitement for everyday life, and yet among the brightest weeks he remembered. The natural man within him was taking possession of his rights now, and if he did so a little more precipitately, a little more feverishly than would have been necessary, this was chiefly attributable to the long time he had been kept from them. Beside the wrinkled baby face even Wasylya's features began to fade, while day by day new graces were discovered in the baby's mother, by an eye determined to discover them. Once again he could stand at the altar without that black spectre of suspicion by his side, and without feeling that his share in the guilt made him unworthy to stand there. 'The Pope's voice has grown clearer,' the peasants said to each other after Sunday

Mass; 'he sings everything now as though it were a Hallelujah.'

Other people besides the peasants noticed the change. Hypolit Jarewicz was not among the last to do so. It was in the street of Lussyatyn that they met for the first time since the day on which they had brushed past each other in Gregor's garden.

These two weeks, which had been to Gregor so delicious, had been for Hypolit the worst two weeks in the history of his quite illogical passion for Zenobia. Although outwardly his family noticed only that he was in a somewhat more biting humour than usual, these fourteen days had, in fact, been one long paroxysm of masked rage. To remember the part he had played that day under the nut-tree was to writhe in impotent fury. Why was it that this woman, of all others, should possess the power of so utterly overthrowing a self-control which knew itself to be far above the average? of making him feel so pitiably small, and slight, and incompetent, both physically and morally? A sense of personal humiliation had always been mixed up with his passion; and now, when he thought of the way he had walked away at her command, 'positively like a whipped dog,' he said to himself, and with that open-mouthed child's face by the paling seeming to add the last touch of ignominy to the situation, he ground his teeth and clutched at his temples. He knew for certain that he had done nothing to be reasonably ashamed of, nothing that Friedrich

Nietsche could have disapproved of. What was it, then, that made him feel so desperately small?

And he had nothing to say for himself either; every word he had stammered might have been brought out by the veriest schoolboy gasping in the grip of his first calf-love. Oh for the means of satisfying his mangled vanity! of taking revenge where it was due!

It was with these thoughts in his mind that he met Gregor in the street, and immediately noted the new light on his face.

'I am late in presenting my felicitations,' he began, with elaborate politeness, his white teeth gleaming under his thin moustache.

'Yes, he is a fine child,—at least that is what they assure me, though personally I doubt whether I should have discovered it myself'; and Gregor laughed more heartily than was his wont.

'It's quite a change to see you in such good spirits,' said Hypolit, jealously watching the other's face. 'It seems to me that I have a second congratulation to offer. I see that you have at last accepted those principles of philosophy which I have so often brought under your notice.'

'How is that?'

'Why, it is only that I take to myself part of the credit of your present most reasonable frame of mind. Have I not told you all along that it was foolish to let your life be spoiled by a mere idea— and an exploded one, too?'

'I know what you mean now,' said Gregor gravely,

'but you are mistaken there. I was coming to tell you so. We have been on a wrong track, Hypolit, all along,—she did not do it.'

'On whose testimony do you say this?'

'Upon her own; she has given me the most solemn assurance.'

Hypolit burst into his own peculiar, cackling laugh.

'O Gregor! is your simplicity genuine, or is it only put on? You did not expect her to assure you of her guilt, did you?'

'But the way she did it,—her eyes! No, no, I believe her!'

Hypolit went on laughing, under his breath now, but in a way that began to get on Gregor's nerves.

'You mean to say that you can still doubt it, after her solemn denial?' he asked impatiently. 'You can still think that——'

Hypolit looked about him. 'I will tell you what I think, but not here. We are close to our house: come in with me, and we can talk.'

They were, in fact, at only about fifty paces from the Jarewiczs' house. Hypolit led Gregor to the back door, and from there down a passage into his own private apartment, which was likewise a species of im-provised laboratory, where even during the vacation time the medical student eagerly pursued his studies. A mixture of modern luxury and scientific rigour marked the large and airy room, where a carved bedstead, with a flaming orange satin cover, stood in one corner, and a complete skeleton unblushingly occupied another, where French novels lay side by side with ponderous volumes of science, where uncanny-looking instruments flashed out of half-open drawers, and still more uncanny-looking bottles, with mysterious contents, stood ranged upon shelves against the wall.

'Sit down,' said Hypolit, taking off his hat, and sticking it on to the head of the skeleton, where it sat rakishly cocked on one side.

'There is no need to sit down that I can see,' said Gregor stiffly, standing still in the middle of the apartment. 'You cannot have much to say to me, and I have told you that my mind is made up on the subject of my wife's innocence.'

Hypolit took a turn round the room, shutting a drawer here and there, or pushing back a book into its place. 'Can she have told him?' he asked himself, struck by this new primness.

'If you are convinced of her innocence,' he said aloud, after a moment, 'then you must feel that you owe her no end of a reparation. I wager that it is only now that your real honeymoon is beginning!'

'She has certainly never been to me what she is now,' said Gregor simply.

Hypolit's foot at that moment knocked against the elegantly inlaid bootjack, which was lying in the middle of the floor. He kicked it almost savagely under the bed as he replied—

'Then, since it seems that to-day is to be a day of

Q

congratulations, all that remains to me is to congratulate you on the perfection of your childlike faith.'

'Thank you,' said Gregor, with some heat. 'I think that is all we can have to say to each other to-day.'

He walked rapidly towards the door, but before reaching it his step faltered.

'This cannot satisfy me, Hypolit. It is not enough that you should leave me my faith; I want to hear also that you share it. I cannot hope to convince every one, of course; but you, who have been so close to the matter all summer, I cannot bear to think that you should still believe this frightful thing of Zenia.'

'No, she has not told him,' passed through Hypolit's mind, as in silence he continued his uneasy perambulations.

'Why do you say nothing?' asked Gregor, in a tone in which the first note of agitation was to be distinguished.

Hypolit faced round, with eyes from which rage was striking sparks.

'Because I cannot say what you want; because I cannot pretend to believe what I do not believe, nor to disbelieve what I consider to be proved.'

'You still hold her guilty?' asked Gregor, catching his breath.

'My opinion is the same as it was before you spoke to me to-day; not having been formed upon sentimental grounds, it cannot be altered by sentimental considerations, nor by the fact that a wife, seeing that all that is required to gain her husband's faith is protestation, should make that protestation. The prize in view, domestic peace, was surely worth putting one more load on one's conscience ; or do you imagine that a woman who does not stop at killing would stop at lying?'

With a spring forward Gregor reached Hypolit's side, and took him roughly by the shoulder with that wonderful white hand of his, which looked so delicate, and which yet had retained some of the peasant vigour of his forefathers.

'It is you who are lying now! You love my wife, and therefore you would blacken her in my eyes. You cannot—no, you cannot—believe the thing you say!'

'I have never denied that I loved your wife,' sneered Hypolit, as with difficulty he extricated himself from Gregor's grasp. Even the consciousness of the superiority of the other's physical strength which that grip had given him, and even the higher level from which the priest's eyes had looked down upon him, had been as fresh fuel to the consuming rage within him. 'Was it not I myself who first warned you against the value of my evidence? Also you are quite right to put me no further questions, and to ask me for no further proofs.'

Gregor released him abruptly.

'Proofs! Proofs!' he cried, while something of the old uncertain light flared up for a moment in his eyes. 'There never have been any proofs : surmises, nothing but surmises ; it is with these that you have poisoned my ears.'

'Did you not want it so ? Did you not ask, almost implore, my help ? '

'It was a proof I asked for, not these worthless insinuations.'

'And if I bring you that proof now ? '

'A proof ? A positive proof ? '

The two men looked at each other, immovable for a moment, then Gregor turned away.

'It cannot be. Where there is no guilt there can be no proof.'

'But if I bring it you ? ' repeated Hypolit.

'If it is an incontestable proof, then I will—— I don't know yet ; but what are you thinking ? What are you going to do ? '

'The proof shall be incontestable,' Hypolit said, more quietly than he had yet spoken. 'The only question is whether it is procurable. There are difficulties, but there are also possibilities, especially if the costs are not counted.' He was speaking now in an almost businesslike tone.

'I don't understand what you are going to do.'

'Perhaps this day week you will understand, or this day fortnight ; it may take longer than I calculate, but if the thing is to be done, I shall do it. I have to keep my promise, you know,' he added, with the shadow of a smile—'the one I made on the first day of the vacation ; nor have I much time either, since the last day is already in sight.'

'Do your best—or your worst,' said Gregor, as

with rather unnecessary jauntiness he walked again to the door. On no account would he stay here a minute longer, nor listen to any more of this talk, which, although of course it could not shake his newly recovered confidence, must yet have an irritating effect upon his nerves. This, at least, was the explanation he gave himself as he somewhat precipitately made his way into the open air.

CHAPTER XXIV

'IF you will come to me this evening after seven, I shall keep the promise I made to you last time we met.'

This was the note which nearly three weeks later Gregor received from Hypolit Jarewicz. During these three weeks Hypolit had remained invisible, nor had Gregor made any effort to penetrate the secret of his present activity. What he would have liked best would have been to forget that Hypolit Jarewicz existed, and in particular to persuade himself that their last interview had been a mere hallucination of his own excited fancy; but in this, despite much goodwill, he had not completely succeeded.

Now he stood in his room with the note of summons in his hand, and looked down at it irresolutely.

'I shall not go,' he said to himself; but when at the same moment Zenobia entered unexpectedly, he hid the paper away with a guilty feeling, which, if he really meant not to go, was absolutely superfluous.

And when evening came he went, after all,

principally, as he told himself, in order to show
Hypolit that he was not afraid to face whatever
new discovery he might imagine himself to have
made; and having told Zenobia that he had promised to spend the early hours of the night beside
one of his sick parishioners. Why he should have
gone the length of telling a lie, instead of simply
acknowledging a visit to Hypolit, who must now be
on the eve of his return to Vienna, was not quite
clear to Gregor; but the thing seemed to arrange
itself without any effort of will on his part.

The servant-girl had evidently received her orders,
for Gregor was conducted past the door of the
drawing-room and straight to Hypolit's end of the
house. But Hypolit himself was not yet there, the
family still being at supper, as the girl apologetically explained before shutting him into the bedroom laboratory, in company with the skeleton, who
again wore one of Hypolit's hats, and seemed to be
grinning hospitably out of his corner as to an old
acquaintance. The striped curtains of some oriental
stuff had been let down to the ground, and, sus-
pended from the middle of the ceiling, a lamp
burned under a pale green shade, which shed a
sickly, subdued light over every object in the room.
The French novels appeared to be bound, not in
yellow but in green; the skeleton might have been
that of a man recently pulled from the bottom of the
sea, and still covered with the pale green slime of
the deep; while even the flaming orange of the satin
bedcover smouldered now in subdued gleams, like

that of a fire on to which a pail of water has been emptied.

Gregor looked about him, with a curious tightening of the heart which he had not been aware of at his first visit. The flasks upon the shelves, mysterious even by daylight, seemed under the present illumination almost directly to suggest the Black Arts. He was aware, too, of an odour—no, of several odours—of which one undoubtedly was some sharp flower-scent, but of which others, with which it was struggling, and which apparently it had been used to disguise, bore an unpleasantly chemical character about them, reminding him of a doctor's waiting-room in Lemberg in which he had once passed half an hour. With a certain sense of trepidation he probed the shadowy corners of the room ; was not this a magician's cave into which he had been lured for his own undoing ? Astonishment at his presence here mingled with the trepidation. What was it, after all, that he had come for ? Would it not be better to retire before Hypolit came in—to miss the tryst, and to remain for ever in ignorance of whatever it was that Hypolit had summoned him to hear ? Probably there would still be time to go before the family left the supper-table. He looked at the door, but instead of going towards it he sat down on the chair beside him, and impatiently took up the first book that lay within reach, ‘*Lettres de Femmes*, par Marcel Prevost.’ He could not even read this much, being totally ignorant of French. He took up the next—a solid volume this, both in appearance and contents—'*An Inquiry into the Effects of Contaminated Air on the Functions of the Breathing Organs.*' Gregor put it down almost as precipitately as the other, but at the same moment bent again sharply forward. Among the litter of books stood an enamelled tray filled with loose photographs, and in the topmost and most conspicuously disposed of these he had recognised the portrait of Wasylya, the same portrait he had seen in the *Matrimonial Album* of the seminary. For a moment he remained in his bent attitude, staring at it fixedly, while the blood mounted slowly from his heart to his head. It seemed to him almost as though he had been abruptly transported back into her presence, and that his first movement might disperse the vision. Then, slowly and cautiously, he stretched his trembling fingers towards the tray, and with bent head looked at the picture, as one looks at a treasure one had never hoped to see again. It was long, very long, since he had met those laughing eyes, even in counterfeit; for his own copy, bestowed by Wasylya's own hand, he had, on the eve of his marriage with Zenobia, destroyed, from a scruple of conscience. How that white rose in her black hair carried back his thoughts to those cruelly brief weeks during which he had scarcely ever seen her without a flower somewhere about her person.

He was still sitting thus, with bent head, holding the picture before him with both his hands, and wondering why it was beginning to grow blurred, when Hypolit came in.

Gregor did not hear the door, nor Hypolit's step upon the soft carpet, and started back to consciousness only when he felt a hand upon his shoulder. Then he quickly threw the picture into the tray, but not before Hypolit's quick eyes had marked it. He said nothing, but the gleam in those small, restless eyes looked remarkably like satisfaction. Was it possible that that topmost photograph had not been quite accidentally disposed?

'You are punctual,' he remarked, more gravely than was his habit. 'It is I who should have been waiting for you.'

Gregor got up in a sudden flurry. So deep had he been in thoughts of the past that for a moment he had lost sight of the object of his visit.

'It is nothing,' he said confusedly. 'I came only to say good-bye—and in answer to your note,' as he seemed abruptly to remember what he was here for.

'Sit down again ; there will be time enough to say good-bye when we have done our talk.'

Defiance stood plainly written in Gregor's blue eyes as he asked a little disdainfully—

'You have something to say to me?'

'I have something to show you.'

'Be quick, please, then, for my wife is expecting me home.'

The unusual gravity, almost solemnity, of Hypolit's manner somehow put him out of his calculations. He never could have supposed that the absence of that delicately derisive smile, without which it was so difficult to imagine Hypolit, could be so disconcerting as it proved to be at this juncture. It was as though he had to do with a stranger, and not with Hypolit at all.

'I shall be as quick as you desire, and I trust also as clear.'

As he spoke, Hypolit had walked to the door and turned the key in the lock.

'It is as well to guard against interruptions,' he said, in reply to Gregor's glance of inquiry. Then, while the other's eyes followed him, he went to a small side-press, and, taking a key from his watch-chain, unlocked it. When he came back to the table he was holding a folded paper in one hand.

'Read this,' he said briefly, putting the paper into Gregor's hands.

Gregor, still standing beside the table, took the paper as he was bid, and held it beneath the lamp. It was not hard to read, being written in an exceptionally clear hand. The stamp upon the paper was that of a chemical institute at Lemberg, and the signature that of the director, while the contents consisted of the attestation that arsenic, in such and such a proportion, had been found in the human remains sent in for analysis, the quantity being such as unavoidably to have caused death.

Gregor read it all through to the signature without any especial sensation, because without comprehension, and then, with an automatic gesture, handed back the paper to Hypolit.

'Why do you show me this?' he asked dully. 'It is one of your medical things.'

'You don't yet understand. It was I who sent in these human remains, Gregor!'

Something in his tone cut Gregor like a knife.

'You?' Then, after a moment, during which a surging sound began to grow in his ears: 'Where did you get them from?'

'From the churchyard at Hlobaki.'

Gregor's gaze became almost a glare before he said, in a voice which made you guess how dry was his mouth—

'You cannot mean—you cannot mean that——'

'Yes, I do. I told you that the thing was difficult, but that, if it did not prove impossible, I would do it. Well, it has not proved impossible.'

The other had fallen on to the chair beside him, sideways, and taking hold of the back with his two hands, on which the strained skin and whitening knuckles betrayed the convulsiveness of the grip, laid his forehead against the carved wood. A sensation, not so much of horror as of pure physical sickness, kept him helpless for some moments. When he looked up at last, his face appeared of as ghastly a green under the lamp-shade as did the skeleton in the corner.

'The family consented?' he asked very low.

'I did not ask whether they did. I managed without anybody's consent.'

'It is not possible!' said Gregor, still speaking faintly.

'Oh yes, it is. At this season the nights are long, you know,' added Hypolit, attempting to fall into

his customary flippancy of tone, perhaps because
he felt that the seriousness of the subject might
otherwise become unbearable, but not perfectly
succeeding. 'It was not exactly child's play, but
human ingenuity can do much, and money can do
more; and fortunately for my plan, the old Hlobaki
gravedigger is a man inclined to listen to reason,
especially when reason paves the way to *wódki*.
The season, too, is favourable; when leaves are falling so thick, any slight disturbance of the ground
is less likely to be noticed.'

With his two hands planted on his knees, Gregor,
still deadly pale, sat like a man stupefied. At
Hypolit's last words a shiver ran abruptly down
his back. A series of hideous visions started up
before his inner eye. Was this creature he was
speaking to a man like himself, or some ghoul of
the night, such as he had read of in the tales of
his childhood?

'I had never doubted that I should find arsenic,'
pursued Hypolit, as he somewhat nervously smoothed
his small moustache; 'and I found it, too, without
difficulty. But my testimony alone would not have
been enough to convince you, I knew that, therefore
I sent the—the stuff to Lemberg, where, fortunately,
I have a friend in the chemical institute. Without
his aid I would never have got the result so quickly.
The chief risk was bringing on an investigation,
but I think I have averted that danger by asserting
that it was a case of suicide, and that the family
was anxious, for especial reasons, to ascertain what

poison had been used. The answer is here,' and he indicated the paper in his hand.

Gregor was looking up at him with twitching lips and haggard eyes.

'Hypolit,' he said, in a broken voice, 'is there anything you believe in?'

'Why do you ask?'

'Because, if you believe in anything, either in heaven or upon earth, I would ask you to swear by this thing that you are not deceiving me; that this testimony really applies to—that which you tell me it applies to, and not perhaps to something quite different; in one word, that this is not all a farce. You have learned so much, and I have learned so little, that in this matter I feel entirely at your mercy.'

'I do not believe in anything but science and the principles of Friedrich Nietsche,' said Hypolit, after a moment's deliberation; 'but I love my father— certainly more than Nietsche would approve of. Will it convince you if I swear to you by my love to him that every word I have told you is true? Besides, although in one sense you say truly that you are at my mercy, in another way I am entirely at yours. If you are convinced of the falseness of my statement, you have only to insist on an exhumation, an official one this time, made in all form, and the absence of all traces of poison would at one blow prove the groundlessness of the accusation, and would betray my own unauthorised act, on which, of course, the law lays a heavy penalty. There is nothing to pre-

vent your adopting this course,—if you believe that
I am lying.'

With one elbow resting on his knee, his body
bent, his face shaded by his hand, Gregor had fallen
into the immobility of deep thought.

'This much is proved, then,' he said presently, and
almost quietly; 'but this does not prove everything.
She was poisoned—but by whom?'

'You know as well as I that there is only one person
who could have an interest in her death. Suicide, I
presume, you will admit to be out of the question.'

Dropping his hand Gregor threw a long glance
towards the photograph on the tray, and slowly
shook his head. Wasylya and suicide! The two
things would not agree.

'An accident?' he suggested, catching at the first
thing that came into his mind.

'If you will question Justina Mostewicz, you will
find that she never, on principle, kept rat-poison in
the house. The only other poison procurable would
have been phosphorus—by breaking off enough
match-heads and infusing them in milk or spirits;
but it was not phosphorus which the analysis
revealed, it was arsenic.'

For a moment longer Gregor sat silent, his eyes
still upon the photograph on the tray, then, getting
up slowly, he began to look about for his hat.

'You are going?' asked Hypolit, watching him
curiously.

'Yes, I am going.'

'And what will you do?'

'I don't know; nothing, I think.' The voice expressed only a profound exhaustion, both physical and mental. He had found his hat by this time, but still stood on the same spot, looking towards the table.

'Do you admit that I have kept my promise?'

'Your promise? Yes, yes,' said Gregor, in what seemed a sudden access of absent-mindedness. 'Hypolit,' he added, in the same tone, 'would you mind letting me have that picture? It can have no value for you.'

He put out his hand as he spoke, and took hold of Wasylya's photograph with fingers which evidently did not mean to give it up again.

The miniature Mephisto had never looked his part so thoroughly as, with a just perceptible gleam of his white teeth, he answered—

'Oh yes, you can have it, if you care. It is like her, I think. Here it is, and here is the attestation too,' he added, with an affectation of carelessness, as he put both the things into Gregor's hands.

And Gregor went home that evening with the suspicion which he had thought dead, come back to life in his mind, and with Wasylya's photograph in his pocket.

CHAPTER XXV

TO fall a prey to a mortal disease is almost the worst evil that can befall us mortal men; but worse than this is to believe ourselves cured, and to awake one morning with the horrible consciousness that the illness is there again,—has been there all the time, only in a latent state instead of in an active one; to recognise the old symptoms, one by one, and to know that the cure has not been a cure at all, but only a stage in the illness.

This was what happened to Gregor, but not until next morning. On the evening of his return from Lussyatyn he had been too tired in body and mind to do anything but lie down and pray for the sleep which, thanks to the exposure to the sharp night air, mercifully came. It was daylight which brought him the full recognition of his state; daylight, and the first sight of his child. As he passed through the room where Zenobia was giving it its morning bath, he stood still, according to his habit, to watch the small red legs churning up the water, and the expression of foolish beatitude in the working of the wrinkles on the indiarubber face. The sight had been one of his daily pleasures for seven weeks

R

past, but to-day, at that sight, he surprised in himself a sensation akin to physical repulsion.

'He is getting quite difficult to hold,' said Zenobia, and one could guess from her voice that she was smiling. 'I think he will be stronger than you, Gregor.'

Getting no answer, she turned round, and caught sight of Gregor's face. In that instant she knew that something was wrong, although she did not immediately guess the truth.

'I have not said good-morning to you,' she said, not yet quite sure of her observation, and wanting to put it to the test. She held up her face as she spoke, as she had grown accustomed to do lately, and Gregor, also according to a new habit, stooped and kissed her on the cheek, but so coldly and hastily that Zenobia knew now that she had been right.

'Has anything happened?' she asked, with a dawning anguish in her eyes; but she knew already what was wrong—it was the old trouble come back again. She made no effort to retain him as he passed out through the second door, but presently, the child being bathed and put to sleep, she rejoined him in his private room. This time, at least, she was determined not to let that dreadful barrier of reserve, which had made of the whole summer so dreary a farce, grow up again between them. She would stand up for her happiness, no matter at what cost to her pride.

In his room Gregor was sitting before the table with his head in his hands.

'Gregor,' she said, making no effort to control the

deep vibrations of her voice, 'I don't know what has come to you since yesterday, but I see that you have again begun to doubt—what I told you after the birth of the little one.   You said I was not to speak of it again, but I see that I must.   Do you want me to repeat my assurance?'

Gregor raised his haggard face from between his hands, and looking at her with eyes that were as fiercely keen as knives, quivering to lay bare her inmost soul.

'Explain to me, rather,' he said hoarsely; 'explain instead of assuring!   It has been proved to me—do not ask me how, but proved beyond doubt—that Wasylya died by poison.   What other hand can have given it her?   Tell me only that!'

'Poison?' said Zenobia, steadying herself by the edge of the table, while her eyes seemed to grow in her white horrified face; 'that has been proved?'

'Yes.   Suggest to me some possible explanation of the mystery.   Zenia, I beg of you, suggest it!'

She remained silent for a minute, her black eyebrows drawn into a single dense line, while his savagely penetrating gaze jealously watched every shade of her expression.

'I can suggest nothing; I know of no explanation, and I am not clever enough to invent one.   I know only that it was not my hand which gave her the poison.   You believe me, Gregor!—say only that you believe me!'

'I am trying to,' said the unhappy man, as he

turned his face from her to the window. 'God knows that I want to believe you!'

The discouragement in his tone was to her almost worse than the coldness.

'Not like that, Gregor! do not say it like that!' she cried, feeling how her happiness was slipping from her grasp, as plainly as one feels a chain slipping through one's fingers, and telling herself that with one last effort it might yet be held back. 'I cannot bear your coldness; I have borne it so long, and I love you too much for that,—at least you believe that I love you, do you not, Gregor?'

'I wish I could forget it!' he broke out, turning his flashing eyes back upon her. 'It is the very thing you should not remind me of, if you were wise!'

And as Zenobia noted the convulsion of his features, she knew that, despite all her efforts, the barrier would again grow up between them, that, in fact, it was already standing in its place.

Within the next days and weeks she knocked herself against it more than once, painfully yet fruitlessly. She was neither an ingenious nor an inventive woman, and always rather slow in working out an idea; she stood by helpless, watching the consummation of her undoing.

Soon Gregor's last state showed itself as far worse than the first. 'It was not because my reason was convinced,' he said to himself, 'that I believed her, it was because I wanted to believe her, but now I have lost that power.' Rack his brain as he might for some explanation of the death by poison, which would be conceivable and would not imply Zenobia's guilt, he could find nothing. It was no use saying to himself that Hypolit's motives were apparent; that jealousy and passion had driven him to the hideous expedient adopted. Of course the motives were apparent, but so also were the proofs; and against all that staring array nothing to stand but Zenobia's word—the word of a woman who, if she had not stopped at murder, would certainly not stop at falsehood, as that diabolical Hypolit had truly said. No, it was the half-confession made on the day after her father's death which was the true one. She had said then that she had been wicked, and had suffered for it; how could the other assurance accord with this?

During these terrible weeks the convulsions which tore Gregor's inner man began to be apparent on the outer one. His mouth grew harder, his eyes wilder, while his abruptly shrunken cheeks and his upright hair, of which the bright ruddy gold began to be tempered by a premature sprinkling of silver, made him almost alarming to behold. It is not jealousy alone which wears the constitution and gnaws the bosom with the 'aspics' tongues' which preyed on Othello; suspicion can do as much, and more, with certain natures. It seemed to Gregor that even jealousy, the common human jealousy, would have been easy to bear in comparison with this. Had she proved a faithless wife, had she betrayed him for Hypolit's sake, the Slav's lenient manner of viewing any weakness of the senses would have moved him to forgive her; but the one supreme crime,—no, it was too hard a punishment which had come over him, to be mated to a female Cain!

His anxiety to surprise her into a confession developed in him an unsuspected cunning. He would watch her from ingeniously devised hiding-places, so as to note the difference of her expression when she believed herself alone; whole nights he would lie awake, hoping to catch some word dropped in her sleep.

Once during these weeks, having been summoned to Hlobaki on some business connected with Father Nikodem's death, he found himself alone in the orchard behind the house, and standing beside the old grave monument, on which the mildewed Matka Boska still faintly smiled. The branches overhead were naked, and the ground whitened by a layer of snow, thin and even as skin, through which the dead grass blades pricked in ungainly fashion, like so many bristling hairs. Nothing could be more unlike that May day so long ago, when he had knelt here on the then flowering grass with Zenobia and her sisters, and yet the sight of the spot carried his memory back forcibly to that moment. He remembered now how near he had been to speaking directly to Zenobia then; that alone might have altered the whole course of after-events. Pledged personally, and knowing himself deeply loved, he would never even have glanced at the other sister, and that which had happened would not have happened. Oh, for a word of warning at that crisis of his life! Could not that stone image have opened its lips to speak the word? 'Betrayed! betrayed!' he groaned, as, with a gesture of senseless reproach, he stretched his two clenched hands towards the impassively smiling Matka Boska.

His only comparatively happy hours now were those in which he shut himself into his room, in company with Wasylya's photograph. The mere possession of the picture had once more revealed to him the existence of the unquenchable passion, from which he would probably never be entirely delivered. Even the joy in his child, as he now recognised, had only been an interlude; for with him affection was as tenacious as suspicion, as impossible to root out, as narrow, but also as deep. The longer he gazed into that seductive face the further away he felt from his wife; and it was the laughter in Wasia's eyes, quite as much as Hypolit's evidence, which prevented him from reading the truth that stood in Zenobia's.

Once, when dusting the room, Zenobia came upon the photograph, hidden away under a book, where he had pushed it when surprised by her entrance. At sight of it something like a revelation came over her.

'That is what he does when he shuts himself in,' she said to herself, taking up the picture with timid curiosity. 'This is why he cannot love me. Was she really so much more beautiful than I am? Why is it that I cannot gain his love as well as she? Perhaps because I have never really tried; I have been content only to love him. But if he loved me he would believe me,' she mused to herself, with that feminine instinct which has nothing to do with logic.

And on that same evening Zenobia did her hair in a different fashion, and, because at this season she could get no flower to put into it, she took one of the blue bows off the baby's baptismal robe, and nestled it among her thick plaits. But Gregor did not even appear to notice it, which perhaps was lucky, as the pale blue colour made her skin appear almost swarthy ; for Zenobia was one of those women who do not know how to make the most of themselves—an art which Wasylya had understood in a supreme degree.

But she did not lose courage. 'After all, he is a young man and I am a young woman,' she said to herself in her despair ; 'it cannot be impossible to make him feel something for me.'

And, by the efforts to which she stooped, she did succeed in making him feel something for her, but it was not the affection she had hoped for. Perhaps it was exactly because she knew how to love that Zenobia was so completely ignorant in the science of making love ; what should have been an artistic and imperceptible throwing out of nets, became in her downright and far too passionately earnest hands a manœuvre palpable to even the least acute masculine eye. Her heart was far too deeply implicated in the matter to let her head keep the government, with the result that Gregor, guessing her aim, shrank yet further from her, with a new sense of horror.

'Does she want to kill my conscience through my senses?' he asked himself indignantly. 'She sees I cannot believe her, and therefore she would draw me into her own sin; we are to let the past remain the past, and to enjoy the fruits of the crime which nothing can undo. My God, preserve me from falling so low!'

CHAPTER XXVI

THERE came a day, choked with a white mist, which, weighing on the world, seemed to have suffocated every sound and almost every movement, and spent, in part, by Gregor by the side of a dying man. Owing to the smallness of the windows, shadowed by overhanging eaves, it was almost dark in the low space. By degrees only, as his eyes grew accustomed to the subdued light, Gregor came clearly to read the features of the moribund peasant, who had been installed on the place of honour: the broad, flat top of the brick baking-oven, where he lay propped up with pillows, and with a red bead rosary wound in and out of his skin-and-bone fingers. Ripe for death he undoubtedly was, this old man, with his white, tangled mane, in which single black threads still lingered, his brown leather cheeks bristling with grisly hair, and his black, sunken eyes, in whose depth just now an uneasy yellow fire was burning. Neither was there much lamentation going on around him; not because his grandchildren and great-grandchildren did not love him, but because they acknowledged in their hearts that it was time for him to reap his reward. To grudge him the

266

hard-earned rest would scarcely have been quite Christianlike, the less so as there could be no doubt of his reaching the right place, seeing that Michal Skowron had lived a life acknowledged by the village to be almost a model one, showing as it did the smallest record of drunkenness and wife-beating, and the largest of church-going, known for miles around. His family had been proud of his life, and were prepared to be even prouder of his death. Therefore it was only the children who, not wise enough to perceive the advantages of the arrangement, snivelled foolishly in corners, while the men and women went about with grave but calm faces, and if they wiped their eyes at all, tried to do so unnoticed.

Just now they had all crowded into the little entrance behind the door, and, but for the presence of two speckled hens who shared the family's winter quarters, Gregor was alone with his penitent. What with the hens, the many sheepskin coats which went out and in there, and the many garlic-scented breaths drawn within the hermetically closed space, the atmosphere was enough to knock down many a strong man, but not the seasoned Gregor. Beside the fleecy whiteness of the mist which lay against the tiny windows as thick as cotton-wool, the oil-lamp before the holy image in the corner burned of a dusky orange. Yellow bunches of maize hung from the rafters, where they had been put to dry, the spot beneath being much frequented by the hens in hopes of fallen grains. A deal table, and a bare wooden bench running round the wall, completed the furniture of the space, of which the enormous brick oven occupied nearly a quarter. The oven was not high, yet high enough to force Gregor, when sitting, to raise his face towards the sick man. The unquiet light in the depth of those eyes had puzzled him from the first ; it could not be regret for life—he had never met the sentiment in any of his parishioners past sixty—and it was not pain, for physically he was suffering nothing. Now, alone with Michal Skowron, he was to learn the cause of this unusual expression.

'You would say, Reverend Father, that I have lived as good a life as my neighbours?' Michal was asking in that peculiar hollow tone which generally means that the end is near.

'A better life than most of your neighbours,' said Gregor in his mildest tone, for the deathbed of this virtuous old man was no place for a display of severity ; 'and you are soon to reap your reward.'

Something rattled in Michal's throat, scarcely possible to recognise as a laugh.

'That is what you think, and what the neighbours think, but I have made fools of you all along. Look at my hand! Do you see anything upon it ?' And, with an effort, he freed one of his hands from the rosary, and held it feebly towards Gregor.

'I see nothing,' said Gregor astonished, and in fact there was nothing to be seen but the blisters and scars of hard labour.

'Not? Then you have only the eyes of a man,

not of God. You do not see the blood upon it?
But it is there! it is there!'

From the poor shaking hand to the burning eyes,
watching him from under ragged, white eyebrows,
Gregor looked back in sudden alarm. When one
of the women put her head into the room in order
stolidly to inquire whether it was not time to bring
the blest candle, he could answer only with a negative
sign. For a minute longer, nothing but Michal's
laboured breath was heard, then he began to speak,
slowly and painfully.

' It is so long ago that not more than half a dozen
men in the village remember it; you, Reverend
Father, will never even have heard of it, for it was
all over long before you were born. His name was
Piotr Ranek, and his ground and mine lay together,
down by the river, where Gawril Lucyan had his
potatoes last summer. He was an aggressive sort of
man, and always ready to pick a quarrel. We had
had a few disputes, because of cows straying over
the border, but never anything serious. One day
towards dark I came to my field, and caught him in
the very act of displacing the stone that stood on
the boundary, pushing it farther to my side, of course.
It began with words, bad words, of course, and it
finished with our hands. I don't think I quite lost my
head until I saw Gawril feeling for his knife. I had
no knife about me; there was nothing near me but
the stone. I did not know how strong I was until
I saw Gawril topple over on to his back; the big,
flat stone had hit him on the side of his head. When

he did not move, after a minute, I began to understand. What was there for it? Why, the river, of course, so deep, and close by. It was nearly dark, and nobody in the fields. I saw in a minute what I must do. I went home, wondering whether I should be arrested next morning. But neither next morning or on any other morning did any one trouble me, not even with so much as a question. The whole village knew that Gawril drank, and when his body was found a mile down the river, every one thought it quite natural that he should have ended that way, and the head had been so battered against the rocks that the first mark could not be seen.

'I was quite young when it happened, and now I am older than I can count. All the rest of the time I have lived respectably, and all have wondered at my keeping so straight; they do not know what it is that has kept me straight: the fear of what I had done, and the hope of washing out the sin. It was possible to live like that, but I find that it is not possible to die like that. I have done no man harm by keeping silence, since no one was suspected; but it is the silence itself that I cannot bear to take with me into the ground. Though nothing is easier than to tell lies so long as a man is on his feet, when once he comes on his back for the last time, it is the truth only which can help. No one forces me to speak, and yet I am forced to speak. There is something in lying here, and in knowing that one will not stand up again, that seems to tear open the lips and to sting the tongue into saying the words. Death and truth—death and truth—they seem to belong together.'

With many pauses and checks, and interrupted once by another opening of the door, and another inquiry regarding the blest candle, Michal Skowron had brought out his tale, and now lay still again, breathing heavily, and searching Gregor's face with his uneasy eyes.

'Is there pardon for me?' he asked timidly, startled by the hardness in the priest's fixed gaze. 'Can I yet die with the candle in my hand?'

'Death and truth!' murmured Gregor, his eyes still fastened to the mud wall opposite, as though they would look through it. Then, as a movement of the moribund caught his attention, he pulled himself together.

'There is pardon for all repentant sinners,' he said hastily, grasping at the first of the customary phrases that came to his memory.

A quarter of an hour later the family filed in again, and the blest candle was placed in Michal's hands. Gregor motioned them all to the bench by the wall.

'He has something to say to you,' he explained briefly, as he stood beside the brick oven; 'but do not press upon him. He does not want to die with any veil between you and him.'

'Nor that you should think better of me than the Almighty does,' whispered Michal; and then, gathering up the last remnants of his strength, he repeated to them the story which he had just told to Gregor, and which, though they had passed their lives by his side, not one of them had suspected. Gregor, from his post beside the oven, could follow every shade of expression upon every face, old and young, ranged in mixed order round the room, the red-cheeked faces of children alternating with the wrinkled visages of middle-age, just as they had sat down at haphazard. He could watch the transition from blank, gaping wonder to curiosity, to agitation, and finally to unmistakable consternation, differently expressed according to the age and individuality of the hearer —but all unanimous in one particular: condemnation of the sinner. Bloodshed! The crime of crimes! By the light of his own thoughts, Gregor could read theirs, without faltering or doubt, and knew that for these simple, yet rigorous people, eighty years of an apparently blameless life had in one instant been outweighed by the revelation of that one black moment.

And yet in the eyes of the old man on the top of the oven the uneasy light no longer burned; quiet and obviously happy he lay there, with the blest candle painfully propped between his fingers. The dumb condemnation of his human judges could no longer disturb one who felt himself so near to another judge, one so much better acquainted with the holes and corners of the human heart, and so much greater a proficient in the dispensation of mercy.

*   *   *   *   *

As Gregor walked home through the blinding mist which drowned the brown roofs as in a sea, and

hung in flakes upon the mottled palings, he seemed
to take with him in his eyes the picture of all those
silent, condemning faces, and in his ears the sound
of Michal's voice.

Truth—yes—truth; how difficult it was to reach
it; it would not be possible to live much longer
without reaching it; he knew this by a new excitement within him, born beside the deathbed he had
just left. His face betrayed him to Zenobia the
moment he entered.

'Gregor, what is it?' she asked, rising instinctively; 'you look ill.'

'No, I am not ill, but I have seen a man die;
perhaps that has unnerved me a little.'

'Michal Skowron? But it is not the first time,
Gregor.'

'No, it is not the first time, but I think it has been
the worst. It has taught me some new things; the
difference, for instance, of doing a thing in life, and
of doing that same thing when death is staring you
in the face. Death and truth—death and truth—
yes, they belong together.'

He was pacing about the room with his eyes on
the floor, speaking more to himself than to her.
Suddenly he stood still before her.

'Zenia,' he said, in the voice of a man who has
come to a resolution, 'this cannot go on. I cannot wait for death to bring me the truth; I must
have it now, while we are both alive.'

'I have told you the truth.'

'Will you tell it me again—more solemnly, more

S

emphatically? Will you swear it to me by the salvation of your soul?'

'If that will help to quiet you——'

'Then come with me; put something round you and come with me quickly!'

His gesture was so imperative that, without asking a question, she took up her shawl and wrapped it round her shoulders.

Gregor had turned to the wall, where on a nail hung the bunch of clumsy keys belonging to the church.

'Come quickly!' he said again, as he preceded her out of the house, and led the way down the short bit of lane, and across the piece of waste ground which surrounded the church, whose round towers loomed like unreal things out of the suffocating mist. Not a living thing met them on their short road; for any sound or movement in the silent lane the world might have been lying dead around them, choked by the mist that weighed upon it, and they the sole survivors.

Gregor went straight to the little side entrance which led to the sacristy, and, with steady fingers, fitted the key into the lock. Inside, still without a word, but with an evident strain upon his set face, he took down his surplice from the wall, and before the eyes of the wondering Zenobia, quickly passed it over his head. Then he looked about him, as though in search of something.

'What is it?' she ventured to ask, beginning to shiver with a sense of impending solemnity.

'The matches,—a candle must be lit.'

He found the matches under a discarded altar-cloth, and taking one of the heavy bee's-wax candles that stood in a corner, lit it and put it into Zenobia's hands.

'Come!' he said for the last time, and taking the book of gospels from its case, he advanced into the church.

Here everything lay as though under a veil; the mist which pressed against the windows seemed to have followed them in by the door, which Gregor had forgotten to close behind them, and to have laid a film even upon the bright gilding and the gaudy colouring of the holy pictures.

'Kneel down!' said Gregor, in a stern whisper; and Zenobia knelt down obediently before the altar, the candle in her shaking hand raining wax on to the carpet which covered the steps.

'Take it into your left hand, and lay the right upon the Book.'

She did so, recognising now the particulars of the ceremony in use when one of the peasants takes the pledge of sobriety, and which she had often witnessed.

'And now speak after me—

'I swear by the salvation of my soul, and by the hope of that salvation which is contained in this Holy Book, that I am innocent of the death of my sister Wasylya, and know nothing of the cause of her death.'

When her last trembling words had died away in

the corners of the empty church, there was a moment during which neither of them moved. Zenobia, still shivering with excitement, did not yet venture to raise her eyes to Gregor's face, for fear of what she might see there. It was only when beside her she heard a breath drawn—it sounded like a breath of relief—that she found courage to look up. The strain seemed gone from his features, as he stood with bent head before the altar.

'You can go,' he said more quietly; 'I shall follow presently.'

And she went, leaving him alone in the church, and praying in her heart that peace might have come to him at last.

The mist was melting into dusk when Gregor reached his room. Groping about for a light, the photograph came into his hands, but he put it aside resolutely.

'I should destroy it,' he said to himself, 'now that I am convinced; and also that villainous paper, which has done all the harm, and which, as likely as not, is a forgery: that devil Hypolit is clever enough for anything.'

He had made a light by this time, and unlocking a drawer, took out the attestation of the chemical institute. He had already made up his mind to push it into the stove, where Zenobia's forethought had lit a crackling fire to welcome him; but instead of doing so on the instant, he unfolded the paper once more, and, driven by an irresistible impulse, began to look it over,—for the last time, he told himself. He had been standing when he began to read, but after a moment he sat down, and having come to the end, remained in his chair, frowning at the sheet before him. No, that could be no forgery; it bore the stamp of genuineness even on the texture of the paper. Truth, a matter-of-fact, businesslike sort of truth, stared back at him from the official stamp. But then—but then——

Gregor fell forward with his head upon the table. Another sham cure! The evil was there again; not even the oath before the altar had been able to conjure the disease. What could an oath—the most solemn of oaths—mean to a woman who had committed the supreme crime? Even an assassin could not be more than damned. Had not Michal Skowron said that nothing was easier than lying, so long as a person was on his feet? And on his knees it was probably not much more difficult, so long as the body feels strong enough to stand up again.

When Zenobia found him thus, she understood even before he had spoken.

'Not yet?' she asked reproachfully, a shade which looked like sulkiness, but which was but wounded pride settling upon her face. 'You do not believe me yet?'

He shook his head without speaking.

'But what more can I do than swear upon the Holy Book?' she cried, in one of her rare bursts of anger.

'I know you can do nothing, but I also can do nothing; it is too strong for me. I shall continue to doubt until death brings truth with it. If you die before me, and if on your deathbed you still have the courage to protest your innocence, then I shall believe you, but not before. Life and lies can live together comfortably side by side—I learned that to-day; but death and truth belong together.'

Then for a moment husband and wife looked at each other across the table, and in each of their hearts the thought of the life before them seemed to stretch like a long, featureless waste.

CHAPTER XXVII

A FEW days before the Christmas Day of the Greek Church, Gregor's sledge, with both Gregor and Zenobia in it, went to Lussyatyn. It was almost the first time that they found themselves in a prolonged *tête-à-tête* since that afternoon visit to the church. The situation had now come to be tacitly acknowledged by both to be so strained that Gregor preferred to come in late to meals, and that Zenobia, too deeply discouraged for further efforts, was even thankful for these respites. But to-day there was no help for it; it was high time for Zenobia to make her Christmas confession to Father Urban, who, since her marriage, had become her standing confessor; and Gregor, whom ecclesiastical business called into town, had no chance but to accompany her.

The cold wind, which drove the snow into their faces, and made the covering up of one's ears a necessity, and the opening of one's mouth almost an impossibility, was, despite its keen edge, welcome to both husband and wife, who spent the half-hour in the sledge almost in silence, though side by side.

'Shall I drive you straight to the church?' asked

Gregor, when they had got into the streets of Lussyatyn.

'No; I have to buy some flannel first; I need some more wrappers for the baby. Please put me down at Fiderer's. I shall go to the church on foot. It is early still, and Father Urban will not yet be in his confessional.'

'Very well; I shall try to catch him at home, so as to get my business over with him.'

Zenobia was accordingly put down at Fiderer's, and Gregor took the sledge to the Jarewiczs' house, where he found Father Urban shivering before a crackling stove, and with a second comforter round his neck in addition to the one which he invariably wore in winter.

'My throat again!' he sighed softly, in answer to Gregor's inquiries. 'And to think that in half an hour I shall have to go over there!' He jerked his shoulder disconsolately in the direction of the window, from which the church was visible. 'The girls are right in saying that these wooden churches are nothing but boxfuls of draughts. Ah, if I had my new brick church ready! That one will be air-tight, I warrant you! Just listen to that wind! Do you think that one rug will be enough for my legs, or hadn't I better take a second?'

On several chairs around the stove a miscellaneous collection of articles of clothing were ranged, as though for exhibition, but with the true object of absorbing as much warmth as their constitution allowed of; a long fur-lined coat, a pair of tall felt boots to be pulled over the leather ones, a striped rug, and yet another comforter of thick, knitted wool; this was the arsenal destined to defend Father Urban from the chilly church atmosphere.

'If I had known it was going to turn out such a day as this I would never have given notice; but there is no help for it now; every one knows that I am to be in my confessional this afternoon, and really it's getting too close, as it is, with the Christmas confessions.'

He smiled at Gregor as he spoke, a smile of wistful resignation. In truth, his face looked so ghastly, and his whole small person so frail, that the idea of tearing this feeble old man out of his sheltered nook struck Gregor as almost inhuman. With the sole thought of compassion in his mind, it became almost inevitable to say—

'Could I not replace you?'

Over Father Urban's fragile features there passed a gleam of hopeful surprise.

'You? But you have your own work; I have no right to take you from it.'

'I am not wanted at Rubience to-day; I have heard all the Christmas confessions.'

'Dear me, how lucky! But I don't know whether I can conscientiously accept,' said the old priest uncertainly.

'I think, on the contrary, that you cannot conscientiously refuse. If you go to the confessional to-day it is almost certain that you will not be fit to sing High Mass on Christmas Day, and I shall not

be able to replace you *then*.　It is for Christmas Day
that you should nurse your throat.'

Gregor spoke with sudden animation, for all in an
instant he had caught sight of an amazing possibility.

Father Urban's washed-out blue eyes travelled
wistfully to the window, against which the snowflakes
were rushing in intermittent gusts, and wistfully lent
his ear meanwhile to the porcelain stove, in which
was to be heard simultaneously the comfortable
crackle of the wood, and the howl of the wind up the
chimney.

' Really, my son, it may be that you are right,' he
murmured, as he settled himself a little deeper in
his easy chair.

When, a little before the lapse of the half-hour,
Gregor, clad in Father Urban's fur coat, which was
undoubtedly warmer than his own, reached the
church, a small crowd of penitents was already
assembled ; but, peer about him as he would, he
could not catch sight of Zenobia. A few heads
were turned towards him, as he went quickly towards the confessional, and a few whispered com-
ments passed, but Father Urban's parishioners were
too much used to these incidents to feel any great
surprise.

The cold was indeed deadly in the church, and
the breath that came from praying lips floated
visibly in the air, more conspicuous often than the
lips themselves ; for the darkness of the weather had

wrapped the inside of the building in a dusk which was premature by at least two hours. Gregor, taking his place behind the wooden trellis, felt that his teeth were chattering, but knew at the same time that it was not with the cold. What was it exactly that he was going to do? Why had he sought to gain the shelter of the confessional so quickly, before too many eyes had marked him? Why was he so glad of this gloom, which hung an almost tangible veil between every two faces? Again, what was he going to do? To fulfil a simple act of neighbourly service, or to commit a great treachery? He was not quite clear, knowing only that if it were wrong, then, perhaps for the first time in his life, he was going to do wrong with the consent of his whole will. That he could not do so calmly was proved to him by the wild heart-beats which greeted every new penitent, by the almost unbearable strain with which he listened, with face carefully shaded, for the first accents of every fresh voice that began to speak at the other side of the wooden trellis. Not yet; old and young, sin-stained and almost innocent, they came in mixed succession; the trembling accents of scrupulous souls alternating with the indifferent drawl of those to whom the whole affair had become a mere matter of habit,—but among them all she came not yet.

The strain, because of its very prolongation, was beginning perforce to relax, when at last, through the thickening shadows, the voice he had been waiting for seemed to tear a passage. It was almost impossible that she should see his face, and yet, at the very first accent, he shrank guiltily together, spreading his hand more elaborately and letting the handkerchief he held fall in looser folds about his features.

When she ceased speaking his position did not change. What he had heard was but a common-place list of very ordinary offences ; but there might be more to hear, and for that it was necessary to question. It was for this that he was trying to steady his nerves.

When several movements had passed without his speaking, the penitent made a discreet movement, as though to arrest his attention, then, after another pause, remarked timidly—

'My confession is ended, Reverend Father.'

With cold fingers Gregor pressed the handkerchief closer to his face. It was time to speak if he would not betray himself, and even if in so doing he betrayed himself, it was time to speak.

'Is it truly ended?' he inquired in a whisper, which nervousness made incisive. 'Does no other sin, some sin of your former life, press upon your conscience?'

There was a pause of surprise, before the well-known voice came back again—

'Of my former life? But I confessed myself three months ago.'

'Yes, but before so great a day it is good to look back even beyond the last absolution——'

He ceased abruptly, for at the other side of the

trellis there had been something like a cry, choked at the rising.

'Gregor!' said Zenobia, almost aloud. 'It is you? Oh, my God!'

'Hush! hush!' was his instinctive word, as in the agitation of the moment he dropped the shielding hand, and husband and wife looked into each other's widely distended eyes, from between the primitive wooden bars. It was the shielding hand itself which had been the traitor. Zenobia had not seen his face, nor recognised the disguised voice, but that wonderfully shaped, delicately white hand, so well known to her and visible even in the shadows, had abruptly told the truth. And to think that the mere precaution of putting on a pair of gloves might have averted this! His nails were blue with cold, as it was, and yet, so great was his mental absorption, that the idea of the gloves had never even occurred to him.

Zenobia's eyes flared up, right through the gloom, and her lips moaned, as though she were going to say more, but no sound came, and before he had spoken again she had risen and was gone, not only out of the confessional but out of the church, where, wrapping her cloak about her, she began to pace about in the shelter of the wall, as though in wait for something, and heedless of the flying snow, or more truly speaking, grateful for its coolness upon her burning face.

When in the dusk, almost in the dark, Gregor at length came out, he found her on his path.

'Listen,' she said, while the wind which took the words out of her mouth made it appear as though she were speaking in gasps; 'this must end somehow,—it is more than I can bear. It was to surprise me that you went into the confessional to-day; you hoped to force some secret from me.'

Gregor might have answered with literal truth: 'It was to replace the sick Father Urban that I went,' but he answered without hesitation, and in that same tone of exasperated excitement in which she spoke—

'Yes, that is what I hoped.'

'And now that you have not succeeded, are you satisfied at last that there is nothing to hear?'

'No, I am not satisfied.'

'But you heard my whole confession?'

'You had recognised me before you began, or at least before you ended; I am sure you had recognised me.'

'But listen——'

'There is nothing to listen to; I know what you would say!'

'But, Gregor, this life is becoming unbearable!' she cried aloud, with the sharp ring of despair in her voice.

'Unbearable!' he echoed, and laughed more like Hypolit than like himself as he added: 'And yet it has to be borne.'

She walked some steps forward, and turned again.

'Where is the sledge? I cannot stay here; I must go home at once.'

'You can go,' he said, after a moment's reflection; 'but I shall stay; I shall not be done with my business to-night.   Father Urban will let Fedor drive you.'

The thought of the drive home and of the long evening before him had suddenly come over him as something which he did not feel equal to face.   Any pretext which allowed him to spend the night at Lussyatyn was good enough, and by to-morrow perhaps something might have occurred to him which could make the situation more endurable.   Such as it was, it could not long remain.   Zenobia was right when she said that this must be ended somehow.

CHAPTER XXVIII

NEXT morning, very early, Fedor was back with the sledge. It was so early that Gregor, who had spent the night in the Jarewiczs' house, was awakened by finding Fedor himself standing beside the bed, and shaking him by the shoulder.

'You are to come at once,' he was saying in his broad peasant's accents; 'the Popadia is ill.'

Gregor sat up, scarcely well awake, blinded by the flame of the tallow candle which Fedor was holding all aslant in one hand, for it was still an hour and more from sunrise.

'I am coming—I am coming,' he said hastily, using the words he was accustomed to speak when awakened in the night by a summons to the dying. Then, after a moment, during which his brain began to clear—

'Who did you say was ill?'

'The Popadia, your wife.'

'The Popadia? But she was well yesterday. Has she sent for the doctor?'

'No; she said she did not want the doctor, but only you, and you were to come quickly.'

'It is what they call an attack of the nerves,' said Gregor to himself, as in the light of the candle he began to grope about for his clothes. 'The continuation of the scene of yesterday; oh, my God, how is this to go on? Another bandying of empty words; and yet I cannot but go, if it is only for shame before the servants.'

He left the house without having seen any one else astir, and, taking the reins from Fedor's hands, began to fill the still sleeping streets with the tinkle of his sledge-bells. There were no lamps on the sledge, but the two whitenesses, that of the approaching dawn and that of the freshly fallen snow, were enough to show him his road, though in a spectral and unreal fashion, making the white fields appear to melt away into the white sky, and the round-headed willows in the hedgerows look unpleasantly human. Without hurry he drove; what was there to hurry for? He felt heart-sick already at the thought of that which awaited him.

It was daylight already—a dull, colourless, sunless daylight—when he went up the steps of his house. The first thing that met him was a sound—a sound which, even without having yet identified it, he recognised as associated in his memory with something terrible. He stood still to listen; it came from the bedroom over there, and,—yes, it was the voice of a woman weeping, loudly and without restraint, as uneducated people weep,—as Hania had wept on the day of Wasylya's death. Pushed by a sudden intense curiosity, rather than by any clearly defined feeling of anxiety, he went towards the room.

T

Zenobia, in the same clothes she had worn yesterday, and with only her dress unbuttoned, was lying on the top of her bed, looking towards the door with the same keenness of expectation as she had gazed towards it on the day when he had found her lying here with her new-born baby beside her—but not with the same face—oh, my God, no—not with that face! Even physically these drawn and discoloured features were scarcely to be recognised as the same. This lividly yellow skin, these fearfully sombre eyes, these contracted muscles of the forehead, did they belong to the happy mother of that day? To Gregor it seemed almost impossible, and as though arrested by some physical force, he stood still at two paces from the bed. It was not Zenobia's sobs he had heard, then. In a corner, with her apron over her head, Jusia, the servant-girl, was uttering those muffled howls which had carried his thoughts back to the catastrophe of last year. He noted the circumstance without looking in that direction. No, Zenobia was not weeping; she had even attempted to smile as he appeared in the doorway—a smile that was fearful to behold. Now she stretched towards him a hand in which the fingers curled irresistibly towards the palm, as they do in moments of physical pain.

'At last!' she said, and the words came out thickly, as though her tongue were lamed or swollen. 'Come here, Gregor! I have done it; you will have to believe me now.'

The wild light which had flickered up in her eyes

died down suddenly as she hid her face in the pillow. Under the blanket which Jusia had flung over her, Gregor, rigid on the spot where he had first stood, could see her body writhing. When she looked up after a minute, her face was more ghastly than before, and her voice weaker.

'You said that if on my deathbed I should still declare I was innocent, you would believe me; well, this is my deathbed, and I tell you again that I am innocent. Is that enough?'

'But you are not dying!' cried Gregor, awaking out of his stupor with a rebound of his whole being. 'You cannot be dying!'

'I know I am. Look at that glass beside the bed; smell it, if you like.'

A tumbler, clouded with milk, and with a few drops of milk still at the bottom, stood beside the bed. Gregor took it up automatically.

'It smells bad.'

'And it did not taste good,' said Zenobia, with a grimace that was partly of pain. 'But there was no other means of getting what I wanted. It took fifteen boxes of matches to make the concoction; I did not want to begin a second time.'

'Phosphorus!' said Gregor incredulously, as the name of the smell which had puzzled him came suddenly to his lips. 'You have drunk poison?'

She nodded in silence, turning her face again to the pillow.

'Unhappy woman! But there is still time,—the doctor! Why did I not bring the doctor with me? The horse is still in the sledge—where is Iwan?'

He stormed from the room, and was back again, breathless, in two minutes. Zenobia still lay as before.

'It is too late for that now,' she said with a dreadful calmness.

His clasped hands went up to his forehead.

'But Zenia, Zenia, you repent?—say only that you repent! Think of the sin!' and he threw himself upon the bed, grasping her hands and dragging them to his breast, as though the better to be able to look deep into her eyes. The husband, the lover, the doubter, they were all dead in him at this moment, and only the priest remained alive, and saw before him a sinner whom perhaps a few minutes separated from eternal damnation.

'You repent, do you not?'

'How can I repent? There was no other way.'

In the pressing need of the moment, he shook the hands he held, almost roughly.

'Say that you repent!'

But Zenobia's eyes, harder than ever he had seen them, looked back into his, unmoved.

'It is you who should repent; it is you who have killed me—with that cruel doubt. You wanted to be a better priest than the others, and you have been a worse one, because you did not understand how to trust. But now you cannot escape me—I have forced you to believe,—say, have I not?'

'Yes, yes—I believe—of course I believe!' he said

almost unthinkingly. The question of belief or disbelief seemed all at once to have become entirely unimportant, a mere trifle of detail which shrunk to nothing before the horror of the thing that was accomplishing itself before his eyes. But was it really accomplishing itself? It still seemed to him hard to believe. Everything around him—the very furniture and carpets and bedclothes—looked so commonplace and so familiar as almost to preclude the idea of anything so completely out of the common; even the smoke-stained face of the old clock upon the wall, which Zenobia had brought with her from her home, and even the patches upon the carpet, which had been applied by her diligent fingers, seemed to be looking at him with a reassuring smile, as though they would say, 'Be quiet—it is not real—presently you will awake!' It did not seem possible that in this everyday frame, with so little pomp and ceremony, and with so much sordid and everyday detail, anything so terrible could really be happening.

'And yet I am not quite innocent,' Zenobia was saying, while a look of deep fatigue began to settle on her face; 'I will tell you all before I go to sleep —it is strange that I should feel sleepy now—I did not do it, but I *thought* of doing it. During those weeks—you know which—my heart was very black. I would have taken you from her if I could ; I was even foolish enough to go to a woman who pretended to sell love-charms; but I could not get myself to follow her advice ; I hoped for something else, I did not know what; there were moments when I wanted her to die—when I even *prayed* for her death, and when it came I felt as though it was I who had killed her with my prayers or my curses, —I did not know which. O Gregor, what a misfortune to be able to love like that! and I don't even know why I have loved you so; you were not worth it,—no, I see now that you were not worth it!'

Sunk on to his knees, with his face upon the bed, Gregor neither moved nor spoke. The man in whom spiritual pride had undermined charity, in whom an earthly passion had killed heavenly love, felt too deeply abased to utter a word. Surely, ah! surely this was the woman whom he ought to have loved, —this one and not the other. This was she whom he ought to have honoured and held high, instead of torturing her to death with that cruel doubt!

What had become of that doubt he did not know until late that night, when he found himself holding vigil at the foot of the same bed, at the head of which now burned two wax tapers, and where reposed a stiff, white form. Until now his soul, buffeted between a wild remorse and a yet wilder rebellious upleaping against fate, had found no moment to go to account with itself. Now only, alone with the dead, he knew at last that when he had said, 'I believe,' it had not been only with his lips, but that he actually believed, fully and completely, without understanding, and without even wishing to understand. The proofs which spoke for her guilt were there the same as ever, but they had abruptly lost their value. The truth was not there; but here upon this bed, pillowed side by side with death,—they belonged together inseparably, exactly as Michal Skowron had said.

In the first hours after the accomplishment of the catastrophe it had not seemed possible to escape despair. If it had not been for the child, Gregor would probably not have escaped it. It was that wrinkled, red face that abruptly showed him the only means of atonement still open to him—that of bringing up his son in the conviction of his mother's innocence, so as to stand ready armed against the calumny which could not fail to reach the ears of the man. From his cradle he should learn to revere her memory as that—if not of a saint, yet most assuredly of a martyr.

EPILOGUE

ZENOBIA had said there was 'no other way,' but she had been wrong, for there was, after all, another way; a way so simple that human perspicacity had blundered past it, leaving its detection to what some people call Providence, and others Chance.

Two months had not yet passed since the sensational death of Zenobia Petrow, when in one of the grim, bare-walled spaces of the *Landesgericht* at Lussyatyn, the whole—anything but complicated mystery—came abruptly to light. It was not so much the curiosity awakened by this second remarkable death as the indiscretions of the old grave-digger at Hlobaki which had set the stone rolling. The desecration of a grave was an idea so profoundly offensive to the popular religious taste, that the moment Pawel Prokup began to grow loquacious, as he was apt to do in his cups, the alarm caught like fire on dry wood, and grew and spread, until the authorities found the necessity of an investigation pressed upon them.

The desecration once verified, there unavoidably arose the question of motive; thence a further investigation, and the plain proof of poison having been used. By whom? The popular mind thought it

knew, and also that the culprit had put herself
beyond the reach of Justice. But Justice herself has
a habit of at least attempting to form her own conclusions. A lengthy examination of all the persons
concerned was the only means at her command, and
among those persons was Hania, the servant-girl
still attached to the widowed Popadia's household.

Until this moment no evidence of any interest had
been elicited, or rather, everything had appeared to
bear out the popular assumption.

' You are quite certain that your mistress never gave
you rat-poison to use, or perhaps fly-poison, to put upon
a plate?' the officiating functionary asked, severely
fixing the girl through his gold-rimmed spectacles.

Hania, despite her evident nervousness, was quite
certain of this.

' And you declare that Zenobia Petrow, then
Zenobia Mostewicz, was aware that Ursula Adamicz
sold white powders which could kill?'

' She was aware of it.'

' Through whom?'

' Through me,' murmured Hania, casting a terrified glance towards the Popadia, who having under-
gone a similar interrogatory, had taken a seat in the
background of the room. It was evident that neither
time nor catastrophes had diminished the terror of
her mistress, in which Hania chronically existed.

' And Zenobia Mostewicz visited Ursula Adamicz?'

' I think she did; I am not sure.'

' Did she ever send you to fetch anything from
Ursula Adamicz?'

' No. never.'

'But you were seen entering the hut,' remarked the inquisitor, with a sharper glare of his spectacles.

Hania's pink doll's face became scarlet.

'She did not send me.'

'Then you went on your own account?'

Hania pulled desperately and in silence at her woollen gloves.

'I warn you that by any prevarication you are exposing yourself to suspicion. If Zenobia Mostewicz did not send you, and you did not go on your own account, then why did you go?'

'Because I was sent—by the other one,' blurted out Hania, with another deprecating glance towards her mistress.

Among the attending functionaries there was a stir, slight but significant.

'Which other one?'

'Panna Wasylya.'

'What did she send you for?'

'For a powder for her face. She had got a rash, and had tried everything for it, and when I told her that Ursula Adamicz sold beauty powders which made the face beautiful in a few days, she would have some at any price, but no one was to know it; so she gave me money, and I had to go in secret.'

Every one had drawn a little nearer now; even the clerk who was taking down the evidence stopped writing to stare at Hania, while upon her chair in the background Justina Mostewicz stiffened suddenly into an attitude of close attention.

'And what was the powder like which you brought?'

'Quite white, and it tasted bitter, for I put some on my tongue.'

'And Wasylya Mostewicz took it?'

'Yes, she took all the three powders at once, for she hoped the rash would go before she went to church.'

The spectacled functionary leaned back in his chair, passing his handkerchief across his brow, as though after a severe exertion.

'I think the investigation will give us little further trouble,' he remarked, looking round at his colleagues, while gratified complacency began to temper the severity of the official manner. 'Every one knows what these "beauty powders" are, of which, unfortunately, so free a use is made by our ignorant populace. What made you not speak before?' and with a fresh access of fierceness he glared again at the agitated witness. 'What made you keep your errand to Ursula Adamicz a secret?'

'I had gone without leave,' said Hania, ducking her head, almost as though to dodge a slap on the cheek, or a box on the ear.

But her mistress was not thinking of her just then; her thin lips had parted in what looked like a smile of triumph, and her brown leather face seemed illuminated in a way which the foolish little servant-girl could not in the least understand, as little as she understood the reason of the sensation which she saw about her,—and all caused, it would seem, by her evidence. After all, it had only been beauty powders which she had fetched, and not that other deadly powder of which she had told Zenobia. To expect of her intellect that it should discover any relation between these two differently named wares was putting too great a demand upon it.

Nor did she ever quite understand. To her and to many other primitive minds the verdict of : 'Death by an accidental overdose of arsenic,' said nothing, and could not alter the fact that Ursula Adamicz sold two kinds of powders, of which one claimed to dispense beauty, and the other death.

Among those who understood was Hypolit, and he did so with a sensation that was far more like disappointment than remorse. So she was not exactly the woman he had taken her for! Might not this discovery, made earlier, have succeeded in cooling that passion whose bitter force had driven her to her death ?

The greater part of the public made the same remark : ' So, after all, the mother is right !' Whenever the words reached Gregor's ears, his bowed head bent lower. Yes, it was the mother who was right, not because she was cleverer than the others, but simply because she could believe no evil of her child. If he had been able to love her as the narrow-minded Popadia had loved, then he would have believed in her, as the Popadia had done—stupidly but faithfully, without understanding and without doubting.